I0739002

Also by *Karla Brandenburg*

The Epitaph Series

Epitaph

The Twins

The Northwest Suburbs Series

Cookie Therapy

Return to Hoffman Grove

Living Canvas

Touched by the Sun

The Mist Trilogy

Mist on the Meadow

Gathering Mist

Rising Mist

Other Novels

Intimate Distance

Heart for Rent, with an Option

Epitaph 2: The Twins

Karla Brandenburg

Acknowledgements: Nurse Paula for stepping out from behind the curtain, Tom Riley, founder of TapCloud, for a really cool tool and for taking the time to take me on the app journey, Dan Lang for his woodworking expertise. Cheryl Bouschard for her physical therapy knowledge and assistance. Sue Cleary and Cynthia Standley for their friendship and for sharing their journeys with me. Beth Dertz for helping with scary ghost stuff. Thanks to Sue and Mike Schrader for the photos of "Mrs. Sumner's" house. As always, thanks to my critique group, Terry and Steve, the crew at Booklover's Bench and my editor, Kelly Lynne, who makes me laugh with her supportive comments. "Squicked?"

 # Chapter 1

RAIN HIT THE WINDSHIELD, the consistency of corn syrup. Jared Pierce checked the thermometer on his dashboard. Thirty-one degrees. The drops might not look like snow, but he'd bet his last dollar the roads would be freezing soon, if they hadn't already. He was thirty miles from his destination, and counted himself lucky the weather had held this long. Winter in Illinois.

He'd been on the road more than twelve hours, making only necessary stops along the way from Vacherie, Louisiana, to Edgarville to flip his great aunt's house.

No one seemed to know what caused the rift between his Grandma Margaret and her sister, Lily, but his mother and his aunt agreed there was something odd about Great Aunt Lily Sumner. Jared had never heard of her until his Aunt Melinda breezed into town and insisted Jared's mother step up to the plate and deal with the sale of her house. Aunt Melinda transferred executorship to Jared's mother, who promptly passed the ball to him. "She thinks the house might be haunted," his mother had told him when he asked why she wanted Jared to go, and not his brother, Troy.

A car sped by on Jared's right, and he instinctively tapped the brakes. His car fishtailed, sending his pulse racing. He'd never driven in ice and snow. Jared took his foot off the gas and his car straightened. Good time to decelerate. He hit his signal and eased into the far right lane, tightening his grip on the steering wheel while he checked the road signs for his exit.

More cars crowded around him, making him less sure of his driving skills in foreign weather.

"In point five miles, take exit, on right," the GPS told him.

"Okay," he replied as if it could hear him, squinting between the wipers and the raindrops for the turnoff.

"In point two miles, take exit, on right," the GPS told him a minute later.

"Got it," he said. He activated the signal and took his foot off the gas once more to slow down. "That doesn't look like the right direction," he told the GPS. He must be getting punchy if he was talking to an inanimate voice.

"Take exit. On right."

Who was he to argue? And the GPS was right. He wasn't going the right direction because the exit was a cloverleaf. Jared drifted into the exit lane and steered into the loop. A speed limit sign told him to drop to 30 mph instead of the 40 he was doing, so he tapped the brake and sent the car into a spin. Reflex made him stomp the brake. The brakes pulsed under his foot, but the damage was already done. With his heart in his throat, Jared tried to straighten the car. The rear quarter panel hit the guard rail with a jolt and spun the car around. He closed his eyes, knowing he'd lost control. *Please don't die, please don't die.* The front of the car hit something. The airbag deployed and his car rolled down the embankment in the center of the cloverleaf.

When he came to a stop, he was upside down. Jared saw stars and raised one hand to stop a trickle snaking its way across his face. He looked at his hand as if it belonged to someone else. Blood. Not good. Where was his cell phone? He'd left it in the cup holder, but once he'd gone into the spin cycle, no telling where it might have landed. *Please, somebody call for help.* He looked out the broken passenger side window, past the roof that now reduced his headroom by half. Should he unfasten his seatbelt, or would that make matters worse since he was wrong side up? He tried to turn, to position himself to slide through the window on his side, but he couldn't move.

A fresh wave of panic hit when a second car slid down the embankment toward him. The last thing Jared remembered was the impact of the second car as it hit his passenger side.

Chapter 2

Three weeks later

I love my mother.

The nurse's aide wheeled Jared through the halls of the rehab hospital toward the parking lot, where his mother would meet him with the getaway car. He was finally being released.

The five-minute wheelchair trip to the outside world was the first moment of silence he'd had since his mother had arrived this morning. She'd flown in to spend every weekend with him since the accident, and her visits to the hospital—and then to the inpatient rehab facility—tended to be filled with tears and nonstop babbling.

The doctors had told Jared not to travel for the next three months, which left him stranded in Illinois. His at-home recovery could be done at Great Aunt Lily's house. His mother had offered to stay with him but Jared, at six-foot-four and just shy of 200 pounds, would crush his mother in an instant if he lost his balance, not to mention the way his skin crawled every time anyone asked him if he was all right. He'd lost track of how many times his mother had asked him already this morning.

Yes, his hip had been broken. Yes, his face was bruised and scarred, but he was an otherwise able-bodied, thirty-year-old man. He was perfectly capable of taking care of himself. They wouldn't be letting him out of rehab if he couldn't.

Today was Monday. His mother should already be gone, but she'd insisted on seeing him home to Great Aunt Lily's. How many hours until she left for the airport?

The aide remained blissfully silent, as if she, too, was exhausted by the incessant chatter. "Is that her car?" the aide asked.

Jared ducked his head to see through the automatic doors. He didn't recognize the car, a rental, but he recognized the driver. "Yes, ma'am," he replied.

The aide pressed the handicap button to open the doors and a blast of cold wind met them. Even wrapped inside the parka Jared had purchased before the trip, he shivered. The thin fleece pants he wore didn't provide much protection against the cold, but he'd been advised to stick with loose fitting pants.

The aide opened the car door for him, helped him out of the wheelchair and handed him his crutches. "Butt first," she told him, "then swing your legs in, like the OT taught you."

Which was harder than he'd anticipated. Eyes closed, holding his breath, Jared ducked his head and backed into the car. He paused to catch his breath as he landed on the seat, then tucked his legs in.

The aide handed him his crutches once more and wished him "good luck." Her smile and the glance she gave his mother spoke more loudly than her words did.

Jared was grateful, and he continued to remind himself of that fact. He was alive, even if he was hampered somewhat. As his mother pulled away, he bowed his head. "Thanks for all you've done for me, Mama."

"I can't get over it," she said. "I nearly lost my baby boy. When I got that phone call…"

And every time she said that he cringed. He cut her off before she reminded him he'd been an inch from death, whether it was the truth or not. "I'm okay, Mama. Let's look ahead. I'll be good as new in no time. But right now, I'm real tired. Do you mind if I rest for a bit?"

"Of course not. Oh, Jared…"

Except he wasn't tired. He was antsy to get on with his life, but he had eight weeks of physical therapy ahead of him and at least another month after that before they'd clear him to travel back to Louisiana. Plenty of time to assess Great Aunt Lily's house. "You never did tell me," he said, hoping he didn't regret opening another conversation. "What's the house like? Did you meet any ghosts, like Aunt Melinda advertised?"

His mother pursed her lips. Closed them. Refused to speak. Now, that was interesting.

"Mama?"

"Tell you the truth, I haven't been inside yet. Your brother flew in yesterday to install everything you need for your recovery, a raised toilet seat, a bathtub seat..." She stared straight ahead in a deliberate attempt to avoid meeting his eye.

"I thought you were staying at the house."

"It's the perfect layout for your recovery," she went on, avoiding a response. "Everything you need is on the main level. You should be able to amble around just fine. And I can continue to come on the weekends to help. I'd stay longer, but I have to get back to work, you know."

"No need to spend your money on more plane tickets, I can manage. Where have you been staying?" he asked.

"One of those hotel suites. It has a fully-stocked kitchenette."

Jared straightened in his seat as she rounded a corner and hissed as streaks of pain shot through his groin and down his leg in spite of his meds. "Do you believe Aunt Melinda's stories?" he asked. "That the house is haunted?"

"Are you okay?" she asked.

"The house," he said through clenched teeth.

"I'm not comfortable staying in strange places." She nodded her head to convince herself, another avoidance of the question, which said 'yes' to him.

"And yet you have no problem with me moving right in." Another check in the plus column. If she was afraid to stay there, she might leave him alone.

"Well, it makes sense, don't you think? With you living there for the next two months, you should know what needs to be taken care of. Then you can work with the real estate agent to sell the place." She glanced at him. "Oh, baby, if you aren't ready to be on your own, I can try to get a leave of absence until you can come home."

Jared grimaced. He'd had people hovering over him for three weeks, taking his temperature and his blood pressure, asking if he needed anything to the point of distraction. "I'll be fine, Mama. You don't have to go to the trouble or the expense to take care of me. Even on the weekends. I have the app they gave me at the hospital to monitor my post-op progress, and I know how to dial 911 if I run into trouble." She didn't need to know he'd added 'aggravated by maternal attention' to his 'how do you feel?' word cloud in the app.

"Maybe Troy can stay with you for a while. Since he's already here."

Bills and jobs played in his head. With Jared out of circulation for a while, Troy would have his hands full keeping up with their contracting business, to pay the insurance premiums that would fund Jared's rehabilitation. To make happy customers who would keep coming back and refer new business. "Can't spare him," Jared said.

He glanced out the windows, at the dark, skeletal trees and snow-dusted lawns. The architecture here was different, no antebellum houses or plantations. Lots of one-level ranch houses and two-story cape cods, all of them with garages instead of the carports he was accustomed to seeing.

His mother steered the car into a driveway beside a bungalow that featured an enclosed porch across the front of the house. Summer screens had been replaced by storm windows. This was his Great Aunt Lily's house? In his experience, older people who lived alone couldn't always care for their property the way they should, but this house looked to be in good repair and the yard was neatly kept. "You haven't been inside?" he asked again.

"No, I gave the keys to Troy so he could get things set up for you." She turned off the ignition, but made no move to get out of the car. She wrung her hands and stared at the house.

"You do believe what Aunt Melinda told you," he guessed.

"She stayed here one summer, you know."

"No, I didn't know. The two of you have been very quiet about my great aunt." Granted, it might not be unusual not to know relatives from Grandma's generation, but there seemed to be more to the story. "Who does she think is haunting it?"

"She said she never actually saw a ghost." His mother got out and walked around the car to open his door. "Your Great Aunt Lily taught Aunt Melinda to sew. That's a good thing, right? She was a good person. That's what we need to remember."

Another news flash. Not that he kept up on all the family business from Nebraska, where Aunt Melinda lived, but generally something like that, something the family did to help each other, would have been mentioned. Aunt Melinda was a tailor. If Great Aunt Lily taught her, wouldn't that be a significant detail to brag about?

Jared pivoted his butt in the seat so he faced the door, closed his eyes and held his breath while he bent his legs enough to get out of the car. The snow had melted off the sidewalks and the cement driveway, no shiny layer of ice to trip him up.

His mother handed him his crutches and led him up the front walk, to the porch steps.

"One at a time," she said. "Hold onto the railing."

"I know how to do the steps," he barked. They'd told him in rehab not to bear weight on his left leg. Each step made him grind his teeth against the pain. He hated being so weak.

His mother reached in front of him and opened the porch door.

What time was her flight?

Inside the porch, the door to the house opened and Troy looked him over. "You look rough," he said.

Jared scowled at his brother. "Then you can imagine how I feel."

"Troy, honey, can't you stay with him a week or two?" his mother asked.

"Can't spare him," Jared said again, meeting Troy's gaze.

"Sorry, Mama," Troy said. "He's right. Besides, who wants to sit with this bear while he's recovering? You know how surly he gets. He's gonna be just fine. Aren't you, Jared?"

"Just fine," Jared repeated, searching the room beyond his brother for a place to sit.

"Reclining hip chair, with arms," Troy told him, stepping aside. "Like Mama said you'd need. And you got handles on the raised toilet seats to help you get up and down."

Jared nodded. Grateful, he reminded himself. "Any sign of the ghost?"

"Jared!" his mother scolded him.

Troy chuckled. "No ghost. At least not that I've seen. Then again, it might prefer to come out at night. I've only been here a couple of hours. Need me to stay tonight and hold your hand?"

Jared flipped Troy off as he eased into the chair.

"Jared! That's not polite," his mother said. She glanced around the room as if she expected something to pop out at her.

"Sorry, Mama," Jared said, with a sideways glance at Troy to let him know he wasn't sorry. "What time is your flight home?"

"Oh, dear, we do have to leave soon," she said. "And I have to return the rental, too. Now listen. I sent food over with Troy, and the woman Aunt Melinda was dealing with said the neighbor lady is very nice. If you need more groceries, you ask her to help you. You hear me?" She dug through her purse. "Here. The woman Aunt Melinda met is named Amy Benson, and this is her number. And the neighbor is Helen Brown. This is her number." She held the piece of paper out of Jared's reach. "I hate leaving you here all by yourself, so far from home and family."

"I've been living on my own for a long time," Jared reminded her.

"We could call Ivette to come stay with him," Troy said, a wicked smile on his face.

Jared gave him a chilling glare, tempted to give him another one-finger salute despite his mother's presence. "I haven't dated Ivette in months, and it's for damn sure she won't want to come up here in the winter to help me put my socks and shoes on."

"But she loves you," Troy said with a mocking tone.

"Hard enough to get rid of her the first time."

His mother ignored that part of the conversation. "Your assistive devices, isn't that what they call them? Are right here on the davenport. Sock puller, grabber stick, dressing stick, shower sponge." She sighed. "How are you going to get along all alone?"

"Visiting nurses, in-home rehab until I can bear weight again. I'll be fine, Mama." Grateful. "Your flight?" Jared asked again.

"We've got an hour before we need to go," Troy said, still smirking.

Jared returned the smirk that told his brother it was Troy's turn to deal with their mother's fretting. "I'll tell you what, give me a tour of the place. Let me get the lay of the land before you go."

"Truth? Everything looks good on the surface," Troy told him. "Great Aunt Whoever seems to have been on top of things. Oh, and I found some tools in the basement, antique looking chisels and gouges. I brought them up in case you needed something to do with your hands, and I bought a box of wood blocks for you."

"Lily," his mother said. "Great Aunt Lily."

"The one nobody wants to talk about," Jared added. He nodded to Troy. "Thanks."

Troy nodded in return.

Jared pushed up and balanced on his crutches. "Show me around."

"Small rooms," Troy said, taking the lead. "Living room, dining room, a pocket door you can close to the kitchen if you choose. Enough room for what you need, not too big to worry about cleaning." He let Jared pass into the kitchen. "Alcove with laundry facilities," he pointed out.

A hallway ran parallel to the living room and dining room, one bedroom on either end, and a bathroom in the middle.

"The bedroom in the back looks like it was used for storage. It's full of boxes. The one in the front looks like the one Aunt Lily used," Troy told him. "That's the one I set up for you. There are two more bedrooms upstairs, along with a full bath with a shower. Converted attic." Jared had thought the door between the dining room and the hallway was a closet, but when Troy opened it, steps led to the second floor. "Basement door in the kitchen."

"I'll have to take your word on the attic and the basement. No skeletons waiting to pop out of the closets?" Jared shot his brother another glare. Troy wasn't beyond a practical joke.

Troy held up his arms. "Hey, I need you at work. I have no intention of impeding your recovery."

The bed or the chair? Jared balanced between the two rooms, trying to decide if he wanted to pass out or distract himself from the pain.

The hip chair won out. "Television?" he asked, as he settled in.

Troy turned on the small set in the corner of the room. "No cable, but you get the local stations."

"Internet?"

"You'll have to use your phone."

His mother was wringing her hands again. "I just don't feel right leaving you like this. I should stay at least another night."

She glanced around the room, and he knew she was thinking about the haunted thing again. "Go home, Mama. You've done so much already. And you also know I can handle anything that comes my way."

She checked her watch. "We really should go, then. We have to return the rental car, you know."

"So you've said," Jared sent Troy silent signals to get her moving.

"Your meds are on the end table, there," she pointed out. "Do you know what time to take your next pain pill?"

"Yes, Mama."

"And the other meds. You know when to take them?"

Jared cocked his head toward the door. "Yes, Mama."

"And you'll call me? Every night?"

Jared closed his eyes and rubbed his forehead. "If you need me to."

She hesitated, Troy's hand on her arm. "Then I guess we should be going. I made some casseroles for you to heat up. You put those in the freezer, didn't you, Troy? The instructions are taped to the top."

"Yes, Mama. He'll be fine," Troy said, escorting her to the front porch. "And he knows how to call for pizza if he runs out of food."

She broke free, knelt in front of Jared's chair and gave him another hug, then patted his cheek. "I love you, baby."

"I love you too, Mama."

"Are you sure…"

"He'll be fine, Mama," Troy said, re-establishing his hold on her. He glanced over his shoulder. "Anything else you need, Jared?"

Jared shook his head. "Nothing that doesn't require a lot of down time. Sorry to leave you in a lurch like this."

"At least it's off season," he said with a smile, one foot out the door. "You know one of us will be on the next plane if you need us."

"Just need me some peace and quiet so I can finish mending," Jared said.

His mother poked her head in one last time. "And you'll let me know if you encounter any ghosts?"

Jared bit his lip. "You'll be the first to know, right after me."

As the door shut behind them, Jared picked up his phone and opened PHM, the hospital app. Timers were set to remind him when to take his meds. Might as well do his check-in before he drifted off into a drug induced haze.

He clicked on Breathing Exercises. Did you use your Incentive Spirometer? Yeah, yeah. Whatever. Jared clicked 'Yes.' Daily Walking. The app outlined his expectations, including his weight-bearing limitations, and then asked, Did you complete your therapy today? Yes. He clicked on Physical Therapy. Did you complete your exercises today? He flexed his ankles and clicked Yes. He clicked on How are you feeling? This was the part he hated most. Those stupid smiley faces that were supposed to measure his pain on the scale of 1-10. Forget the numbers, he looked at the faces. What did he imagine his face looked like? Jared winced and clicked on 8. That last PT session before he'd left rehab had been a bitch, even with pain meds. When he hit submit, the app took him to his word cloud. All the symptoms that went with his condition, his meds and his state of mind. He grinned at the one he'd added, the 'aggravated by maternal attention' one. Okay, he was going to miss his mama. He browsed the rest of the words in the cloud and selected 'Tired,' 'Supported,' 'Incision Pain,' and stopped cold on 'Morning Erection.'

"What the hell?" he muttered.

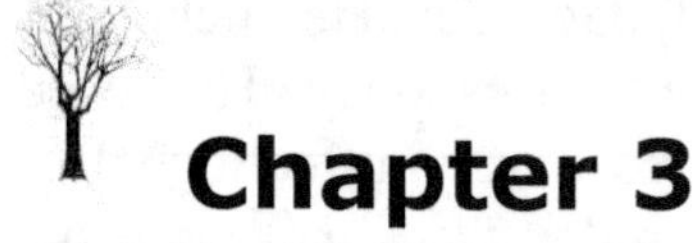

Chapter 3

SIOBHAN MCCORMICK STROLLED TO her office from the hospital cafeteria. The food at St. Francis was better than she'd been used to. The launch of Patient Health Monitoring—PHM, the new post-operative monitoring app—had provided her the perfect job opportunity, as if fate had stepped in to encourage her decision to stay in Edgarville. Her new position still had some nursing responsibilities, but now she'd have regular hours and she didn't have to wear scrubs.

What if the app didn't catch on the way they expected it to? Not all patients who were offered the app signed up. What if this job, instead of being a step toward the future, failed? Siobhan shrugged. Wouldn't be the first time she'd made a bad decision. She liked to think she was done with those.

"Excuse me." A nurse stopped Siobhan outside the administrative offices. She looked young, 19 or 20. Siobhan checked the nurse's name tag. Ariel, LPN.

"How can I help you?" Siobhan asked.

The nurse stared at Siobhan's name tag with a familiar look of confusion.

"It's pronounced Shi-VAWN," Siobhan said. When she'd first been capped, she'd put "Shevy" on her nametag, her brother Kevin's nickname for her, but that garnered as many questions as her given name, so she'd reverted to the name she was born with.

The nurse exhaled a relieved sigh. "Thank you. I wasn't sure how to pronounce it, and they told me to bring these to you. I'm Ariel." She pointed to her own name tag before she handed Siobhan a stack of charts. "These are the patients who were discharged today who are using the new app." She cleared her throat. "Do you know if they'll be training more people to do monitoring? I'd heard it would be a regular program, like visiting nurses."

"That's my understanding, as PHM usage becomes more widespread." Siobhan took the charts in one hand. "Are you planning to be an RN?" she asked.

"Would I need that to apply for the program?"

"I'm afraid so." Siobhan held up her free hand and counted off her qualifications with her fingers. "I worked the ER, surgery, recovery, telemetry, critical care." She ran out of fingers. "In other words, I have a lot of experience in a lot of areas."

Ariel blushed and lowered her eyes. "It sounds like an interesting job."

Siobhan smiled at her. "It is fun to be on the cutting edge of technology. With this information, we can spot issues that might result in readmissions before they become problems, but I miss the smile on someone's face when they're able to gain a step in their recovery. The terminal patient who wants a hand to hold."

"The bitter old ladies who call you stupid and useless?" Ariel said with a laugh. "If you ever need any help." She shrugged. "I might learn something, huh?"

"I'll let you know. Thanks for the charts."

Ariel beamed. Young. Fresh. Optimistic. Siobhan had no doubt the young nurse felt like she was saving the world, one patient at a time.

Siobhan set the new charts on her desk and checked on her virtual patients, reviewing incision photos, making sure their word clouds were within appropriate positive/negative parameters, checking for patient-added notes or other triggers that required attention. Most patients didn't bother sending anything more than the app requested. Answer the questions and be done with it. One patient left daily notes, thinking she had to chart the way doctors did. She detailed her food and water intake every day and the amount of time she spent doing her physical therapy. Siobhan sent push notifications acknowledging "nice job."

And then there was this new guy. Released from rehab this morning. He'd been keeping up with his progress, but Siobhan hadn't done much with his file while he was in-patient. He'd added words to his "how are you feeling?" cloud like "aggravated by maternal attention" and "planning a jailbreak." He was good for a laugh, but she pictured a grown man-child who spent his days playing computer games. From the way he used his app, Siobhan judged Jared Pierce to be a grumpy patient. Some people didn't do well with slowing the pace of their lives while they recovered. While she checked his progress, she found he'd written a note.

"Who the hell cares if I have an erection when I wake up? Isn't that kind of personal? You going to send a nurse over to jump into bed with me?"

Siobhan laughed out loud and checked his word cloud. He'd highlighted that yes, he indeed had an early morning erection. She sent a push notification through the app. "An erection indicates good circulation and is normal and healthy. If you didn't have one, that would be an indication of a problem."

She continued through her charts and checked off three more of her patients when another note appeared from Jared Pierce.

"You mean there's a real person on the other end of this godforsaken app?"

She laughed again. Definitely a grumpy patient. Behind the technology, her job was to monitor and report. Despite years of coddling patients face to face, in her present position, Siobhan was instructed to point them to their primary physicians with any questions. Personal involvement with the PHM users would diminish her ability to do the rest of her job, and yet she couldn't ignore his question.

"I will be monitoring your recovery and coordinating with your primary physician." As soon as she sent the message, the cell phone dedicated to PHM rang.

The number was the one associated with Jared Pierce. "And who, exactly, are you?" His voice was deep, with a hint of New Orleans.

Credit him for reading through the app screens and finding the number. "My name is Siobhan. I'll be checking your progress a couple of times each day," she told him in her most officious voice.

His voice reverberated like a cat's purr. "So I can call you anytime I start feeling lonesome?"

"I'm a transition care nurse. If you have any critical health issues, you should call 911," she said. "Do you have family helping you during your recovery?"

"Well, now, they've just left me on my own for the remainder of my recuperation period. I feel at a disadvantage, Miss Siobhan. You sound like a pretty girl, and you already know more about me than I know about you. That hardly seems fair."

She'd dealt with flirty patients before, but it concerned her that he had no help for the next couple of weeks. "Are you in contact with your primary physician? Do you need help coordinating home health care?"

"It's all good. I'm fine by myself. I've got a visiting nurse coming tomorrow, and at-home physical therapy, but I am a long way from home and they tell me I can't travel until I'm healed. Sure would be nice to have a friendly voice say hello every now and then."

This was new territory for her. Was it unprofessional to call the app patients? Her contact was supposed to be minimal. "But you do have family?"

"Well, sure…"

"Is there anything else I can help you with today?" she asked.

He chuckled softly, a sound that woke up long dormant nerve endings. "I do apologize for my crass note, Miss Siobhan. Knee jerk reaction. Not too many people ask me if I wake up with morning wood, and I guess I responded poorly."

"It's a standard question," she said, growing uncomfortably warm. She was a nurse, used to clinical discussions about bodily functions. So why was she flustered talking to Mr. Pierce? She cleared her throat. "The words in the cloud are typical symptoms that accompany both your condition and your medications and are designed to ferret out any potential issues that might hamper your recovery."

"Understood. But I do like the sound of your voice, ma'am. I believe it might go a long way toward speeding my recovery."

"This is a business phone, Mr. Pierce, and you may not always get an answer."

"Fair enough. I thank you for your time, ma'am, and I do believe my meds are kicking in so I'll say goodbye and close my eyes now. It's been a pleasure."

"Have a good day." Siobhan disconnected the call with a cheek splitting grin. Pain meds did funny things to patients. Jared Pierce would likely wake from his nap and forget all about their phone call, but she wouldn't. The timbre in his voice was well suited to a phone sex operator, although the way he drawled his folksy Southern "ma'ams" was a bit much. Still, it was good of him to apologize for requesting a nurse in his bed.

Which reminded her how long it had been since "this nurse" had shared a bed with a man. A man with a voice like that could certainly cure whatever ailed her. Siobhan laughed at her wayward thoughts. People rarely aligned with how you pictured them from a phone call. Even if she considered giving in to her wildest fantasies, Jared wasn't physically able to have sex for at least another month, and more likely longer than that. She'd do well to picture him with greasy hair, warts and a foot shorter than she was.

And he'd distracted her from the rest of her job.

The other app patients would have to wait. She had a meeting to get to, charts to validate, and quality control reports to prepare.

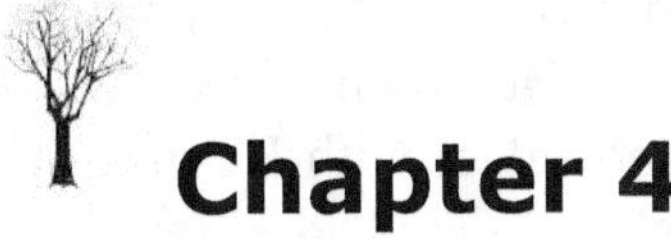

Chapter 4

NOW THAT SHE WORKED regular hours, Siobhan had too much time on her hands. Her brother, Kevin, had advised her to get a life, but she didn't know how, which is how she ended up driving to his apartment once again. He'd given her a key when she'd asked him for a place to escape from their mother, when she'd first arrived in town, and she'd used it regularly.

She found a visitor parking spot and walked up to Kevin's apartment, slotting the key into his door. When she walked inside, she found Kevin, bare-chested, pressing his fiancée, Amy, against the wall and unbuttoning Amy's blouse.

"Oh, for heaven's sake." Siobhan turned away as Amy pulled her blouse closed. "I guess I should have knocked."

Kevin bowed his head, then turned to face her. He held out his palm. "Key."

Siobhan's heart stopped. She glanced at Amy, resentment building. Her idiot brother was whipped. Figured he'd want to marry the first woman he had sex with. Siobhan handed over his key.

Kevin rubbed his hand across his face. He took Siobhan by the shoulders. "I need my space. Me and Amy. I get that you don't know what to do with yourself, but you need to find something. Volunteer somewhere. Walk dogs at the shelter. Serve meals to the homeless."

Amy slipped into the bedroom. Siobhan shook free of Kevin's grasp, her eyes burning. She lowered her voice. "You've only known her a couple of weeks, Kev. You're thinking with your dick."

Kevin's eyes narrowed. "Aren't you the one who told me to go after her? That I was miserable without her?"

"Well, yeah, but I figured you'd get it out of your system. Sex can muddle your brain if you're not used to it."

He cringed. "It isn't about the sex. I love Amy. She's going to be my wife, and you have to respect that. Respect her. Respect me."

He blew out a slow breath. "I'm glad you're home, Siobhan, really, but you can't keep barging in. You have your own place now."

Her own place? More like Amy's place even after Amy had moved in with Kevin. Siobhan stared at her brother, worried that if she blinked the tears would find their way out. Insulting his girlfriend—okay, fiancée—wasn't the right way to recapture the camaraderie she and Kevin had shared in high school. She nodded. "I'm sorry. It's just that you've always represented home to me."

He rubbed his face with his hand again. "Listen. Get some dinner, and then if you want company later, we can stop by and catch a movie on Netflix or something."

Siobhan shook her head. She knew she should be happy for Kevin, be thankful to Amy for subletting her apartment to Siobhan. And Amy was a nice girl. But Amy had taken Siobhan's brother from her, her partner in crime, her best friend. She waved a hand in the direction of the bedroom. "Carry on with whatever it is you were about to do. I can take care of myself." She always had.

Kevin smirked. "You kinda killed the mood."

"Yeah, well, I'm sure you can remedy that." She gave him one last smile. "I really am sorry. I'm still trying to figure out where I belong in the grand scheme of things, you know? I guess I've forgotten how family is supposed to act."

Kevin tugged Siobhan's arm. "Hey. You okay?"

No, she wanted to tell him. She was lost and afraid in a place that should have been familiar. "I'll figure it out. And don't worry about stopping over. I can watch Netflix by myself."

Siobhan walked to her car, grabbed the steering wheel and banged her forehead on it. Coming home wasn't going the way she expected it would, but she'd made the move, and she never did anything halfway. That was the problem. She'd moved to Virginia after high school throwing all her eggs into the Carter basket. Then when he'd dumped her, she'd thrown herself into nursing school and the jobs she'd had to take to pay tuition. Then she'd thrown herself into her job. She hadn't opened her eyes and noticed what was missing until Kevin's life was in danger.

Family. A life.

Kevin had told her she needed to get a life, and she'd come home to find one. Her mistake, this time, was expecting Kevin to help her. She'd pictured the two of them taking on the world, the way they had when they were in high school. She'd come home to fill the gaps in her life. Instead, those gaps seemed to be growing wider.

Siobhan started her car and backed out of her parking spot when her phone rang. Amy. Siobhan took a deep breath and smiled, hoping it would come through her voice. "Hi, Amy. Look I'm sorry…"

"That's not why I'm calling," she said. "I heard they're going to sell Mrs. Sumner's house and I wanted to let you know. Mrs. Sumner's niece told me they plan to flip it. I understand another family member is living there temporarily. If you made an offer before they listed the house, you might get a good price. The family seemed anxious to get rid of it since none of them live in Illinois. If you want, I could take you over. Introduce you."

Amy was so darn likeable. Siobhan needed to make the effort to be friends, at least until Kevin came to his senses. Then she remembered what they'd told her about Mrs. Sumner's house. "Didn't you guys say the place was haunted?" Which probably translated to an underground spring or an overactive imagination. When Amy and Kevin had stayed there, they'd been hiding out from a serial killer.

"It was," she said, "but I'm pretty sure the ghosts are laid to rest now, like maybe it was Mr. Sumner keeping Mrs. Sumner company until she passed. Last time we were there, I didn't sense anything otherworldly."

Amy believed in ghosts. She had Kevin wrapped up all sorts of ways if she was able to get him to believe, too.

"I'll let you know," Siobhan said. It was the best she could do tonight.

~ ~ ~

Jared woke with a start, opened his eyes and glanced around. *Where was he?* He looked for the call button to summon a nurse. Surely he was due for another round of pain meds. Or someone had to check his vital signs.

Oh, wait. He wasn't in the hospital anymore, wasn't in rehab. He was in Great Aunt Lily's house. The alarm on his phone was letting him know it was time for another pain pill. His meds were on the table beside him along with his ever-present cup of water. Check that. An empty cup.

He eased his legs off the recliner footrest and straightened them to the floor. Pain shot across his pelvis, centering on the incision on his hip. Definitely time for his meds. He pushed against the arms on the chair until he was upright, balanced on one leg and grabbed his crutches. Two steps toward the kitchen his circulation returned and the pain eased. Two more steps and he went back for the empty cup he'd forgotten beside his chair. Man, this sucked. He'd never take a simple stroll to the kitchen for granted again.

The more he moved, the easier it became. He took the pitcher of water from the refrigerator and refilled his cup, then crutched—ever so slowly—to the living room and his chair. He eased down and breathed a sigh of relief. Mission accomplished, although if he was smart, he would have gone to the bedroom. It was almost midnight. Jared took his pain killer, then pushed to his feet once more with a new goal in mind. Bed.

Getting undressed was out of the question. Too much work, and he wasn't in the mood. One painful step at a time, he walked the short hallway to the front bedroom and rearranged the extra pillows to elevate his feet. He sat on the bed, like he'd been taught in occupational therapy, and scooted over, trying to lift his legs, but the left leg wasn't cooperating. Every attempt to lift it was met with a protest, and yet he was dying to lie down, would give anything for a decent night's sleep. Where was that nurse when you wanted her?

Jared pulled out his phone and stared at it. There was a live person on the other end of his hospital app, a nurse. A nurse with a soft voice that carried a hint of dialect from somewhere he couldn't place. She'd sure made him feel better when he talked to her earlier, but she did say she was only there during business hours. Did she have voicemail?

How pathetic was he that he was willing to call a woman's voicemail to hear her voice—a woman he didn't even know? And yet he couldn't help himself. Blame it on the pain, or on the meds, but right now, he desperately wanted to hear another human voice, and the one that belonged to Nurse Siobhan was a mighty pleasing one.

He inverted one of his crutches and hooked his foot to lift the uncooperative leg onto the pillows at the end of the bed. He collapsed onto his back, exhausted from the effort and held his phone in front of his face to check his call history. No harm in dialing the number, right? She wouldn't answer. She'd never know he called.

He hit redial.

His eyelids grew heavy, the pain meds taking hold.

"Hello?"

Jared's eyes popped open. That wasn't a voicemail greeting. "Miss Siobhan?"

An intake of air, and then a quietly muttered 'omigod' followed. "I forgot to turn my work phone off," she said. "I shouldn't be talking to you." She cleared her throat. "Did you have a question, Mr. Pierce?"

Just the way he remembered, soft, sweet, with a touch of breathiness that caught a man's attention. "Well, you see, I'm not from around here, but this accident has left me stranded. My first night out of a care facility and I'm all alone in unfamiliar surroundings. I hope you don't mind, I was hoping to hear a friendly voice before I settled in for the night. And I do wish you'd call me Jared."

"I don't suppose there's any problem answering the call since you called me," she said as if she meant to reassure herself. "I'll tell my boss I forgot to turn it off…" She heaved a sigh. "You'd think I was fresh out of school. I don't know where my head is. How are you feeling?"

"Worlds better since you answered that phone, ma'am."

"Do you call everyone ma'am?" she asked.

"Where I'm from, it's the polite thing to do." His thoughts weren't very polite at the moment. "And I hear something in your voice that says you aren't from these parts, either," he added. "Where are you from?"

"I'm from right here in Edgarville," she told him. "I've lived away for the last twelve years."

"That's why I can't place your accent," he said. "And I'll bet you lived somewhere south."

"Virginia."

"Tell me, Miss Siobhan. Are you married? Do I have to worry about some burly man chasing me down for calling his wife at all hours of the night?"

"Do you plan to call me at all hours of the night?" she asked in a sultry tone that sent chills over his body.

Jared repositioned himself, grimacing in spite of the pain meds. "You have the most interesting voice," he told her. "And I notice you didn't answer the question."

"No, I'm not married," she said. "But I need to remind you this is a business phone, and I should turn it off."

"Then call me from a not business phone," he said. "Unless you're willing to give me your personal number. Then I could coax you over here to nurse me through the night. It's my first night on my own, after all."

"You have a visiting nurse coming to see you tomorrow?" she asked.

He yawned. "Yes ma'am. Do you do home visits?"

She chuckled, a deep throaty sound. "No, I don't."

"Now that's just a shame. With a voice like that, I bet you are one beautiful woman."

"You should never make assumptions based on the sound of someone's voice," she said. "I might weigh 300 pounds with stringy hair and leprosy."

"I'll tell you what," he said. "As long as you talk to me in that sweet voice, I don't think I care." He closed his eyes and the world drifted farther away.

"No wife waiting for you in New Orleans?" she asked.

Jared grinned. "Good guess. A bit north of there, actually. No wife." He yawned. "Funny how fate steps in and changes the course of your life, isn't it? One icy road and I get to spend the next three months experiencing winter in Illinois."

"Fate," Siobhan repeated.

"Yeah. Like the voice of an angel who answered the phone when she wasn't supposed to." He grinned again. "Maybe one day I'll get to meet that angel. What do you say?"

"Maybe one day."

"I'm afraid I can't hold up my end of the conversation much longer," Jared told her. "I hate to be rude and fall asleep talking to you, but those drugs are doing me in. I do appreciate your kindness, Miss Siobhan. You have my phone number and I hope you'll call me from your personal phone so you don't get into trouble for using the business phone. It sure is nice to hear a friendly voice." He chuckled. "Did I say that already?"

"I think you did."

"Good night, Miss Siobhan. And thanks for answering the phone." He was pretty sure he'd already told her that, too. Jared ended the call and set his phone beside him on the bed. As tired as he was, he couldn't stop grinning.

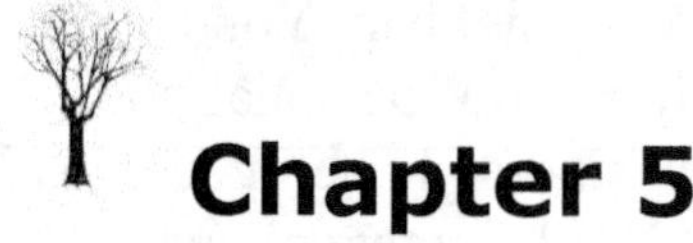

Chapter 5

AS SHE TOOK A seat at her desk, Siobhan powered up the hospital phone, and with it came memories of Jared Pierce, the man with the phone sex voice. He'd sounded lonely and vulnerable—an injured man in a foreign environment. She could relate. She might have come "home," but she felt horribly out of place.

With a cell phone in each hand, Siobhan considered the wisdom of what she'd done last night. Until Jared had called, she'd been tossing and turning, disconnected from the one member of her family she'd always been closest to. When Jared had suggested she program his number into her personal phone, she'd done it without hesitation. Whether due to the late hour or her state of mind at the time, in the stark light of day, she reconsidered her decision.

And what would her bosses say when they reviewed the phone bill and saw she'd used the work phone after hours? Would they even review the phone bill, or was she borrowing trouble? Even if they did, it had been an incoming call. An honest mistake. She'd forgotten to turn the phone off, a mistake she wouldn't repeat. She couldn't afford to jeopardize her new job. St. Francis was the only hospital within a fifty-mile radius.

Jared Pierce had nursing care. A visiting nurse would attend to him today. He didn't require Siobhan's attention and there was no real reason for her to call him. Patients flirted with nurses all the time, so why did this one get under her skin?

Calling him would be unprofessional. Her finger hovered over his name on her personal phone, ready to hit the delete key. In her other hand, the hospital phone buzzed an incoming notification. Another patient posting incision photos. She'd worry about what to do with Jared Pierce later. Siobhan tossed her personal phone into her purse, closed her desk drawer and pulled up PHM on her computer for a bigger screen to look at.

The incision was bright red and oozing between the staples. She immediately sent a push notification to the patient that they should contact their physician, and followed up with a memo to the physician on record.

What other surprises were in store for her today?

She went through the PHM patients who had updated their progress, most of whom were doing well. The journal lady had documented her dinner last night and breakfast this morning along with a "feeling good" comment.

With her first pass of the day completed, Siobhan threw herself into her quality assurance projects, and when her desk phone interrupted her, she was surprised to see it was lunchtime.

"Siobhan McCormick," she answered.

"What are you doing for lunch?" Kevin asked.

A friendly voice. Relief coursed through her that he wasn't angry with her for barging in on him yet again. He'd made sure she couldn't barge in anymore. "What did you have in mind?"

"Well, I know how dedicated you are, so I thought I could meet you at the hospital and join you for lunch in the cafeteria."

Because he knew her well enough to know that's where she'd eat. Kevin was still her brother, after all. "What time?" she asked.

"I'm in the hospital lobby right now. I took a chance and stopped. What time can you get away?"

Siobhan closed the file she'd been working on and locked her computer screen. "Now's good. I'll see you in the lobby in a minute."

She gathered her purse and left the administrative offices. When she walked off the elevator at the lobby, she spotted her brother, standing beside a woman with mousy brown hair. Amy. Siobhan's enthusiasm waned and she exhaled a sigh.

Kevin was facing Amy, wearing a smile Siobhan had never seen before. He held Amy's hand, touched her face and gave her a sweet kiss, one that made Siobhan's heart ache. Kevin looked happy, not like a dog chasing a bitch in heat. Could he have fallen in love so quickly?

He turned his head and smiled when he saw Siobhan, a different kind of smile. More strained as if he wanted to make sure she knew it was important to him that she and Amy get along. Siobhan wanted that, too, if Amy was everything he said she was, but this was new to Siobhan. Her brother had always been there for her, for the rest of the family. He'd made it clear Amy was more important now.

Kevin let go of Amy's hand and hugged Siobhan. "Glad you could take the time."

"Anything for family," she said. Siobhan gave Amy a hug. "Nice to see you. He didn't tell me you'd be joining us."

"I think he was afraid you wouldn't come if he told you," Amy said.

Amy was straightforward. Siobhan liked that about her. If Siobhan wanted to rebuild her relationship with her brother, she had to take the high road. "Of course I'd come. It's always nice to see you, Amy."

Kevin narrowed his eyes, silently asking her what she was up to. Yep, she could still read his every expression, which is why she had to accept that the expression on his face a moment ago, when he'd looked at Amy, was genuine, and not a by-product of lust.

Siobhan waved her arm toward the cafeteria. They filled their trays and regrouped at a table.

"So what brings you here?" Siobhan asked.

"Wondering if you'd given any thought to what Amy called you about yesterday," Kevin said. "About Mrs. Sumner's house. It's a nice place, nice neighborhood, in good condition. Mrs. Sumner's niece had mentioned they were motivated to sell. If you wanted to take a look at it, you should probably move quickly, before they list it."

Siobhan held up a hand. "I appreciate the inside track, but I don't even know if my job is going to last six months, much less if I want to stay in Edgarville." She poked at her fruit salad, not meeting his eye. "Things aren't quite the way I expected."

"Couldn't hurt to look?" Kevin shrugged. "Would be nice to know you're staying, putting down roots. And as for the job, you've never done anything halfway. Even if this app thing doesn't catch on, I'm sure the hospital could always use an experienced nurse."

All good points, but something in her gut was telling her to run away. She'd abandoned her family after high school, and that made her an outsider now. She didn't belong in Edgarville anymore.

"Okay, let's talk about something else then," he said. "Are you coming to Ma's for dinner Friday night? And next week is Thanksgiving…"

Friday night dinners, the tradition that had started after Siobhan left home. She'd been to two since she'd been back, and both times the table had been quiet, as if no one knew what to say. This lunch wasn't going well, either. Why did she feel so out of step? "I'll check with Ma about dinner," she said.

Kevin scowled and Amy took his hand, giving him the old "it's okay" look. Except it wasn't okay. Yes, this was hard for Siobhan, but she'd moved home, and she intended to make this work. Even if the PHM app didn't catch on, Kevin was right. She could get a nursing job. And she was determined to find a way to fit in with her family after all these years.

"Tell you what," she said. "Why don't you find out if I can tour that house? Can't hurt, right?"

Amy bounced in her seat. "Great. I'll call Melinda tonight and ask her to set something up."

~ ~ ~

When the visiting nurse removed the dressing on Jared's incision, she snapped a photo for the hospital app before she put on the new bandage. She prattled on about her kids and Thanksgiving preparations and as much as he was glad to see another live person, his head ached from listening to her squeaky voice.

She took his vitals and pronounced him healthy. The entire visit lasted half an hour, and then she left for her next appointment.

Jared checked the PHM app on his phone and went through his checklist. When he got to his word cloud, he stopped to wonder if the nurses in rehab had checked his crotch on their morning rounds. If they had, they'd been discreet about it. He certainly hoped they'd been entertained. He attributed his morning wood today to a late night conversation with a sultry voice on the other end of the telephone. Would she call tonight? She'd been flustered last night, obviously worried she'd overstepped professional boundaries, and he certainly didn't want to get her in trouble with her boss. While he considered a carefully worded message to invite her to call, his phone rang. Aunt Melinda.

"You find any ghosts yet?" she asked.

Not unless you counted being haunted by a nurse's seductive voice. "No unexplained moaning or rattling of chains," he replied.

"I'm glad you had somewhere to go after the accident. How are you feeling?"

"It's all good," he told her. "I'm doing fine."

"Listen, that woman I met who was a friend of Aunt Lily's, she mentioned a friend of hers might be interested in buying the house. Would you mind if they stopped by?"

"I'm not going anywhere for a while," he said. "I hope they don't mind me sitting around while they take their tour."

"I'm sure they wouldn't mind. I'll let them know. I didn't want to catch you unaware. Your mother says the house looks to be in good repair, and she said Troy thinks so, too." She paused. "And you haven't found anything else we should be aware of?"

He'd already told her he hadn't met any ghosts, the real reason they'd sent Jared and not Troy. "No, ma'am," he said. "But I'll keep my eyes open for anything that needs fixing."

"I know you will. We'll be in touch."

She disconnected and Jared's phone returned to PHM. Oh yeah, the note to Nurse Siobhan. Was it worth the effort? He nodded. He definitely wanted to hear her voice one more time. He'd guess patients propositioned her all the time. He wouldn't trouble her, but she'd seemed to enjoy their conversations as much as he did.

"Visiting nurse sent the photo today," he typed. "Hoping the other nurse calls tonight to discuss acceptable forms of distraction."

Distraction. Troy had left the woodcarving tools on the dining room table, but Jared didn't trust himself to stay alert long enough. The meds still left him fuzzy headed, and he wasn't sure he could concentrate. He'd try tomorrow.

He sure hoped Siobhan would call. He tried to write his note clearly enough to reinforce his request, vague enough that anyone else who might see it shouldn't understand she was the other nurse. Then again, subtlety wasn't his strong suit.

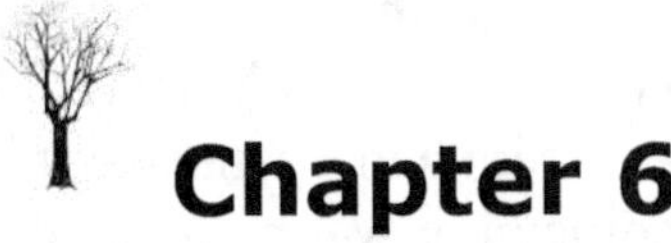

Chapter 6

SIOBHAN DROVE STRAIGHT TO Amy's apartment after work—she had a hard time thinking of it as her place with Amy's possessions surrounding her. The lease was due to lapse in January. She'd have to find a new place to live soon.

If she bought Mrs. Sumner's house, Siobhan would have a place to call her own.

Could she afford to buy a house? Once she did, she'd be committed to Edgarville for the foreseeable future.

As she dumped her purse on the dining room table—minus the dedicated app phone, which was locked in her drawer at work—her personal cell phone rang with her sister's ring tone. "Hey, Kathleen," she answered.

"Hey, Shevy. Do you have dinner plans tonight?"

Suddenly the whole family was worried about her eating habits? "I'm kind of tired. Still getting used to the new job and all."

"How about if I stop over then. I could use some sister time, now that I have a sister again."

Like a sucker punch to the gut, Siobhan bent over, reached for a chair and sat. Their youngest sister, Mary, had been dead a year and a half, but the reminders still caught her unprepared. Siobhan hadn't seen Mary since Mary was eight years old, hadn't made it home for the funeral. Denial was easier at a distance, but now that she'd come home, grief stared her in the face.

"Shev?" Kathleen asked.

"Yeah, sure," she said. "I guess you know where Amy's apartment is?"

"You mean your apartment, don't you?"

"I guess." Except her things were in storage after her move to Illinois. Nothing in Amy's apartment made it feel like it was hers.

"How about I pick up Chinese on my way over?"

"That'd be great." Siobhan hung up and surveyed the apartment. Was she the only one who was uncomfortable around Amy? She couldn't wait to hear what Kathleen thought.

Siobhan changed into pajama pants and a long-sleeved t-shirt, something warm and comforting. The weather in Virginia would still be mild, unlike the approaching winter that reared its head in Illinois. She stood by the patio door, folded her arms and stared across the parking lot at the dark clouds passing over the moon.

What was the Thomas Wolfe poem? You can't go home again, and yet, here she was. But what choice did she have? It was long past time to reconnect with her family. Her cousin, Mick, had been killed by the same person who murdered Mary, and she'd nearly lost Kevin, as well.

Siobhan took a deep breath.

On the reasons-to-stay side of things, she liked her new job. It was interesting—even more interesting since Jared Pierce had called her. Should she call him back? The note he'd written today indicated he was hoping for a phone call. The truth of the matter was she wanted to call him. He'd said he was far from home, stranded during his recovery period. She felt as lost as he must feel. Alone in a strange place. Edgarville hadn't been home for a long time.

Her cell phone was still on the dining room table. She had his number…

A knock on the door changed her mind. Kathleen. With a blush of shame, Siobhan understood why Kevin was angry with her. She hadn't bothered to knock when she went to his place, she'd let herself in, because that's what family did. At least that's what she told herself. And now Kathleen, her sister, her family, was knocking on her door. "It's called common courtesy," she reminded herself. Siobhan opened the door and Kathleen wrapped her in a hug.

This was what she'd missed. Genuine affection.

"I'm glad you came over," Siobhan told her sister.

"I'm sorry to barge in on you," Kathleen said.

Siobhan laughed. Maybe the barging in was a girl thing, but Kathleen had hardly barged. "Anytime," she said. And meant it.

"Listen, I really need to talk to someone, but you have to promise not to say anything to Ma or to Kevin. Not even Liam."

Their younger brother, Liam, had seemed wrapped up in his own life when she'd seen him at Friday night dinners. Aside from soccer games and being scouted by the professional soccer teams, he'd said very little. She doubted he cared about Kathleen's secret.

Siobhan took Kathleen's hand and pulled her into the apartment. "I swear on a stack of Bibles," she said. The same oath she used to give Kevin. They walked into the kitchen and Siobhan pulled a couple of plates from the cupboard, took a couple of forks from the drawer.

"I've been seeing this guy," Kathleen went on.

Girl talk. Siobhan had been so focused on school, and then on work, for the past twelve years, that she hadn't stopped to develop any real friendships. That her sister trusted her with secrets brought a tear to her eye. "So what's he like?" she asked.

They loaded their plates and carried them into the living room. Kathleen told her how she was sure Ma and Kevin would disapprove of her choice of boyfriend, and for that reason, she was reserving details, but according to Kathleen, she was going to burst if she didn't talk to someone about him. She wanted to invite him to Friday night dinner so everyone could meet him, but she was worried about Kevin's reaction. Apparently, Kevin had met him briefly, so withholding whatever Kevin wouldn't like wasn't an option.

Kathleen didn't give Siobhan a chance to respond. Like she'd said, it seemed more that she needed to tell someone than she needed advice, because suddenly she changed the subject.

"Whatever happened with you and Carter?" Kathleen asked. "I remember Da saying the most awful things about what he was going to do to him for knocking up his little girl, but you were never pregnant, were you?"

Siobhan laughed. "No, but I didn't make any secrets about the fact I was sleeping with him, which probably made things worse for you and Mary. Da figured I must have been knocked up in order to move away with Carter's family. Why else would I leave home? Even after I told him I left because I couldn't stand to live here anymore, refused to be a punching bag." Memories flooded back from her rebellious teen years. "It's a wonder he didn't kill me then and there."

"I never heard the whole story. How did you end up in Virginia?"

"Carter's dad got transferred, so they were moving. Carter said something about wishing I could move with them and his mother felt sorry for me—she knew what our home life was like—and told me I was welcome to come with." Siobhan laughed. "She probably should have discussed it with Carter first. He never expected them to agree, never intended to marry me. He suffered from teenage lust. I tried to turn him into my savior." She leaned forward and rested her forearms on her thighs. "No one can save you but you. We are all in control of our own destiny."

Kathleen stared at her a moment and nodded. "Da locked himself in his study for a week after you left. He tried to stay sober for a while."

"Yeah, alcohol's a tough task-master," Siobhan said. It was the closest she could get to excusing her father's behavior.

"And you never got married? Never found someone else?" Kathleen asked.

Regret washed over Siobhan, cold and chilling. "I didn't have much time to develop any real relationships."

"But you have time now, don't you?"

Unbidden, Jared Pierce came to mind, he of the deep, rumbly, phone sex voice. Who better to share secrets with than your sister? "I met a man recently," she said.

Kathleen split a grin, gathered her curly red hair into her hand and flipped it to her back. "And?"

Siobhan understood family secrets. "It's complicated. He's a patient, and that's always a bad idea. They tend to see nurses as gods, the ones who've saved their lives. And then when reality takes over, they're disillusioned. Not to mention dating a patient is unprofessional."

"But this guy's different, isn't he?" Kathleen straightened. "And I thought you weren't interacting directly with patients."

"That's true for the most part, but I do have some interaction." How could she tell Kathleen she'd never met Jared in person? "We don't know each other very well, yet," she hedged.

"But you'd like to."

Siobhan smiled. "Yeah."

"And now you have the time. You aren't getting any younger."

Siobhan punched Kathleen's shoulder. "Thanks. I'm not exactly ancient, little sister. And same goes. You can't tell anyone. I have no idea where this is going, if it goes anywhere at all."

Kathleen drew a cross over her heart. "Swear on a stack of Bibles."

"Okay, so now you need to tell me what you think of Amy."

Kathleen's expression grew guarded. Pay dirt. "Kevin loves her." She pursed her lips. "When he first met her, he described her as interesting. I was kind of happy for him, because he hasn't had a quote-unquote real girlfriend for ages. But there is definitely something different about her. I suppose he told you Amy heard Mary's voice from the grave."

The twinge of grief and regret tweaked Siobhan once more. "I didn't quite understand that whole story, but yeah."

"I think its Amy's eyes. The color is so unusual, like amber, or whiskey. When she looks at you, it's like she can see through you."

"What do you know about the color of whiskey?" Siobhan asked, assuming the voice of authority.

Kathleen held up her hands. "Not me," she said, knowing full well where Siobhan was going with that question. "But, as you know, I've *seen* whiskey often enough."

Siobhan nodded. "Kevin does seem to love her."

"She's nice," Kathleen said.

Siobhan laughed. "Yeah. She's nice. I guess we'll have to get used to her, huh?"

And then Kathleen laughed. "Yeah."

At times like this, all the lost years fell away. When Kathleen checked her watch close to eight o'clock and gasped about losing track of the time, Siobhan's heart tugged. Kathleen had to return to her campus apartment for a date with her secret boyfriend, a date she expected to last all night.

When was the last time Siobhan had had an all-night date? The closest she'd come in recent history was a midnight phone call from a man she didn't know.

A man with a voice that gave her a thrill thinking about it.

The apartment was too quiet after Kathleen left. Siobhan's cell phone seemed to beckon her from the dining room table. What would it hurt to check up on a patient? She gravitated toward the table and picked up her phone.

Her heartbeat raced as her finger hovered over the call button. "Short," she told herself. "Greasy hair. I'm only concerned about his health." She pressed the button.

"Hallo?" he drawled when he answered.

Her breath left her. She didn't know what to say.

Jared hesitated a moment and then asked, "Siobhan?"

"Yes."

"Hey baby. Where y'at?"

She shook her head. "Excuse me?"

He chuckled and her nipples took notice. No man's voice should sound so sinful. "Let me rephrase. How are you?"

"Which was exactly what I called to ask you," she said, assuming her nurse role. She could be professional.

"Uh-uh-uh," he said. "You're calling me from your personal phone. I don't want to talk about my injuries or look at those damn smiley faces to determine how I feel tonight. You aren't my nurse right now. I just want to listen to your voice a while. Talk to me, angel."

"How was your day?" she asked. "I can imagine how hard it must be not to be able to get out and about."

"Well, the visiting nurse stopped in, and tomorrow the physical therapist stops over."

She nodded. "Then you should be a little less lonely."

"I wouldn't say that, but I'm guessing you know what I mean. That's why you called me, isn't it Siobhan?"

Who was the patient and who was the nurse? "I shouldn't have called," she said.

"But you did."

She closed her eyes and drew a deep breath. "I know what it feels like to be new in town without a friend."

"Then let's be friends." The way he drawled melted her through to the core. "How old are you, Siobhan?"

"I'll be thirty on my next birthday."

"Which must be soon since you're already hedging and it's a milestone birthday. When's your birthday?"

"January 29. How about you?" She didn't need to ask, she could check his chart when she got to her office, but that felt dishonest.

"Well, I turned 30 on October 1, so I guess that makes me a year older than you by the calendar."

"And what do you do when you're home, in Louisiana?"

The tone of his voice changed. Was he offended she'd asked about his employment? "I do carpentry work with my brother."

"Must be nice to spend your days with family."

"Some days."

Siobhan laughed. She understood that all too well.

"You have family?" he asked.

"Two sisters, two brothers," she told him, and then amended her statement. "One sister, two brothers. My youngest sister died last year." Mick crossed her mind. He wasn't a sibling, but he'd been raised with them. One more loss in the time she'd been gone.

"I'd give you a hug if I was in a room with you, but over the phone, I can only tell you how truly sorry I am."

Twice today she'd thought of Mary. Siobhan swallowed back the grief she hadn't been able to share with the rest of her family. "What about you? Only the one brother?" she asked.

"Yes, ma'am."

"I thought we'd agreed to dispense with the ma'am."

"Creature of habit," he said. "That's the way we talk in Louisiana." He pronounced it in that lazy way where they dropped the extra vowels. "Something you don't like about being called ma'am?"

"Makes me feel matronly," she said.

He chuckled. "Tell me what you look like? Really?"

Dangerous territory. Siobhan swallowed hard. Jared's phone sex voice made it too easy to get drawn in. "Already told you," she said. "Three hundred pounds and leprosy."

"They wouldn't let you be a nurse if you had leprosy."

"Ah, but I don't have much patient contact," she reminded him. "Hence the app and the phone conversations."

He chuckled. "I'll continue to doubt that part of your story if it's all the same to you."

What did he look like? She had a photo of his incision. A visiting nurse had seen him in his underwear—or less—and snapped a shot of a muscled leg. Siobhan was suddenly envious of that nurse.

"Tell me what you're wearing?" he coaxed, his voice sending tingles to all her girl parts.

Not going there. "Sweat pants and a t-shirt," she told him.

"Now that's not how you play the game."

"And you're not supposed to be thinking about sex for another month," she told him.

He laughed then. "Who said anything about sex? And that's only if you have sex with another person. I do believe I can take care of business on my own in the meantime, can't I, Nurse Siobhan?"

"I'm not having phone sex with you," she clarified.

"And I'm not asking you to," he replied, "although your voice does evoke all kinds of interesting images. None of them three hundred pounds and leprous."

"I suppose if I were to ask you what you looked like, you'd probably tell me you were tall, dark and handsome. Isn't that the cliché?"

"That's what the ladies tell me," he drawled.

"So you're a ladies' man."

"No, ma'am—and yes, I called you ma'am on purpose to be respectful. A man doesn't necessarily want women fawning over him. He appreciates an intelligent mind, good conversation. Someone he can sit on the porch with and hold hands while the sun sets. A woman who won't mind when his hair goes gray and he develops crows' feet around his eyes. And if her cooking gives him a little paunch, well, she appreciates that about him."

Wow. That was the most inviting image she'd had in years. Could he be for real? "That sounds so nice," she said before she realized she'd spoken.

"There's a porch at my house," he told her. "It's cold out, but I expect we could sit out there. If you wanted to stop over."

She laughed. "You're a terrible flirt."

"And as serious as the grave," he replied.

She'd never been so tempted, but did she dare? "Another time," she said.

"I see. You don't date injured men. But I won't always be injured."

"I don't know you," she told him.

"Or maybe you don't appreciate scars. I have several, you know. Occupational hazard."

"I can't say they bother me. On some men, they're a sign you've fought and won a battle."

"A romantic," he said.

Siobhan smiled. "No, a realist. How did you get injured?"

"Car crash."

"And you survived. You won the battle."

"Do you mind if I call you next time?" he asked. "After all, we're friends now, right? Until the day you trust me enough to sit on my porch with me."

Siobhan smiled. "Yes, you can call me." As she said it, her heart pounded. She must be crazy, letting down her guard with a man she hardly knew. Then again, this was one of the reasons she didn't have a life. If she wanted a life, she had to take a chance.

"I'll call you tomorrow? Around this same time?"

Kevin had a life. Kathleen had a life. Everyone had a life but her. Siobhan rolled her eyes. How sad was her life that talking on the phone to a stranger was her best option? If he kept talking to her in that deep, honeyed voice, she was pretty sure she'd take him up on that visit to the porch.

A man was not the criteria for having a life. Still, she found herself answering "Okay."

"Good night, angel."

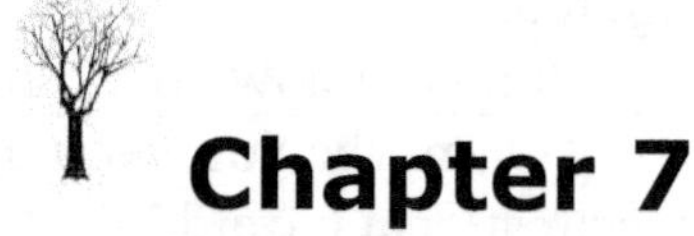

Chapter 7

JARED FOLLOWED HIS VISITING physical therapist, Anton, to the door. A chilly wind passed through his sweat pants, making him wish for his jeans. The temperature had risen above freezing, and the snow that had dusted the grass was gone, but winter was most definitely on its way.

"See you Thursday," Anton told him with a wave over the shoulder as he skipped down the front steps.

Before Jared closed the door, the neighbor lady crossed the driveway toward him. "Yoo-hoo," she called out, waving to Jared.

He had a bad feeling he was about to be mothered. She looked to be about the same age as his mother, maybe a little older, but he managed a smile and a wave with one crutch. "Ma'am," he greeted her. His aching muscles cried out for an ice pack, but he could last another five minutes.

She walked into the front porch. "I'm Helen Brown," she said. "I live next door." She rubbed her arms and hunched as if to ward off the cold.

"Jared Pierce, ma'am. It's nice to know you." He stepped aside. "You're welcome to come in out of the cold, although I'm not good company just now."

Mrs. Brown stepped inside and glanced around. "Your mother told me you'd be staying here for a couple of months. If there's anything I can do for you…"

His mother, bless her meddling heart. "Much obliged, ma'am. I'm getting along fine, and she did give me your number." His good leg ached and the exertion of his physical therapy made him feel as if he'd run a marathon. "Hope you don't mind, but I need to sit."

"Of course," she said. "I won't bother you, but I wanted to introduce myself. Do you have something for dinner? Is there anything I can get for you? Your great aunt and I were good friends. She was a good neighbor."

"I do appreciate your thoughtfulness," Jared said, as the throbbing in his leg grew more demanding. "I think I'm good on food for the moment." He eased into his chair. "Would you get me an ice pack from the freezer, since you're here?"

"Of course." She passed through the dining room and stopped when she noticed the tools and the blocks of wood on the table. "Your mother told me you're a finish work carpenter. Do you do wood carving, too?"

"It's a hobby," he said. "I'm not up to it quite yet."

She nodded and continued to the kitchen, returning a moment later with his ice. "I hope you know you're welcome to stop over any time. I'm sure you'd have lots to talk about with my husband, David, and as I said, we're more than happy to offer you any assistance."

Jared eased the ice beside his hip and closed his eyes. "Once I'm feeling more myself, I promise to stop over."

"I'll let you rest. Feel free to call if there's anything you need."

"Much obliged," he said.

Mrs. Brown let herself out, but he was too tiredre to lock the door behind her. The weakness bothered him more than the pain. He shouldn't be so exhausted after an hour's worth of stretching.

With a fortifying breath, he tapped out one of his pain pills and gulped it down with his ever-present cup of water. Jared leaned his head back and waited for the pill to kick in, blessing his mama for trying to take care of him without hovering over him.

Speaking of which, he owed her a phone call.

As the throbbing subsided, Jared pointed the remote at the television. The weather forecast predicted freezing rain. He'd seen his share of that and wasn't in a hurry to be out in it again any time soon. He clicked the television off and picked up his phone.

"I met Mrs. Brown," he told his mother when she answered. "I do appreciate all you are still doing for me, Mama, but I'm fine. I really am."

"She seems like a nice woman," his mother said. "Someone needs to know you're alive in that house. Speaking of alive, any dead visitors?"

Jared's face shifted into a smile. "Did you set mouse traps before you left?"

"You have mice in the house?"

He chuckled. "That was a joke. No mice, no ghosts. Sorry to disappoint you."

"I suppose that's a good thing," she said. "How are you feeling? Are you in a lot of pain still?"

"I just finished physical therapy. Torture, but I always feel better later."

"Jared, honey, I don't know what to do about Thanksgiving," she said. "You know your daddy and Troy and I volunteered to serve at the shelter, otherwise we'd all come up there. I hate the thought of you all by yourself. Maybe that nice Mrs. Brown will invite you over."

He was fading, losing track of the conversation. "I'll be fine, Mama. Don't you worry. Right now my pain pills are kicking in. Can I talk to you later?"

"Of course. You'll call me if there's anything you need?"

"I surely will." He didn't have to. She'd make provisions whether he called or not, as evidenced by Mrs. Brown, next door.

~ ~ ~

Siobhan did one last check of her PHM patients. Jared had left a note indicating he was stiff and hurting after physical therapy. She sent him a push notification to ice. The rest of his standard responses lined up with forward progress. Should she ask him how he was feeling when he called her tonight?

Would he call her tonight?

He'd said he didn't want her to be his nurse after hours. He wanted her to be his friend. Friends asked how their friends were feeling didn't they?

She was overthinking his condition way too much. If he wanted to share his progress, or lack thereof, with her, she'd let him bring it up. In the meantime, Kevin and Amy were picking her up after work to show Siobhan the house they thought she should buy, and then they were all going out to dinner.

Whoopee.

As long as she was home in time for the phone call from Jared.

If he called.

Funny how much she was looking forward to the phone call. She felt a sort of kinship with Jared. The Society of Displaced Souls.

He was marooned by his injuries and she was struggling to fit into a world she'd left behind.

Siobhan turned off the work cell phone and tucked it into her drawer, pulled out her purse and rose to put on her coat.

"Amy's a very nice woman," she told herself.

"I'm sure she is," a male voice answered behind her. "And who is Amy?"

Heat rose to Siobhan's face. One of the hospital vice presidents, Duncan Phelps, had his coat on and was behind her. "My future sister-in-law," she replied.

"So why do you sound like you're trying to convince yourself?" he asked.

"More like remind myself," she said. "I'm still getting to know her, but she's been very helpful since I got to town."

"You keep telling yourself that," he teased. "Can I walk you out?"

Siobhan took a second look at him. The question sounded oddly like a date. Dr. Phelps was at least ten years older than she was. His light brown hair was marked by distinguished silver patches at his temples. Hazel eyes widened with his affable smile. He was fit, probably a runner if she had to guess. She knew he was divorced, and she hadn't heard any rumors of him hitting on nurses. Then again, as a new hire, the rumor mill might not have shared that part.

And why was she overanalyzing a friendly gesture? She did need to get a life. "Suit yourself." She forced a friendly smile.

He waved her ahead and pushed the elevator button. "How are things going with PHM? We seem to be having excellent results heading off readmissions."

Did he know about her after-hours phone call? They couldn't have gotten a phone bill yet, could they? And she could explain… Siobhan took a breath. Overthinking again. "I'm still finding my way, but the app does seem to be a great tool in that patients will more readily answer a question on PHM that they might find uncomfortable in person."

"Your reports have been great, thanks, and I did see the report on the patient you sent to her physician." The elevator doors opened and again he waved her ahead. "Her doctor followed up with me to thank us for the intervention. I should have shared that with you sooner. Without the app, she was one that might have ended up back in the hospital."

"Don't you worry about census counts?" Siobhan asked. "Not that I want people to be readmitted but it does seem to be a double-edged sword."

"We're more worried about the patient experience here, and the cost of readmissions is actually higher." He glanced at the numbers counting down to the garage level. "Are you settling in okay? No relocation problems?"

"Everything's been great. That sister-in-law I mentioned sublet her place to me, and she also has the inside scoop on a house I'm looking at tonight."

"Amy, the very nice woman?"

Siobhan winced. "Yes." She shot Dr. Phelps a smile. "She really is."

"You're still trying to convince yourself."

Siobhan laughed. "It's simple." Again she was met by Dr. Phelps's raised eyebrows. "No one's good enough for my brother, you know?"

"I get it."

The elevator counted off the last floor with a "ding." The doors opened and they stepped into the parking garage.

"If you find yourself looking for company, I'd love to buy you a drink. Welcome you to Edgarville."

"Back to Edgarville," she told him, before she realized he actually was asking her out. "Are you allowed to fraternize with the hired help?" she asked.

"No strings," he told her. "Just a friendly glass of wine. Cup of coffee, if you'd rather."

Siobhan took another look. Dr. Phelps was a nice looking man, and he seemed friendly enough.

She was here to get a life, and a handsome doctor was asking her out. Siobhan straightened her back and gave Dr. Phelps another smile. "That would be nice."

"What are you doing now?" he asked.

She closed her eyes. Was this her one shot? Didn't matter. Life would provide her opportunities. "Going to look at that house with my brother and his fiancée."

"Another time, then." Dr. Phelps took her hand between his for a moment, smiled, and walked off to his car.

Another plus for St. Francis. Many of the doctors who'd asked her out in Virginia were married or residents who were always on call. The ones she accepted rarely made it to the date. Dr. Phelps had done his time and now worked regular hours. Had his marriage been a casualty of a doctor's schedule? Or was there more to his story? She'd pump Ariel for information tomorrow.

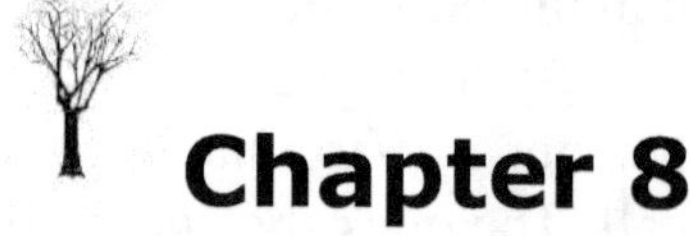 **Chapter 8**

SIOBHAN OPENED THE APARTMENT door to Kevin who was looking at the ground. He met her eyes and smiled. "See, this is how it's done. You knock, the person inside opens the door."

One more degree of separation. "Very funny." She got it. His home was not her home, and that also meant Amy's apartment wasn't quite her home, either, even if she was paying the bills now.

Siobhan slipped on her coat, grabbed her purse, and locked the door behind them. She smiled at Amy. "Thanks again for the inside track on the house. I hope it looks as nice as it sounds."

"It's an old bungalow," Kevin said. "Needs updating, but it seems to be in good shape."

"And obviously, you don't have to feel obligated if you don't like it," Amy added. "But it's worth a look. Mrs. Sumner's family might give you a good deal if they can avoid realtors."

They all climbed into Kevin's car, Siobhan in the back seat. *Where the third wheel goes.*

Amy's a nice woman.

"Working on any good stories?" Siobhan asked Kevin. He'd told her the Associated Press had run a couple of his articles, so she knew he was a good reporter.

"They've still got me on the holiday pieces," he said, "with Thanksgiving next week, and then Christmas coming up."

Amy turned toward him and squeezed his shoulder, a proud smile on her face. "They're testing a syndicated column," she added. "Life through the eyes of Kevin McCormick. He's done a couple of fun pieces on wedding planning from the groom's point of view that have done well."

Wedding planning? "Didn't you want to be a beat writer?" Siobhan asked. "Hard hitting news?"

He met her gaze in the rearview mirror. "I did, until I had to live on the edge for a week. That wasn't so much fun. Found out I'm squeamish when it comes to dealing with murderers. Can't imagine what it would be like to live in a big city where that's a headline every day."

He steered into a driveway and came to a stop outside the bungalow they'd told her about, white siding and in the twilight, the trim looked black. An enclosed porch ran across the front of the house.

A man wants someone he can sit on the porch with and hold hands while the sun sets.

Jared's words rang in her ears, and she felt an affinity toward the house. "This is the place?" she asked.

"The rooms are small," Amy said. "But it's a nice size for a woman on her own."

Siobhan gave her a tight smile. "I like the porch."

"Does he know we're coming?" Kevin asked.

"Yes, Melinda said she'd called him and it wouldn't be a problem," Amy replied.

"Him?" Siobhan asked.

"Mrs. Sumner's nephew is staying here for a while. They sent him to make sure everything was in good shape."

The driveway passed the north side of the house, ending at a one-car garage in the back yard, although in the waning daylight she couldn't be certain of the size.

The three of them got out of Kevin's car and Siobhan's chest tightened. Renewed concerns about job security and being able to make a mortgage payment circled her like vultures.

She was still a nurse. Even if PHM failed, she could find another nursing job. She'd always landed on her feet in the past, no reason to think she wouldn't do so again.

Would Duncan Phelps like sitting on the porch holding hands?

Where had that thought come from?

"You coming?" Kevin asked, halfway up the front steps.

Siobhan hurried to catch up, pulling her coat tight against the November wind. Heating bills flashed before her eyes. And air conditioning. Did a house of this vintage have air conditioning? She glanced around the yard, at the gangly branches of mature trees whose leaves would shade the house in the summer.

Amy opened the porch door, walked inside and knocked on the front door of the house.

"Are you supposed to walk into the porch?" Siobhan whispered to Kevin. "Is that a thing? Or should we knock on the porch door?"

He laughed. "Funny, coming from you." He gave her a squeeze across her shoulders. "It's okay to walk into the porch."

They waited a couple of minutes without anyone answering the door.

"Maybe he isn't home," Siobhan said, more relieved than disappointed.

"Melinda said he might need an extra minute to get to the door," Amy said. "He's recovering from an accident."

"What kind of accident?" Siobhan asked.

"Rolled his car on the Interstate coming into town," Amy said. "He isn't used to driving in snow and ice."

Car accident? Front porch… It couldn't be.

"I'm suddenly getting cold feet," Siobhan said.

"We're already here," Kevin said. "We can wait another minute."

The porch light flipped on and the lock turned. Siobhan grabbed hold of Kevin's arm. "Don't mention my name, okay? Whatever you do."

He turned to look at her, but before he could ask why, a man opened the front door.

The man on crutches was taller than Kevin by a couple of inches, taller than Siobhan by at least three more. He wore sweat pants and a Harry Connick, Jr. t-shirt clinging to broad shoulders.

"You must be Amy Benson," he said in the deep drawl Siobhan recognized. He glanced from Siobhan to Amy, waiting for one of them to confirm.

Amy stepped inside and shook his hand. "And you must be Jared?"

"That's right. Jared Pierce. A pleasure."

Siobhan's heart pounded and spots clouded her vision. *She would not pass out.*

"This is my fiancé, Kevin, and his sister…"

"How do you do?" Kevin interrupted, one eye on Siobhan indicating he could still read her. And he could see something was off.

Meanwhile, Siobhan continued to stare at Jared. He looked as if he hadn't shaved in a week, his dark brown beard rough against tanned cheeks. A bruise highlighted one side of his face, and a fresh scar puckered over his right eye. His chocolate brown hair was tousled, as if he'd used his fingers as a comb, and deep brown eyes sparkled with his smile.

He leaned on his crutches and waved them in. "Pardon the mess. I'm not cleared to do housework yet, but Mrs. Brown, next door, assures me she knows someone who'll come in to help out."

The hip chair in the corner, the assistive devices on the couch. Siobhan struggled to breathe. She was face to face with Jared Pierce. What would he do if he knew who she was? What should she do? She'd crossed over professional lines, unfamiliar territory.

"Please don't feel you have to show us around," Amy told him. "Kevin and I are familiar with the house. We can show his sister around." She shot Kevin a meaningful glance, silently asking him what the secrecy was about.

"That'd be fine," Jared drawled. He looked at Siobhan. "I didn't get your name?"

"Shevy," she told him. "Shevy McCormick."

"That's an unusual name. Is Shevy short for something?"

"Melinda said you'd been in an accident," Kevin said. "We don't want to take up too much of your time, and you'd probably be more comfortable sitting."

Jared narrowed his eyes. "Thank you." He limped with his crutches to the hip chair and eased down, hands firmly gripping the arms, his face screwed up with the effort.

"We won't take long," Amy told him, as she started the tour. "Living room," she pointed out, advancing a couple of steps. "Adjoining dining room. Kitchen behind, with a pocket door if you want to close it off."

Siobhan hardly paid attention, walking like an automaton, nodding her head every time Amy stopped speaking. When they walked upstairs, Amy announced the bathroom at the top, then turned and said in a whisper, "What's going on?"

Kevin raised an eyebrow at Siobhan to indicate he seconded the question.

"He's one of my app patients," Siobhan whispered. "And he knows my name. I'd rather he didn't know my face, too. Not yet."

Amy shrugged.

When they reached the upstairs bedroom at the front of the house, Kevin and Amy lingered an extra moment and clasped hands. And what was that about? Siobhan was too preoccupied to ask.

Kevin continued the tour downstairs, through the kitchen and into the basement.

"This is different," Kevin said. "Everything's been pushed against the wall."

"Maybe he started doing an inventory or something," Amy said. "Everything else looks pretty much the same as when Mrs. Sumner was alive."

"You're probably right." He smiled and kissed her, then kissed her again and drew her into his arms.

"Don't need to see this," Siobhan said, shielding her eyes. Especially not when the man who owned the seductive phone-sex voice was so near. "Can we go now?"

"What do you think of the house?" Amy asked.

What did she think? She'd hardly paid attention. And then she remembered the detail they'd overlooked. "And your so-called ghosts?" she asked. "That would drive the price down, wouldn't it?"

Amy looked to Kevin. "I don't feel anything, do you?" she asked.

"Not like I did when we stayed here before," Kevin replied.

Amy smiled at Siobhan. "The ghosts weren't frightening. A little unnerving, maybe."

"The séance was scary," Kevin said.

Siobhan backed to the staircase. "Séance?" Amy could have hypnotized Kevin and called it a séance. Is that how she'd snagged him?

"Yeah, *those* ghosts were scary," Amy said. "That's not something I'd want to do again anytime soon." She looked at Siobhan. "I believe the ghosts who were here are at rest now."

"I'm so glad," Siobhan said sarcastically. "Can we go now?"

Kevin huffed. "It's not a bad house."

"No," Siobhan agreed, following him up the stairs. "It's not a bad house. At least what I've seen." Which wasn't much considering the shock of seeing Jared Pierce, live and in person, had pretty much robbed her of all her senses.

In the kitchen, Siobhan cast a glance at the living room, the chair where Jared sat. He filled the room with his presence. His head was tilted back, his eyes closed. If she wanted to give the house a real assessment, she should see her living space. "I want to see the bedroom again," she said quietly. "And the bathroom on this floor."

She hesitated in the dining room. He had blocks of wood and tools on the table. A hobby to occupy his time? She tiptoed to the hallway, peeked into the bathroom with a tub, no shower. Jared had told them to pardon the mess, but everything was neat. Not even toothpaste in the sink. The toilet had a raised seat, one of his precautions until his injuries had healed. She took the dozen steps toward the front of the house, to the bedroom.

The queen-sized bed was unmade. Siobhan pictured Jared laying there, dark hair against the pillow, talking to her on the phone.

"It's very comfortable," Jared said, his deep voice waking up all her nerve endings. He stood behind her, braced on his crutches. "I'm sure you'd enjoy living here."

Siobhan turned to look at him, hoping he didn't notice the flush that burned her cheeks. "It seems like a nice house."

"I'm especially fond of the front porch," he said, the hint of a smile curling his lips.

She swallowed hard. "I imagine there's good air flow when you put screens on in the summer. Does the house have air conditioning?"

"Tell you the truth, I haven't checked. No need for it this time of year. But the thermostat's right here." He shifted, flipped on the hallway light and hunched to look at the thermostat. "Doesn't appear so, but you could check out back to be sure, for the unit."

"That's okay," she said, her voice breathless. What was wrong with her? She cleared her throat and forced a smile. "We'll be on our way." She stuck out her hand. "Thanks for letting us look around."

Jared closed his hands around hers, similar to the way Dr. Phelps had, and held her gaze. "Pleasure to meet you, ma'am. Let me know if you need another look around. It'll be at least another month before I list the house, and I'll likely be here another month beyond that."

"Thank you. I'll let you know before then. We'll go out the back way so I can have a look at the yard."

"You make yourself right at home, and feel free to stop by anytime. Y'heard?"

He smiled, just when Siobhan didn't think he could be any more attractive. She'd been wrong.

"Right. Got it." She licked her lips, which were suddenly too dry. "Kevin?" Siobhan left the intimacy of the hallway in search of her brother and found Amy and Kevin waiting in the dining room, arms loosely draped around each other. They had to stop being so touchy-feely. It made her fingers itch, especially with Jared Pierce oozing testosterone a few feet away. "Back door," she said. "I want to see the yard."

They passed through the kitchen, out the door, to a rear porch that was large enough for two lawn chairs, down the steps and into the yard. More mature trees stood guard, two of them conjoined by a branch across the middle.

"Look at that," Amy said. "I've never seen trees grow together like that."

"It's called inosculation," Kevin told her. "I did an article at the arboretum a year or so ago and learned all kinds of fun tree facts."

"I wonder how it grew that way." Amy reached up and laid a hand on the branch that connected the two trunks. The color drained from her face and she looked as if she would vomit.

"Are you okay?" Siobhan asked.

Amy pulled away from the tree and bent over. She glanced around, searching for something.

"What is it?" Siobhan asked Kevin.

"Do you have a piece of paper and a pen?" Kevin asked.

Siobhan rummaged through her purse and handed a scrap to her brother. He pulled a pen from his pocket and handed both to Amy.

Amy took the pen and began writing. When she was done, she took a cleansing breath, her color returning.

"What was that about?" Siobhan asked. "Please tell me you're not pregnant already."

Kevin shoved Siobhan's arm. "You need to stop."

"What?" She asked innocently and took a step back. "That happens when people have sex, you know."

Kevin ignored her. "An epitaph?" he asked Amy.

Amy nodded. "I think the tree marks a grave."

~ ~ ~

Jared watched her through the kitchen window. "Shevy" had hair the color of his mother's copper cookware, and blue-green eyes that had taken him in. All of him. No, he hadn't missed that fact, and with that coloring and those freckles, he'd bank money Shevy was short for Siobhan, his angel-voiced nurse. Well, well, well. Not quite 300 pounds, like she'd said, and definitely not leprous. No, this Siobhan, if he was right, was very pretty, with curves in all the right places.

She'd looked stunned when he'd introduced himself, as if she hadn't known he was the one living in this house, as if Amy Benson hadn't told her. What kept her from introducing herself proper?

Her brother glanced at the house and waved. Jared waved back, and Kevin walked up the steps. Jared opened the door for him and Kevin pointed to one of the trees in the yard. "Do you know anything about that tree?"

Jared squinted. With only the moon and the porch light to illuminate the yard, he couldn't tell what Kevin meant. "You mean the two together? They look like oak trees."

"They're conjoined. Inosculated," Kevin said.

"Sometimes trees grow that way."

"No family stories?" Kevin asked.

"Not sure what you're looking for," Jared said. "I didn't know my great aunt before she died. Didn't know I had a great aunt, to be truthful. If there's any family story connected with the tree, I'm afraid I don't know it. Is it important?"

Kevin grinned. "No. Thanks for letting us intrude. Hope your recovery goes smoothly." He shook Jared's hand.

"You tell Siobhan I'll talk to her later, y'heard?"

Kevin gave him a crooked smile and saluted. "I'll tell her." He trotted down the steps and joined the women, but he didn't appear to say anything to Siobhan.

They disappeared down the driveway and Jared locked the back door. He checked the clock on the stove. His phone date with Nurse Siobhan wasn't for another two hours. Tonight promised to be an interesting conversation.

Chapter 9

THE PILLOWS STACKED ON the dining room chair raised the height enough for Jared to eat at the table like a normal person. The dishes, however, would have to wait. He wasn't in the mood to stand at the sink, balancing on one foot and his crutches. The physical therapist had tried partial weight-bearing on his left side, had Jared touch his foot to the ground instead of hovering over the invisible egg they'd had him envision in rehab, and Jared had nearly passed out. Not ready yet. He'd have to get that name from Mrs. Brown for a housekeeper to come in once a week.

Jared picked up one of the wood shapers Troy had found and studied it. The set of tools had handcrafted handles darkened with age. He dumped the bag of wood blocks and sorted them by size. Enough to carve a set of chess pieces.

He carried one of the chisels and a block to his chair. As he carved the piece, his hands worked from muscle memory until he forgot about the pain in his leg, the throbbing in the scar over his eye.

When the alarm on his phone rang, he had to blink to place the sound.

His call with Siobhan.

Jared set down the piece he'd been working, a rook, took a sip of water, cleared his throat and placed his call, counting the rings. Siobhan's voicemail picked up. Was she avoiding him? The recorded voice definitely matched "Shevy," the woman who'd walked through the house. He left her a message at the beep. "Maybe I do look more like the Frankenstein monster than I thought, but I do hope you'll call me back anyway."

Siobhan had been the one good thing that had happened to him since he'd been stranded in Illinois. This recuperation period was going to be mighty long without her friendly voice, not to mention the lovely Irish complexion and sweet figure that went with it.

He pushed to his feet once more, retrieved the remaining tools on the dining room table and stuck them in his pocket, then crutched to his chair. As he resumed his seat, his phone rang with Celine Dion's *My Angel*—the lovely Siobhan McCormick. He knew her last name now.

"Hallo?" he answered.

"Sorry I missed your call."

"I was worried I might have scared you off, with all my bruises and bandages and scars."

She was silent a moment.

"Siobhan?"

"I'm here," she said softly.

"Why didn't you tell me who you were?"

"How did you know it was me?"

He smiled. "Well, I didn't place your voice at first, but that silly nickname you used was close enough to put it all together. If you'd have said your name was Miss McCormick, then I might have had a more difficult time."

"Shevy's not a silly nickname. My brother calls me that. And my sister."

"Sounds more like a car, and darlin', you don't look anything like a car." He closed his eyes to picture her. No, she was sweet, and pretty and he sensed a bit of feisty that would make things interesting, but best not to go there right now, not while his bones were still mending. "So you want to buy my house?"

"I haven't decided if I'm ready to take that step."

"I noticed you lingering in the bedroom. Something about that appeal to you?" Nope, nothing wrong with his circulation. Jared shook his head, frustrated once more by his injuries.

"The closet didn't look very big," she said, but her voice held a teasing tone.

"I'll make it bigger for you," he said.

She laughed. "I think I already told you I'm not having phone sex with you."

He opened his eyes wide, then chuckled. "Well, that one's on you, ma'am. I was actually referring to the closet. I'm a carpenter by trade. What were you referring to?" Not so Frankenstein-ish after all if her mind was going to those places.

"The closet, of course," she replied, that breathy hitch in her voice.

"You want to have sex in the closet?" he asked. *Say yes.*

She giggled. "You're a terrible flirt."

"Tell me what else you liked about the house, because you know I can't have sex for another month, and you're killing me here." He took hold of the rook and rolled it around in his hand.

"My brother says the house used to be haunted. Have you run across any ghosts?"

"No, ma'am. And did you say used to be?"

"His fiancée claims to be something of a ghost whisperer. She says whatever spirits were there are at peace now that Mrs. Sumner has gone to her eternal reward."

"Is that so? And what do you think? Did you meet any ghosts while you were looking around?"

"I don't believe in ghosts. Please don't tell me you do."

He stared at the rook in his hand. "Well, now, that's an interesting subject. Where I'm from, you have to believe. There are plenty of things on this earth we can't account for."

"Most of which can be explained by science," she argued. "And overactive imaginations."

"That may be so, but I'm not one to dismiss things so lightly."

"Dismiss science?" she asked.

"Try to apply things I understand to things I don't. It doesn't always work. Either way, your brother's fiancée appears to have blessed the house as free from spirits, so that shouldn't stand in your way."

"So you're superstitious?" she asked, a healthy note of skepticism in her voice. "Coming from Louisiana, should I assume you believe in voodoo and zombies and magic potions?"

Jared chuckled. "If I practiced voodoo, we wouldn't be talking on the phone, you'd be sitting in this room with me, giving me a pretty face to look at in addition to your angel's voice."

"Laying it on a bit thick, aren't you?"

She sounded insulted. Jared pinched his eyebrows together. "Have I said something to offend you?"

Siobhan sighed. "I'm just tired of the whole ghost thing." She sighed again. "It isn't you, I'm having a hard time adjusting to my brother's fiancée. It happened so fast, under unusual circumstances, and there's something about her…"

"She has very unusual eyes," Jared said. "And you don't believe she can see the dead?"

"Well, that's the thing. The only dead person she claims to have been able to see is my little sister, Mary. But then she says she hears voices. She heard something when she touched the tree in your yard."

Jared cast a glance toward the kitchen. "Is that why your brother came back to ask me about it?"

"Voices inside trees." She sputtered. "Nonsense. Whoever heard of such a thing?"

He'd heard stranger stories in Louisiana, but Siobhan wouldn't want to know those things. Best to steer clear of that for now. "So you don't approve of your brother's choice for a wife."

Another sigh. "Amy's a very nice woman."

A line she'd obviously practiced several times over. "I'm sure she is. Now about that closet…"

Siobhan laughed, which brought a smile to his face.

"There y'are," he said.

"How about the weather," she said. "That's a safe topic. I hear we're supposed to get an ice storm tomorrow. I sure didn't miss those when I lived in Virginia."

Jared's muscles tightened, bracing for the impact of the crash one more time. His breathing grew shallow and pain took over. *Relax,* he told himself, taking measured breaths.

"Jared? You okay?"

"Yes, ma'am," he said between clenched teeth. If he could relax, the pain would go away.

"At least you don't have to go out in the bad weather."

He closed his eyes, focused on his breathing, and his muscles loosened. "That's right."

"Are you in pain? You don't sound so good."

The last thing he wanted was to be helpless in front of this woman. "I did tell you not to nurse me, didn't I?"

"And I asked you not to call me ma'am. Want me to point out how many times you've said that tonight?"

Yep, she sure was feisty.

"Jared, I'm not nursing you. You're the one who said we were friends, didn't you? Friends look out for each other."

Was she putting him in the friend zone? And yet he'd been the one to open that door. Is that what he wanted?

"Jared?"

He turned the rook in his hand once more. "Do you play chess?"

"No, I never learned."

"You interested in learning?"

"Chess?" she repeated.

He smiled. "Something to pass the time. I could teach you."

"I can stop over this weekend, if you like, but I do have a job. I can't afford to while away my days like you."

Whatever reason she came over, he wanted to see Siobhan again. In person. "When you come by, you can show me how big you like your closets."

She laughed. "Do you always travel with a chess board?"

"Well there's the thing," he said. "I don't have one. You'd have to bring it. But if you wanted me to show you how to play…"

"We can talk more about that tomorrow. You sound like you could use some rest."

She was right, but he liked talking to her, hearing the sound of her voice. "Whatever you think would be best," he said with a sigh.

"Sleep well," she told him.

"You too, angel."

Chapter 10

SIOBHAN GLANCED OUT HER office window, at the hospital parking lot. The predicted ice storm had arrived right on schedule.

When she'd mentioned the weather to Jared last night, his mood had shifted noticeably. Jared's accident had happened on a night like this. If Siobhan had thought a second more, she might have realized he was probably still dealing with the trauma.

Her fingers itched to call him, to make sure he was okay. She'd never crossed the line between nurse and patient before, although Jared had insisted he didn't want to talk to her as a nurse. Was her conduct unprofessional? What would her bosses say if she told them she'd been consulting with a patient after hours? Okay, not consulting. What exactly was she doing with Jared Pierce?

She jumped when Dr. Phelps called her name. "Siobhan?"

"Dr. Phelps." And now she felt like a kid who'd been caught misbehaving. Her heart hammered.

"Call me Duncan, please? I didn't mean to startle you. The weather looks pretty nasty. I guess tonight isn't the right night for that glass of wine either?"

She smiled. "I think you're right."

"How did the house hunting go last night?"

"Great. Well, maybe. I don't know." She took a deep breath, closed her eyes and tried again. "Sorry. It was a great house, but since I wasn't ready to start looking yet, I guess I'm not sure if I'm ready to buy." She winced. "Am I rambling?"

"A little. Is the reason you don't like the house because that 'nice woman' suggested it?"

Great. And now the whole world knew she was uncomfortable around Amy. "She really is nice," Siobhan said.

"So you've said. If we can put something on the calendar, you can highlight the rest of her attributes over that glass of wine."

"On the calendar." Dr. Phelps seriously wanted to date her? *Get a life.* "Tomorrow night," she said. "I don't have anything tomorrow night."

He shook his head. "Tomorrow's Thursday? Doesn't work for me. I have a meeting. Friday?"

Friday. Another uncomfortable dinner night at Ma's. Siobhan had gone too long between dates, and she'd had dinner with the family last week. If she wanted a life, it was time to take a leap. "Okay."

"How about right after work? We can leave from here."

She nodded. "Sounds good."

He smiled and returned to his office.

Dr. Phelps, who was smart, and distinguished, and good-looking. He'd been married once, so he knew how relationships worked. Siobhan had plenty of relationships in high school, right up until she ran away with Carter. The last several years had been a litany of "sorry I couldn't make its," both on her part and on the part of those men who'd asked her out. Now she was gauche and inexperienced, a complete turnaround from her slutty high school days.

And Dr. Phelps had asked her out.

What if things went badly? Would she lose her job? Wait. Was he harassing her and she was too stupid to realize it? "Overthinking," she said under her breath.

She went through her PHM patients. Jared hadn't done his check-in today. The app sent automatic reminders every night, but Jared usually did his early in the afternoon. Should she call to check on him? Emotional trauma sometimes set an accident victim's recovery back, and she'd reminded him of his accident.

His house was on Monroe Street, on her way home. She could stop by to check on him.

But he didn't want her to nurse him.

She wouldn't be able to concentrate until she was sure Jared hadn't suffered a setback. Siobhan dug her phone out of her purse and called. When the call went to voicemail, her concern grew. What if something was wrong? He was all alone in that house, and he was barely out of rehab. She tried to make her voice sound nonchalant.

"Just checking to make sure you're okay," she said. "Anything I can bring you, other than a chess board?"

She rolled her eyes at her pathetic message and hung up.

What if he'd fallen and couldn't reach his phone? Was the visiting nurse due to stop in today? Would they reschedule with the weather?

Siobhan stared at her phone for ten minutes, and when she didn't get a call back, she packed up her desk. The parking deck had saved her car windows from a coating of ice, and within minutes, she was on her way to Jared's.

Tree branches encased in ice glittered in the waning sunlight. Salt crunched beneath her tires. A salt truck passed on the other side of the road, shooting tiny pellets against her windshield, which smeared when she turned on her wipers. Winter in northern Illinois. No, she hadn't missed this. The traction light came on in her car a couple of times along the way, making her more nervous.

She found the house and veered into the driveway, only then realizing she was grabbing the steering wheel as if it would fly away. The house was dark, not a good sign with the sun disappearing below the horizon. Siobhan got out of the car and slid her way up the sidewalk. As she reached for the front porch railing, her feet went out from under her. She landed on her butt. Hard.

"You gonna sue me?" Jared drawled from the porch door, leaning on his crutches.

Siobhan narrowed her eyes, pushed to her feet and took hold of the railing, mounting the stairs carefully. "You didn't answer your phone."

He glanced over his shoulder. "It's on the charger. I didn't hear it ring." He grinned. "You were worried about me?"

She stepped into the porch, to safe ground. "Your lights aren't on."

"The ice snapped the power line in the backyard."

"How long before they can fix it?"

"I don't know. Do they call you to tell you here?"

"There's a number you can call." She rubbed her aching backside. "They give you an estimated return to service time."

"Would you like to come in and keep me warm?" He nodded to where she massaged her bruised butt. "I can do that for you."

Siobhan pushed past him, into the house. "You can't stay here with no heat."

"I'm not about to go sliding on the ice with you." Jared broke into a wide grin as he settled into his chair. "You sure are cute when you're bossy. The way your nose turns up at the end like that, and your freckles all stand out. Sure would be a shame if you had leprosy and those freckles all kinda flaked off."

She laughed. His smile grew wider and something inside her pinched. Something warm and wonderful. Something scary she'd kept buried all the years since she'd left home.

Even with a bruise on his face and a scar on his brow, Jared Pierce was a handsome man. She'd been joking when she'd asked if he was tall, dark and handsome, but there he was, if somewhat battered around the edges.

She stopped at the table beside his chair and picked up a tiny wooden castle, not more than three inches high. Another piece was the head of a horse, the details of the mane beautifully carved. A third piece looked to be a man wearing a crown. Automatically, she looked at the dining room table. The wooden blocks were lined up by size. "Did you make those?" she asked.

"Yes, ma'am. I find whittling keeps my mind off the pain when I'm not sleeping."

She set the castle down and wrapped her arms around herself. Even in her coat, she was chilly, and Jared was in sweatpants and a sweatshirt.

"How do you plan to keep warm?" she asked.

"You could stay and cuddle with me," he suggested.

She laughed. "As nice as that might sound to you, it would likely be very painful."

He winced. "You sure know how to hurt a guy's feelings."

A loud crack shook the house. Siobhan squeaked a startled cry and ducked.

Jared shuffled to the kitchen. She followed, glancing over his shoulder when he opened the back door. The moon cast a glow that made the world look as if it was encased in glass. Power lines sagged across the lot line.

"This ice is too heavy," Siobhan said.

The conjoined tree broke apart with another loud crack, a large branch sparking against the power lines. Siobhan gripped Jared's arm with a gasp.

The brooding look on Jared's face rivaled his broadest smile for most handsome expression. What was it about this guy?

He tilted his head and pushed the door open. "Hey, kid. You okay?" he called out. "Where's your coat? You wanna come inside and warm up?"

Siobhan squinted into the backyard. "Who are you talking to?"

Jared pointed. "That little boy." Lines of concern tightened around his eyes. He opened the door once more. "You okay, kid?"

Siobhan leaned forward, trying to see the boy. "There's no one out there. Close the door. You'll lose what heat you have left."

Jared pointed. "He's right…" And then his arm fell to his side. "Well, I'll be damned."

~ ~ ~

If Jared told her he'd seen a ghost, Siobhan would think he'd taken one too many pain pills, but damn if that kid hadn't evaporated into thin air.

It seemed he had been the right person to send on this trip after all.

He closed the door and looked at Siobhan, who was giving him a clinical once over. Jared ambled to the living room and tugged on his parka. She was right. The house was cold.

"Don't suppose you brought a chess board with you," he said, trying to get rid of the worried look on her face. He settled into his chair and winced with the effort.

Siobhan pulled a candle from the bookshelf, a book of matches beside it. Hell, if he hadn't been wrapped up in carving his king, he might have noticed those same candles. She lit the wick and the sulfur from the match was replaced by something spicy— sandalwood.

Someone knocked on the front door. Siobhan pointed to him. "Stay."

Bossy, too. He liked that.

He recognized Mrs. Brown's voice. "I heard the crack and I was worried. Are you the visiting nurse?"

Siobhan stepped aside and let Mrs. Brown in. "Yes, I am," she said, sending a no-nonsense look at Jared.

Well, damn.

"I saw the tree in back," Mrs. Brown said to him. "And your power is out? You'll have to come to our house. We have a fireplace, at least. You can't stay here without any heat."

He flashed a look at Siobhan. So much for extra blankets and overnight guests, if she'd even be willing to stay. Based on the look on her face, that was out of the question.

"Do you have a young boy staying with you?" Jared asked his neighbor. "I swear I saw a kid standing in the yard."

"No, our children are grown and gone. Maybe you saw one of the other neighbors. How old was the boy?"

"Eight? Ten? I'm not a good judge of age. I don't know many young kids."

Mrs. Brown shook her head. "No, I don't know of any children that age around here. C'mon. Let's get your things together and you can come over to my house."

He shot a glance at Siobhan. "The sidewalk looks a might slick out there. Not sure walking outside is what I should be doing right now."

Siobhan rolled her eyes. "Let me call the power company and see how quickly they expect a return to service." She disappeared down the hallway. Interesting she seemed so drawn to his bedroom. He had no problem with that, aside from the fact he was currently disabled.

And damn again.

"Do you happen to own a chess board?" he asked Mrs. Brown.

"Well, yes. I do." Her eyes moved to the table at his side. Like Siobhan, she picked up the rook. "These are beautiful. And your knight. The details on this horse are stunning."

"Thank you, ma'am. Maybe you'd let me borrow your game until the weekend? I'd like to carve a few more pieces and having a board set up would keep me on task."

"I didn't realize you were so artistic," she went on. "You know, my husband, David, teaches at the high school. They do night classes for the community, and I happen to know they need someone to teach woodworking. And they teach classes on Saturdays at the woodworking store. You could help out while you're here."

"I have a job in Louisiana, ma'am," he told her.

"Yes, but your mother says you can't travel." She set the rook down. "Listen to me, going on. You're not going anywhere until you heal, and if you were, it would be home. Once you're back on your feet you could fill in a night or two. Think about it and let me know. In the meantime, you concentrate on getting better."

Siobhan reappeared under the arch that opened to the hallway. "They expect power should be restored by seven o'clock tonight," she reported.

"Would you like me to stay with you?" Mrs. Brown offered.

"I told Nurse Siobhan I'd teach her to play chess. This might be a good time for that. What do you say, Miss Siobhan?"

Siobhan's face flushed cherry red. Flirting with her wasn't so different from his chess strategy, and he'd just scored a move.

"You shouldn't be driving in this weather," he added, "and you're already here."

"I'll dash over and get the chess set," Mrs. Brown said, "and be right back."

"Watch your step on the ice," Siobhan called after her.

"You don't mind, do you?" he asked.

"What if I have a date?" she challenged.

The idea hit him like a two-by-four to the head. He shook it free and reminded himself he was less than a man at the moment. Crippled and as good as impotent. "Hazardous driving conditions," he pointed out. "But don't let me interfere."

Something softened in her face. "Your accident," she said. "What happened?"

He pinched his brow. "Lost control coming off the highway. Rolled my car and another car followed me down."

"I'm sorry."

He didn't want her pity, but before he could say anything more, Mrs. Brown reappeared with the chess set. "Much obliged," he told his neighbor.

Siobhan lit several more candles, giving the room a soft glow. He hadn't realized how dark it had gotten.

"You'll give me a shout if you need anything?" Mrs. Brown said to Siobhan. "Men are so independent. He hasn't let me do anything for him."

"If I see anything before I leave that you can do, I'll let you know," Siobhan told her as she walked Mrs. Brown to the door.

Siobhan by candlelight. Her skin glowed. And the scent, sandalwood.

If there were spirits in this house, the sandalwood might draw them out. Maybe he should send Siobhan away. He ruffled his hair, feeling more frustration than anything else.

Siobhan opened the chess board and looked from the plastic pieces to the pieces he'd carved. "Is that what you're making?" she asked. "Chess pieces?"

"Yes, ma'am," he replied sullenly.

She glanced at the dining room table. "You don't have enough blocks of wood for two sets, do you?"

"No, ma'am. Didn't decide what I was making until after my brother left. The tools, they appear to have belonged to my great uncle. Troy thought I might need something to do until I could walk again."

"I can bring you more blocks," she said softly.

Still that pitying tone of voice. And she hadn't complained about his use of the word ma'am. "Wouldn't want to keep you from your date," he said, trying hard not to sound disappointed.

"I don't have one. Not tonight."

A qualification. Did he want to probe that comment? No, he decided. He forced a smile. "So did you check the closet while you were in my room?"

And the blush was back. He'd won another piece off their virtual chess board.

"I'm sure the closet would do fine," she replied. She set up a second tray table for the chess board and pulled in a chair from the dining room. "Okay, sensei. Teach me."

He showed her the pieces as he set them on the board, had her set up her side to mirror his. Explained to her how each piece moved. Her faced screwed up into a mask of concentration.

"That's a lot to remember."

"You'll get it," he assured her. "Let's give it a try." He moved a pawn and she followed his lead. As the board opened up, she touched her knight.

"This one moves in an L?" she asked.

"That's right."

She moved the knight and he captured it. "And this one," she said, hand on the rook. "It goes straight, but I can move it all the way across the board?"

"That's right." She was a quick study.

She grinned and took his bishop, then looked to him for approval. If she wasn't the most beautiful woman he'd ever seen right at that moment. He wasn't sure he'd ever enjoyed a woman's company out of bed quite so much.

Within fifteen minutes, he'd cornered her king. "Checkmate."

"Okay, I get it now," she said. "Let's go again. I bet I beat you this time."

Before he could tell her how unlikely that was, the lights flickered and came on.

Siobhan rubbed her hands together. "I forgot how cold it was in here! Do you want something warm to drink?"

Jared hadn't noticed the cold either. Or the pain. "Don't trouble yourself."

She checked her watch. "Oh. I should go." She glanced at him apologetically. "Now that the heat is on again."

He nodded, not quite sure why he was speechless. Another first. He didn't know what to say to her.

"If you like, I'll call to say goodnight," she said.

"That way I'll know you got home safe," he replied. "I'd appreciate it."

"Can I do anything for you before I go?"

He shook his head.

She smiled, leaned in to kiss his cheek and was out the door.

He might never wash that cheek again.

Jared pushed out of his chair and blew out the candles. A fresh stab of pain reminded him to take his meds and he swallowed down a pill.

He eased into his seat and picked up a new block of wood. This one would be the queen. One with shining copper hair? Jared glanced at the hallway. Siobhan seemed to gravitate to his bedroom, but she was so careful to avoid sexual innuendo. He'd never had any trouble sweet talking a woman into his bed, but he sensed Siobhan fought for control. Of herself? He could easily imagine her as a hellcat in the bedroom.

Irrelevant. He was out of service for at least another month. But he could watch her squirm.

He shrugged out of his coat as the house returned to a moderate temperature before he concentrated on his work once more. A crackle of static electricity reminded him this house needed a humidifier in the winter months. He looked up and was startled to see the boy from the backyard standing between the living room and the dining room. "What's your name?" Jared asked. "Are you lost?"

The boy shook his head, shimmering against the dark background.

Shimmering?

"Can you help me find my brother?" the boy asked, his voice hollow, barely a whisper.

And then the boy vanished, the same way he had outside. Jared fumbled for his phone and called his mother.

"How are you?" she asked in that annoying worried voice.

"I believe I've just seen a ghost."

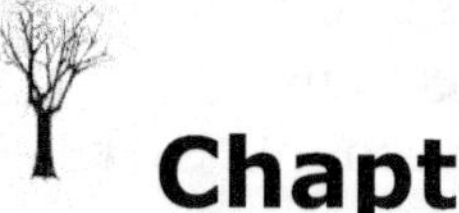

Chapter 11

SIOBHAN CHECKED HER PHM patients one more time, then turned off her work cell phone and tucked it into her drawer. She'd been religious about turning it off since that first night in case the vice presidents analyzed the phone bill. Certainly they would allow her the one rookie mistake.

A mistake that led to nightly phone calls with a patient.

Siobhan had learned a lot about Jared over the last couple of nights, about his brother, his mother, and the new things he was learning about his aunt and his great aunt. In return, she'd probably shared more than she should about Kevin and Kathleen, Liam and her mother. Thankfully, they hadn't gotten into the conversation of how she left home.

Rule number one in dating. Don't talk about the ex.

But she wasn't dating Jared, and she did have a date with Duncan Phelps. Why did that make her feel like she was cheating on Jared? She scoffed. Jared was a shameless flirt, and equally harmless. At least for now. Once he was cleared to travel, he'd go back to Louisiana and she'd likely never see him again. Until then, she could be a friend. By the time he left, she'd have new things to occupy her time.

Dr. Phelps came out of his office buttoning the wool coat that hit him mid-hip. "Ready to go?"

Siobhan nodded and pulled her purse out of the drawer. He met her at the closet and helped her into her parka.

"I can drive," he offered.

Except it was a first date, and she didn't want to be at his mercy if things went badly. *What could go wrong on a date with a doctor?* He'd been friendly since he'd initially asked her out, hadn't come on to her in the office or said anything inappropriate, nothing to indicate he wanted anything more than to get to know her, and yet she was uneasy. "I can meet you. I'd rather not make a second trip to the hospital later," she told him.

"Is *Oliver's* okay? If you're hungry, we can have dinner, too."

Her stomach growled. She put a hand to it and grinned. "Sounds good. I'll meet you there."

Dr. Phelps guided her to the elevator with a gentle hand in the center of her back. "I've been looking forward to this all week," he said. "I don't usually date people from the hospital, but I don't know how to meet people these days. I thought since you're new in town, you wouldn't mind…" He rubbed his forehead. "The truth is I've only been divorced six months and I'm out of practice at this dating thing. I hope you'll forgive me if I do anything awkward."

Siobhan smiled. "I won't bite."

They parted ways in the parking garage, and along the drive to the restaurant Siobhan reconsidered her decision to go out with the doctor. He was nice looking and he seemed genuine, but he was much older. While that shouldn't matter, she considered her psychology classes and the whole father-figure scenario. She'd long ago given up on the idea of finding someone who could provide parental love. She had Ma, even if she'd blamed Ma for their discordant family life. Ma had welcomed her home with open arms, and they'd come a long way in repairing the rift between them. So why was she going out with Duncan Phelps?

Oh yeah. She needed a life. Except in the last couple of days, she'd stopped by the animal shelter and volunteered to walk dogs and socialize the cats, and she'd stopped at the extended care facility associated with the hospital and offered to play games with the patients there. Did she need the entanglement of a relationship?

If her phone calls with Jared proved nothing else, they reminded her how long it had been since she'd had sex, and she liked sex. Jared's voice had woken up those dormant hormones.

Sex with Dr. Phelps? The idea held little appeal. When she'd been in high school, she hadn't been discerning. Then again, in high school, she'd been searching for love, for someone to rescue her. She didn't need a man to save her anymore. The next man she slept with, assuming she would have sex again in this lifetime, would be a man she wanted to sleep with for a reason other than he wanted to sleep with her.

Duncan—she had to think of him that way if they were on a date, Dr. Phelps was too distant—was waiting for her when she arrived at *Oliver's*. A first date was way too soon to assess him as a sex partner. She'd have a drink and see how things went from there.

They were escorted to a table and Duncan ordered her a glass of wine before she had a chance to glance at the menu. Okay, maybe he knew what was good, but shouldn't he ask her preference first?

She opened her menu and glanced over the entrees. Duncan put a hand on the top of her menu.

"Don't trouble yourself trying to decide. The salmon is excellent."

Now she was getting annoyed. "I don't like salmon," she told him, even though she did.

He straightened with a look a surprise. "Please, get whatever you want."

Was he apologizing? Or giving her permission?

The waiter brought her wine, a Shiraz. She thanked him and ordered a glass of whiskey, neat, to go with her dinner. She went on to order a petite filet mignon. Duncan ordered the salmon, and when the waiter left, Duncan fussed with his napkin.

"My wife always wanted me to order for her," he said. "Old habits die hard."

Probably an apology. Siobhan would give him the benefit of the doubt. "I understand you're an oncologist, that is, before you moved into the vice president spot," she said, changing the subject. Evidently he didn't know the first rule of dating.

Duncan perked up and went on to tell her about his residency at Johns Hopkins, continuing with the rest of his resume. She did the math. He was at least sixteen years older than she was, definitely out of her dating pool unless she wanted to be a trophy wife.

She didn't.

He circled back to his marriage, how he'd taken the administrative position after his wife said he didn't spend enough time at home. He had two children, the oldest of which was Liam's age, seven years younger than she was.

Siobhan checked her purse, made sure she had enough money to cover her dinner so he wouldn't think she owed him anything. Duncan continued to regale her with his life history.

By the time coffee arrived at the end of the meal, she was exhausted, the way she felt when she'd worked a double shift.

Duncan reached across the table for her hand. "But I've been doing all the talking. I'm so sorry. I need to get out more."

She pulled her hand away. "That's fine."

"I'm not sure where the night goes from here. I'll leave that to you."

He wasn't seriously expecting her to go home with him? Or vice versa? "I think this is where we say goodnight," she said.

He glanced down, disappointed or embarrassed? "Can we do this again?"

He sounded so pitiable, but this was absolutely not what she wanted on her quest to find a life. He needed a friend, like Jared did, except Duncan didn't realize that. Her one-hour assessment told her he was interviewing for the next Mrs. Dr. Duncan Phelps. "I have an idea," she said. "What would you think about the whole administrative team getting together once a month for a night out?"

He chuckled. "I have to admit I was hoping for something more intimate."

Her smiled turned apologetic. How could she turn him down gracefully? "I've had a lovely evening, but I generally date men closer to my own age." *Men like Jared.* And why was she still thinking about Jared? She squeezed her eyes closed and put a hand to her forehead. Tact had never been her strong suit. "That didn't sound very nice."

"But it was honest," Duncan replied. "What a shame, because I like you."

"I like you, too, but I like my job better." She reached into her purse and offered him her share of the bill. "I think it's time I said goodnight."

He waved off her attempt to pay her part. "My treat. No strings attached." His smile turned sheepish. "And this dinner isn't tied to your job. Thanks for letting me practice on you. At least now I can say I've been on a date. You can give me advice on what to do better next time."

"Rule number one. Don't talk about the ex," she said, and gave him a wink.

~ ~ ~

When Jared asked Mrs. Brown if she knew of any children who'd lived in the house, she'd told him what he already knew, that Aunt Lily and Uncle Charlie had never had children, and they were the only occupants the Browns had known.

So where did the ghost come from?

He'd checked the electronic records online at the county's website and found the owners prior to Great Aunt Lily had been Stanley and Iris Mason. Unfortunately, the record of ownership didn't supply census information, like if Stanley and Iris had a child.

He called Amy Benson under the pretense of wanting to know more about his great aunt and she'd agreed to stop over this morning. He'd overheard her telling Siobhan the house was no longer haunted when they'd done the house tour. She was wrong, but at least Amy believed in ghosts. Siobhan had made her opinions on the subject crystal clear. By the time Siobhan was due to arrive this afternoon, Amy should be gone and he wouldn't have to trouble Siobhan with conversation she wouldn't appreciate.

While he waited for Amy, he carved another chess piece. He'd finished six of the sixteen pieces, and ordered Palo Santo wood blocks online to complete a second set. He'd also ordered supplies to craft a chessboard. In another week or so, he and Siobhan could be using the new board, and when he left, he'd give it to her so she'd have something to remind her of him—and the Palo Santo would provide good juju for her whether she believed in the magic or not.

Jared shouldn't have been surprised when Amy knocked on the back door instead of the front. He set aside his project, grabbed his crutches and hobbled through the kitchen. Kevin had come with her and was inspecting the large tree trunk, now on the ground after the power company had restrung the lines. He made a mental note to call someone to clear the tree away while he opened the door and invited Amy and Kevin in.

Kevin shook his hand. "I suppose I should tell you I forgot to give your message to my sister last time we were here."

"It's all good," Jared replied. He let them pass into the house and closed the door behind them.

"She's your nurse?" Kevin asked.

Jared thought about that a moment. "I guess she is. I tend to forget there's a live person on the other end of the app. I record my progress every day and send it off to be collected somewhere. She's the one with the catcher's mitt."

"How did you know my sister was that person?"

"She sent me what she called a push notification. Caught me off guard, so I called the phone number on the help screen and she answered." He made his way to his chair, inviting Kevin and Amy to sit on the sofa.

"That must be why she was worried about maintaining professionalism," Kevin told him. "The reason she didn't want us to tell you who she was."

"Oh, I knew who she was," Jared said. "After talking with her every night, I'd recognize her voice anywhere."

Kevin and Amy exchanged a glance. "You talk with her every night?" Amy asked.

"She took pity on me. We talk after work, so as not to interfere with her professional responsibilities. She makes my nights not quite so lonely, a stranger stranded in unfamiliar surroundings."

Again his guests exchanged a glance.

Time to get down to business. "Listen, I didn't know I had a Great Aunt Lily until my Aunt Melinda sent me to flip her house. I was hoping you might tell me more about her. What kind of person she was."

"She took us in when we were in trouble," Kevin said. "She had a great sense of adventure, liked the excitement."

Amy laced her fingers with Kevin's and they shared a smile. "Mr. and Mrs. Sumner ran the florist shop in town," Amy said. "My family runs the monument shop, so we did business with them on a regular basis, but I didn't know them personally until after Mr. Sumner died, when Mrs. Sumner invited us to stay for a couple of days. That was right before she died."

Amy's expression turned wary. She pulled her hand out of Kevin's and crossed her arms. She was leaving something out. If he wanted answers, he'd have to get to the point.

"You'd told me this house was haunted, that the spirits had moved on. Who haunted it?"

"Whatever ghosts were here seemed to be attached to Mrs. Sumner," Amy said. "When she passed, they guided her home, in a manner of speaking." Another secretive glance passed between Amy and Kevin.

"I've seen a ghost," he told them. "A boy, about ten years old."

Amy sat on the edge of the sofa cushion and reached into her pocket. "Something happened when we were here the other night." She glanced at Kevin. "I'd never noticed the tree in the backyard. If it marks a grave…" She withdrew a piece of paper from her pocket and concentrated on it.

"He's not going to make fun of you," Kevin told her. "In fact, it sounds like he believes in ghosts."

Amy pursed her lips. "Mrs. Sumner was an extraordinary woman, to quote her words. She did some fortune telling, more as a lark, but she had the gift. Most people didn't know that about her. They knew her as a shrewd businesswoman and a good neighbor. The reason I know about Mrs. Sumner's gift is that I have one too." She rose and handed Jared the slip of paper. "When I touched the tree, a voice spoke to me."

Jared unfolded the paper. "One becomes two, two become one, forever joined," he read. "What does it mean?"

"I don't know," she said.

"She hears epitaphs," Kevin said. "The last thoughts of the dead."

"You hear the dead?" Jared asked Amy.

She nodded. "Like I'm tuned into a frequency they talk on."

"I don't understand."

"I'm not sure you can," Kevin said. "The words don't mean anything to you?"

"No clue. The boy. He asked me to help find his brother." Jared scrubbed his face with a hand. "So what do I do now? I don't know who the boy is or where his brother might be."

"A séance?" Kevin asked Amy.

"No," she said firmly. "Not doing that again. Ever."

"I'd bet Mrs. Sumner would be your spirit guide."

"No," Amy said again.

Jared shook his head, not sure he'd heard correctly. "Séance? In this house?" It was a wonder there weren't dozens of spirits trapped here if they'd opened a portal to the afterlife with a séance.

Amy rose to her feet. "There has to be another way. Surely one of the neighbors has been here long enough to know who owned the house before the Sumners did."

"I've already checked the county website. I have a name," Jared said. "But someone who knew them would be more helpful."

Kevin wrapped an arm across Amy's shoulders. "We'll look into it."

Chapter 12

AFTER JARED OPENED THE door for Siobhan, he crutched away without a greeting and eased into his chair. His face was tight, as if his thoughts weren't organizing themselves properly.

"Something wrong?" she asked, closing the door.

He shook his head, but didn't say anything.

"How's the incision? Are you in pain?"

"Don't nurse me," he said in a low growl.

"Technically…"

"Yeah, and I forget you're my nurse most days. I don't like folks fussing over me."

Siobhan raised her eyebrows. She'd bet a large part of his grumpy mood was due to being cooped up inside the house all day every day. "When do you start outside therapy?" she asked.

"Monday."

"How will you get there?"

"You're still nursing me," he said, shooting her an angry glare.

"No, you're being oversensitive. What's going on?"

He turned his head away, chewing on his irritation. "Taxi," he said.

"Taxi?" she asked.

"The physical therapy place sends a taxi to pick me up and drive me back after."

She nodded. "I see." She put her hands on her hips.

This was why nurses didn't get involved with patients. His mood produced an uncomfortable twinge in her chest. "Maybe I should leave." She held her breath waiting for his answer. The scenario felt too much like a break-up.

Jared pinched the spot between his eyebrows. "Sit down. Please." When he looked up, he wore a forced smile. "Let's play chess."

Siobhan hesitated. *What was she doing?* He was a patient, albeit an unorthodox one. He was also going home to Louisiana after he regained his strength. She'd agreed to be his friend, but the lines were blurred between professional and personal, as much as she tried to convince herself otherwise. Hadn't she been thinking about Jared while she was on her date with Duncan? Comparing the good doctor with the grumpy patient?

She massaged the cramp in her chest.

"Look, I'm sorry," he said.

What was she supposed to say to that? *Sorry, I forgot my place,* or *You're not allowed to be grumpy when you're in pain,* or *Who am I going to talk to when you leave?*

"Siobhan?"

"Chess," she said. She had to pull herself together. "And don't expect me to feel sorry for you, either. I'm going to beat you."

His smile brightened. "So you think."

She slipped off her parka and dropped it on the sofa beside her purse, then set up the chess board on a tray table and pulled up one of the dining room chairs. "What time is your appointment on Monday?"

Jared raised an eyebrow. "Three o'clock."

"I'll drive you."

"Don't you have to work?"

"I can take a late lunch, or leave early." And why was she offering? "It might be difficult for you to get in and out of a taxi," she said, as much to convince herself as him. "And it's supposed to snow. A cabbie won't help you up and down the front stairs."

"And you can? If I slip, we both go down."

She moved her pawn. "I'm driving you. Are we going to play or talk?"

"You're just afraid I'll win if I distract you."

Score one for the nurse. Her cajoling had brought out the personality she'd come to know. "Your move." She nodded at the chess board.

He crooked a finger, inviting her to come closer. "I need you to check something for me, Nurse Siobhan." He turned his head and pointed to a spot behind his ear.

She rose from her chair and leaned over him, but when she got close enough to see what he was pointing out, he turned his face to meet hers and steadied her with a hand behind her neck. He pressed his lips to hers.

Rookie mistake. Other patients had tried that move before. She'd never fallen prey to it before. Did she want to kiss Jared?

Obviously.

He held her an inch from his face, studying her with dark, brown eyes. "I apologize for being tetchy," he said quietly, his deep southern drawl cloaking her like a down comforter.

A fraction of an inch was all that stood between Siobhan and another kiss, a deeper, hotter kiss. She braced her hands against his solid chest. Yes, she'd thought about Jared on her date with Duncan because Jared was the one who stoked her furnace, not Duncan. Jared who inspired fantasies that had lain dormant for too long.

Jared who was physically unable to bring those fantasies to life. Was that the attraction? She was safe with him?

~ ~ ~

Siobhan straightened and returned to her chair.

She hadn't slapped him. That was a good thing, right? Her cheeks were flushed and her eyes shone, a look he knew well, and yet she didn't step into the opening he'd given her. Damn, but he wanted more of her!

"Just a friendly kiss," he said cautiously, trying to read her. "That peck you gave me on the cheek was nice, but I do like the taste of a woman's lips. Are you angry with me?"

"No," she said too quickly.

Then he wasn't the only one who felt the attraction between them. He didn't believe for a minute he'd fooled her with his ploy, so why did she pull away? "I'll let you take me to therapy on Monday if you want to," he said.

Siobhan laughed. "I might be confused, but who's doing who the favor?"

"Most assuredly it would be you doing a favor for me. I'd be much obliged, but I hate to impose on you during the work day."

"Then make your appointments for after five o'clock," she told him.

Appointments. Plural. He liked the sound of that, and it promised him more time with her. "I can do that. If it's no bother."

"It's not a bother."

Jared moved a chess piece. But he was bothered. Hot and bothered. "You don't trust me," he said.

"I wouldn't say that." But she didn't look at him, reinforcing his initial impression that she didn't trust herself. Siobhan fingered another pawn and moved it one space.

"Then what would you say?" he asked.

Her lips curled into a wry smile. "More attempts to distract me? I'm a natural at this game. You're worried I'm going to beat you."

He made his next move. "Did it work?"

"You're awfully sure of yourself." Still she didn't look at him, her concentration focused on the board.

He shifted in his chair. "I guess I am. I'll make you a wager."

"I'm not the gambling type."

"No money," he said.

Siobhan sat back and folded her arms, meeting his gaze. "What then?"

"The winner of the game gets a truth or dare question. What do you say?"

Her pupils dilated. His attention was drawn to the pinpoints on her sweater. Siobhan raised her chin. "Deal." She moved another piece.

He couldn't resist raising the stakes, teasing her more. Could he break her defenses? "Would you like to know my dare?" he asked as he captured one of her pawns.

"What? And take all the fun out of waiting?"

Jared's surprise made the scar in his eyebrow twinge. Siobhan knew how to flirt with the best of them. "Anticipation."

"And if I win?"

He leaned forward, despite the shot of pain in his repaired hip. "You want a truth? Or a dare?"

Siobhan's eyes gave away the passion she held in check, a challenge Jared couldn't resist.

"I haven't decided yet," she replied. "Which scares you more? Telling me a truth, or performing a dare?"

"Oh, the truth, surely, although that isn't nearly as much fun."

She captured one of his pawns and smiled with her triumph. "How about every time a piece is captured the victor asks for a truth until the king is taken. Then you can have your dare, provided you win, of course." Siobhan glanced at him, and her eyes betrayed a moment of uncertainty.

Jared captured another of her pawns. "Truth, then. Did I offend you when I kissed you?"

Siobhan huffed and studied the board. "No." She pursed her lips, then assessed the move he'd left open for her. She was indeed a quick study at this game. She captured his knight and looked up triumphantly. "My turn. How many women have you tricked into kissing you?"

"Tricked?" he asked, assuming an air of innocence. She hadn't been fooled when he'd kissed her, but if she wanted to pretend she was… "Did I trick you?"

Her cheeks flamed red again. She raised an eyebrow.

A gentleman wouldn't point out such a weakness, especially to a woman he wanted to impress. "Okay," he conceded. "One."

She scoffed. "I doubt that."

"Truth," he said. "And that's assuming I believe I was able to trick you." He moved another piece and watched for her reaction. Another piece for her to take, one that would leave her king vulnerable.

She narrowed her eyes, seeing the move he'd given her. "Maybe this isn't such a good idea. If you want me to ask you questions, we could do that without a chess board."

She thought he was throwing the game? Which meant she didn't understand strategy as well as she thought she did. "You don't have to ask a question," he replied. "I've already told you I'm not fond of the truth parts of this game."

"Something to hide?" she asked as she captured another pawn.

He advanced his rook and captured her bishop. "Chess is a game of strategy. Sometimes you have to sacrifice to gain an advantage." He wrapped her bishop inside his palm. "Truth."

Siobhan sighed. "Go ahead."

Something to throw her off the scent. "Why don't you like your brother's fiancée?"

Siobhan backed away. "What makes you say I don't like her?"

"Truth," he reminded her.

She took a deep breath. "My brother and I have always been close. Amy adds a new dynamic to the mix, and I guess I miss being the one he talks to. Having him available to talk to me."

"You don't let many people close, do you?" he asked.

She pursed her lips, studying the board. "No, I don't."

"They let you down? People?"

Siobhan slid another piece across the board. "I suppose."

Jared made another move and knocked over her king. "Checkmate."

"Already?"

He watched her face closely, but she didn't look up. "Distraction is an effective way to win." Which left him to collect. Surely she would be expecting his request. "Do I need to phrase it as a dare?" he asked.

Siobhan licked her lips, then raised her gaze to meet his. "Depends on what you're looking for."

He smiled. She wasn't going to make this easy. "A kiss."

She stared at him, her body humming with energy. Damn, he wished he was whole.

"Siobhan McCormick, I dare you to kiss me, and I'm not asking for a peck on the cheek."

"Why?"

His smile slanted. "Because I think you are about the most beautiful woman I've ever met, and because you keep me on my toes. You don't giggle and titter the way most women do. You're feisty, and I like that."

"Feisty?" she narrowed her eyes. "I think you said that once before."

"Then it must be true. You going to pay your debts?"

Bingo. He'd found the right approach. Truth or dare was a stroke of brilliance. The stubborn look on her face showed she wasn't one to back down from a challenge. Siobhan rose from her chair and leaned over him.

"Be careful what you wish for," she said.

She had no idea what he was wishing for. A kiss was only the beginning, and the breathy catch in her voice increased his desire for her.

Siobhan touched her lips to his and breathed a gasp. Jared opened his mouth against hers, meeting her in the middle. He cupped her face, deepening the kiss and she placed a palm against his chest for support.

The woman stole his breath. Jared stroked her cheek as the kiss ended and rested his forehead against hers. "Damn, woman. You kiss like nothing or no one else."

She nodded, dazed?

"I've got an idea for another dare," he said, his voice tight with need. "You ready to lose a second time?"

She backed away. "Jared…"

She was still afraid then. "Relax," he whispered. "I'm perfectly willing to skip another game if you'll kiss me like that again."

"Not a good idea," she said.

Maybe he couldn't make love to her, but there were other things they could do that didn't require him to bear weight or strain his injuries. "I know you like my bedroom. Let me show you how big that closet is."

She laughed and surveyed the room. "I think we need a change of subject. Are you really going to sell this house?"

He grimaced and shifted in his chair. "The family has no need for it." He locked eyes with her. "You want to buy it?"

She shrugged.

"I'll sell it to you cheap, with the ghost as a lagniappe."

"A ghost? As a what?" she asked.

"A little something extra thrown in."

Her hands went to her hips. "Did you say a ghost?"

"Yes, ma'am."

She tilted her head, scowling. "You don't believe that. Even Amy said any so-called ghosts who might have been hanging around are gone."

"I'm afraid I do. It appears Amy was mistaken."

Siobhan dropped into her chair. "I pictured you as intelligent, with your feet on the ground."

"I'm not allowed to bear weight on my left foot just now," he joked, but she didn't laugh. Not even a smile.

She shot a glance at the front door. Siobhan closed her eyes and exhaled a sigh. Her mood had shifted.

"You're not laughing at my joke," he said as he tried to read her.

"Which joke in particular?" she asked. "The one where you believe in ghosts?"

Jared steepled his fingers under his chin. Oh. That. "You did ask for the truth, didn't you? Tell me what you believe in, Siobhan."

"Wow. No beating around the bush with you." She got to her feet, turned away from him, took a step toward the dining room, then turned back. She put her hands on her hips. "I'll tell you what I believe in," she said. "Dealing straight with people, not playing games to get what you want. Saying what you mean and not creating an illusion or a façade to hide behind."

Apparently, he'd struck a nerve. "Is that comment aimed at me?" he asked, his eyes narrowing.

She clamped her mouth shut, pressed her lips together.

"Are you passing judgment on me for believing something you don't?" he asked

"Judgment?" she asked.

"Your brother. He's a reporter, right?" Jared asked. "He believes in ghosts."

Siobhan closed her eyes and swallowed hard. "I'm not judging you," she said. "I'm sure whatever he—or you—think you saw can easily be explained by something logical." When she looked at him again, her expression bordered on panic. Where had things gone wrong?

She pursed her lips again. "Can I get anything for you? Water? An ice pack?"

"And the nurse is back," he said with a sigh of exasperation. "Don't hide from me, Siobhan."

"I should probably go," she replied. "I promised to help out at the animal shelter today."

"You promised to play chess with me."

"And so I have."

"Come back tomorrow?" he asked.

Her arms crossed, effectively shutting him out. "Tomorrow is the Bunco tournament at the extended care facility where I volunteer."

Jared rubbed his forehead. "Should I assume you won't be able to take me to therapy on Monday after all?"

"I already told you I would," she groused.

That fell into the nursing category. She was retreating into a safe space, but he'd glimpsed what sizzled beneath the surface. She might rationalize that she was honoring a commitment—thank heaven for that—but he wouldn't bank on her letting him inside her defenses so easily next time.

She grabbed her parka from the sofa and shoved her arms into it.

"I'll call you later?" he asked.

She nodded, clearly flustered, and rushed out the front door.

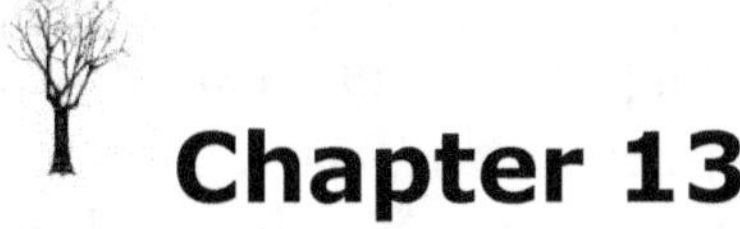

Chapter 13

WORKING WITH THE ANIMALS provided Siobhan with the companionship she missed. The dogs were always happy to see her and the cats chased and curled through her legs, rewarding her with a purr when she scratched their ears. She didn't need a man, she needed a pet. No games, no change of heart. They were happy to have you in their lives, no questions asked. But she couldn't have a pet at Amy's apartment.

Another reason to buy a house, and if she intended to stay in Edgarville, she might as well. Did she want to buy Jared's house?

The man had a tendency to make her stupid when she was around him. She'd toured the house, spent time in it, and she still didn't have a feel for it, aside from her unhealthy fascination with his bedroom. Jared was too great a distraction.

She picked up a salad on her way home from the shelter, and upon arriving, she stood before Amy's bookshelf, looking over the titles for something to read while she forked bits of lettuce and carrots. Many of the authors were familiar to her, something she had in common with Amy. Siobhan pulled a romance from the shelf, carried the book to the living room and sat in the easy chair, tucking her legs beneath her as she opened the book while taking bites of her salad.

The author was one of her favorites, the book, one she hadn't read before. By the time Siobhan had finished her salad, she was engrossed in the story. The hero—tall, dark and handsome—made her think of Jared.

If only storybook heroes existed in the real world.

A hundred pages later, the relationship in the book heated up. Siobhan set the book down and closed her eyes. Okay, a man could be useful sometimes, but how long had it been since she'd met anyone she'd trust to scratch that itch?

Jared certainly inspired fantasies. He'd gotten her attention during their chess game, and she knew, without a doubt, if he'd been able, she would have taken him up on that second game of chess, risked another dare. The kiss had only been the beginning of what he'd wanted from her, and she wanted him right back.

She imagined another challenge as they captured pieces, each piece representing an article of clothing. Strip chess? Siobhan giggled at the thought. Yes, it had been too long since she'd had sex. Fortunately for her, Jared was restricted from home run territory for the time being, and as much as she enjoyed running the bases in between, that wasn't going to be enough. She wanted it all.

Duncan Phelps would probably be happy to oblige her, but she didn't want Duncan Phelps.

She wanted Jared.

That was a problem. She'd met his kind before, dating back to her high school days. Flirting was sexual flattery, and she'd outgrown the need to be flattered. Not to mention Jared was superstitious.

She glanced at the book on the table, needing the break, needing to allow her overcharged hormones time to cool down before she continued reading, except now she had all this excess energy. A quick shower and self-service relief? A run around the block? She could run to the cemetery, prove to everyone that ghosts didn't come out at night, didn't haunt the living.

Ghosts were manifestations of grief. Imagination to give people something to hold onto. That would explain Kevin's belief that he'd seen Mary.

Her phone rang and Siobhan stared at it. She glanced at the clock. Jared.

"Hey baby," he said when she answered.

His words wrapped around her. She'd never been one to appreciate being called baby, but the way he said it was different.

"How are you feeling?" she asked reflexively. Her voice hitched.

She shouldn't have answered the phone. Not while her hormones were still running hot. His voice did more things to her than other men did with a touch.

"I hate the way we left things today," he said.

Siobhan curled up in a chair, wrapped her free hand around her. "How did we leave things?"

"You, upset with me. Me, wanting to make things right."

She wanted to tell him they were just friends, to take away the intimacy, but she couldn't. "I'm not upset with you." She closed her eyes, imagining the way he'd kissed her. "Tell me how you think you could have made things right." *Talk to me in that seductive voice.*

"Would it bother you if I told you how much I enjoyed kissing you? Told you I'd hoped to kiss you again?"

Siobhan's eyes rolled back in her head. Every nerve ending tingled. They may have joked about phone sex, but Jared didn't even have to say something sexually charged to take her where she needed to go.

He didn't have to know that.

"How are the wood carvings coming?" she asked, breathless. It didn't matter what he talked about, as long as he kept talking in that smooth, southern drawl.

She'd asked the right question. He told her what tools he was using, what pieces he'd been working on, what type of wood he was carving, his sultry voice stroking her, memories of his mouth on hers.

She bit her lip, and a moan escaped.

"Siobhan?"

"Mm-hmm?" she replied, not trusting her voice to sound normal.

He chuckled as if he knew where her mind had gone, and damn if that didn't send a fresh ripple of lust through her.

"I don't suppose you'd like to stop back over tonight?"

She cleared her throat. He couldn't give her what she wanted. Not for at least another month. Yes, there were plenty of other ways to satisfy each other, but she'd flown solo long enough. "I'm not sure that's a good idea," she said.

"You keep saying that," he replied. "I'd like the chance to prove you wrong."

"How do you intend to do that?" she asked, afraid of his response.

"You think playing chess would be a bad idea?"

One piece of clothing for each piece captured. She giggled. "Tonight? Yes."

"Straight up chess, no dare?" he asked.

Except she'd be thinking about removing his clothes, one piece at a time, and nothing could come from that. Without the dare, would he kiss her again? Memories of high school flooded in, of the boys she'd spent hours making out with. Why didn't people make out after the relationship included sex? She'd developed a reputation during her junior year, but even the boys who asked her out to find out if her reputation was true started with make-out sessions. After she'd given them what they wanted, the make-out sessions ended.

Those days were long gone.

"Siobhan?"

Jared couldn't go that next step, not for a few more weeks. "It's late," she said finally.

"So stay the night with me. You know you're safe. At least for now."

She was tempted. "What do you want from me?"

"Are we still playing truth or dare?" his voice purred.

"No dare attached. Does that question require a lie?" she asked.

"And now you're unhappy with me again."

"No, I'd really like to know."

"You said no phone sex."

There it was. Everybody wanted a turn with Siobhan the slut. She was over it. No, she wasn't going to talk dirty to him. "That's what you want? Phone sex?" Her tone had switched to accusing.

"I was joking. I want to look at you. That's why I invited you over. I want to see you, and truth be told, I'd enjoy kissing you some more."

A shiver of lust shook her. She was still a slut, even if she hadn't slept with a man in years. "Dream on. And I'm still not going to talk dirty to you."

"You don't have to," he said. "It's that breathy hitch in your voice, the way you say my name. You could recite your mother's recipe for potato salad. I can't help what you do to me."

What was she supposed to say to that? He'd just talked to her about tools and varieties of wood and she was halfway to orgasm.

"You asked what I want from you," he said. "No more than you're willing to give. These late night conversations? They mean the world to me. I'll tell you true. I am attracted to you something powerful, and I'm pretty sure that feeling is mutual. You know my restrictions right now probably better than I do, but that doesn't stop the wanting.

"I enjoy our conversations more than anything, so if that's all you're willing to share with me, I'll take it. If sometimes the sound of your voice takes me somewhere else, we can go on pretending those things aren't happening."

"Jared…"

"I won't tell a soul. Won't even mention it to you, but you did ask for the truth from me."

She smiled, in spite of herself. "When you were in high school, when life was simpler and we didn't know all the secrets that changed the rules, did you make out with your girlfriends? Why don't people do that once they figure out what comes next?"

"Who says they don't?" She heard the smile in his voice. "And I'll tell you what, I could kiss you all day long if that's what you wanted to do, y'heard? That kiss we shared was something special. Siobhan. You are something special."

"I may take you up on that, but not tonight." Tonight she wanted to pretend he was her boyfriend, that sex wouldn't ruin everything.

That he wouldn't be moving back to Louisiana in a couple of months.

~ ~ ~

Jared eased to his feet and balanced on his crutches, grabbed his meds and his phone from the table and tucked them into his pocket. He turned off the lamp and followed the path of nightlights.

He flipped the switch in the bedroom, and the frosted glass ceiling fixture cast an eerie glow. Jared emptied his pockets onto the nightstand and turned on the table lamp. He crossed to the door to turn out the ceiling light before he sat on the edge of the bed, ready for a good night's sleep.

With his crutches settled between the bed and the nightstand within easy reach, Jared lifted his leg onto the bed, smiling that he was able to do it without assistance tonight. When he turned to position his pillow, he noticed an indentation in the second pillow, an indentation the size of a small boy's head.

"Are you here, then?" he asked the empty room.

The pillow resumed its shape and the boy appeared at the foot of his bed.

"Where's my mother?" the boy asked.

"What's your name?" Jared asked the ghost.

"Who are you?" A noticeable chill crept into the room.

"My name's Jared. Your mother doesn't live here anymore. She hasn't for a long time. Can you tell me why you're here?"

"Where's my mother? Where's my brother?" the boy asked. He looked around the room. "Are you a friend of my stepfather's?"

"What's your name?" Jared asked again.

"I won't let you hurt me," the boy said. He flew around the room, followed by a gust of wind that knocked Jared's crutches to the floor, and disappeared through the wall.

Cleansing a house of ghosts was a challenge when he was whole. Hampered as he was, Jared questioned his ability to do the job he'd been sent to do, and now the ghost knew Jared's weakness. He huffed, unable to reach his crutches. He couldn't bend to the floor. If he could get to the living room, he could use his grabber to pick the crutches up, but that meant hopping on one foot, which would produce its own brand of hell.

He'd already asked Siobhan if she'd come back. Would she think he was playing her if he told her he needed help? Jared cringed. The first call was to his father. He'd figure out the rest after.

"It's late," his daddy said when he answered.

"I know."

"Trouble?"

Jared grimaced. "The boy doesn't know he's dead, and I believe he feels threatened by my presence in his house." He glanced at his crutches, out of reach. "Not sure I can do this in my present condition."

"Anyone there you can trust?" his father asked. "Or do you need me to come?"

Amy had experience with the spirit world. Hadn't she said something about a séance? "I'll see what I can do here, first."

"Put the ghost at his ease," his father told him. "He won't move on until he trusts you're telling him the truth."

"And in the meantime?"

"Watch yourself. Don't let him take advantage of your weakness."

Again Jared grimaced. "He already has."

"You need me, then?"

Jared heard his mother's voice in the background. "Is that Jared? Is something wrong?"

"Tell her I'm fine," he told his father. "There's someone who might be able to help me here. Let me try that, first."

He heard fumbling on his father's end and then his mother came on the line.

"Jared, what's going on?"

"Hey, Mama. I dropped my crutches is all. Feeling a little helpless."

"And you called your daddy to pick your crutches up for you? From a thousand miles away? You're not fooling me. I can be on a plane tomorrow."

"I'm fine, Mama. There's no need for you to waste your time. Besides, you don't want to stay here with the ghost hanging around, now, do you?"

He smiled when she didn't respond right away. No, she wouldn't want to stay with him now that she knew there actually was a ghost in the house.

"You call that nice Mrs. Brown," his mother finally said. "She'll help you pick up your crutches. Better still, I'll call her for you."

"It's late," Jared said. He glanced out his bedroom window toward the Brown's house. "But I see a light on. I'd best call them before they go to bed. Love you, Mama." He disconnected before she had a chance to mother him anymore and called Mrs. Brown. At least she wouldn't threaten to stay with him.

"It's Jared Pierce, next door," he said when she answered. "I wonder if you could stop over for just a minute. I didn't secure my crutches, and they fell over. Did you tell me my great aunt gave you a key? I hate to bother you, but if I need to get up in the night…"

"I'll be there in a minute," Mrs. Brown told him.

He set the phone on the nightstand and made a mental note to add his grabber stick to those things he carried around, along with his pills and his phone. He scanned the ceiling.

"I won't hurt you," he said to the empty room.

The front door opened and Mrs. Brown called out.

"I'm in the bedroom," Jared replied.

A wisp shimmered in the corner of the room.

Mrs. Brown peeked in tentatively. "Are you decent?"

"Yes, ma'am. Just a might embarrassed."

She stepped into the room with a smile. "These things happen." She bent over, retrieved his crutches and handed them to him. "It's chilly in here. Is the heat working?"

Jared checked the corner again. The ghost was there, barely visible. "I expect the thermostat adjusted down for the night. I apologize for calling you out at this hour."

"Oh, I'm happy to help. You know you can call on me," she said. She rubbed her arms. "Are you sure you're warm enough?"

"I'm fine." He pushed to his feet and propped himself on his crutches. "I'll see you out."

She waved at the air. "No need. You get some rest, and if there's anything else you need…"

"Thank you, kindly."

Mrs. Brown retreated and a moment later he heard the front door close and the lock turn.

"Can you find my brother?" the ghost whispered from the corner.

"I can try," Jared replied. "Will you tell me your name?"

The boy walked through the bedroom door and Jared followed him, into the dining room, into the kitchen, and then the ghost went through the closed back door.

Jared limped his way to the door and gazed out the window. Ice spiders formed on the single pane of glass. Scattered snowflakes fell from the sky to dust the fallen tree—he reminded himself to call a tree removal service. The boy stood beside the part of the tree that remained intact, his arms wrapped around the trunk.

"Try and explain that away, Siobhan," Jared whispered. Except she hadn't seen the boy when he'd first appeared in the backyard.

Amy had suggested the tree marked a grave. What if the fallen tree had disturbed the boy's final resting place?

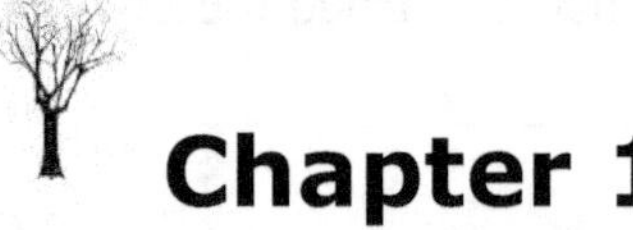

Chapter 14

LAST NIGHT'S SNOW FROSTED the grass, but the temperature was still warm enough that the snow melted when it hit the streets. As Siobhan drove to the nursing home, she contemplated a white Christmas this year. She hadn't seen one since high school. As inconvenient as the weather could be to drive in, there was something magical about waking up to a blanket of white shrouding the world.

First, she had to make it through Thanksgiving. She'd offered to help her mother prepare the meal and been told Kathleen helped with those tasks. So had Siobhan, before she'd left home. Clearly, her mother didn't want Siobhan's help. Siobhan was still a square peg.

She parked in the lot and reached for the prizes she'd brought, one bag with an assortment of the scented soaps the ladies liked, and one with chocolates and sugar free candies that were more popular with the men.

Siobhan found Elsie, the activity organizer, in the gathering room. Elsie stood on a chair hooking Thanksgiving decorations from the florescent light fixtures in the dropped ceiling. Her hair was pulled into a ponytail, and she absently pushed her glasses up her nose as she stepped down from the chair. Some of the residents were already at the tables, most of them in wheelchairs.

"I thought I'd be early enough to help," Siobhan said.

Elsie smiled at her and straightened her smock. "Just about done." She nodded at the bags. "Prizes?"

"Yes ma'am." Siobhan blinked. She'd never in her life addressed anyone as ma'am. And where had that come from? Only one person in her acquaintance addressed people as ma'am, a man who defibrillated her heart with a glance.

"Everyone is looking forward to the Bunco party," Elsie said. "And I'm checking into whether we can use your other suggestion and bring in dogs one day a week to cheer the residents. One of the nurses said she'd heard about nursing homes where they had cats roaming the halls and visiting patients. I'm surprised no one thought to mention it before."

"I volunteer at the shelter," Siobhan told her. "Seemed like a natural fit. They have older cats that would be great hall monitors, as long as nobody's allergic."

Aides and nurses wheeled more residents to the hall. Siobhan carried the prizes to a sideboard and unpacked them, pausing when she heard someone speaking behind her.

"I'd forgotten you lived on Monroe Street," Amy said.

What was Amy doing here? Siobhan turned around to make sure she wasn't imagining the voice.

"Did you know the Sumners?" Amy asked the man whose wheelchair she pushed.

"Sure. We used to play cards together. Good people."

"Do you know who owned the house before them? I think their name was Mason," she said. When Amy looked up, the surprise in her eyes mirrored Siobhan's.

"That's a long time back," the man said to her. "Hard to remember anyone living there other than Charlie and Lily. Of course once my wife grew ill, we didn't see much of the Sumners anymore. And then Charlie passed." The old man shook his head. "I'm the only one left, and look at me. Had to sell the house on Monroe Street."

Amy stopped beside Siobhan. "I didn't know you volunteered here.'"

"Part of my quest to find a life." She forced a smile. "I know it wasn't on Kevin's list, but it's something I used to do."

"And who is this lovely lady?" the man in the wheelchair asked.

"Mr. Burke, this is my future sister-in-law, Siobhan McCormick. She's moved back to Edgarville and, coincidentally, my fiancé and I were trying to talk her into buying Mrs. Sumner's house."

"And you're looking for history on the house?" Mr. Burke asked, taking hold of Siobhan's hand.

"Someone had mentioned something about a young boy who may have lived there," Amy continued.

The ghost Jared had claimed to see? Siobhan pulled her hand from Mr. Burke's and straightened. "Someone?" she asked Amy.

"Who's ready to play Bunco?" Elsie called out with a hand-held microphone.

"Young boy?" Siobhan whispered to Amy. "Are you talking about the so-called ghost?"

Amy grimaced. "We'll talk later, huh?" She turned to one of the tables and explained the rules of the game, demonstrating a roll of the dice.

Siobhan followed suit, helping out a second table. As people caught on, Siobhan stood back and watched.

How did Amy know about the boy? Siobhan had been alone with Jared when he'd claimed to see the boy, which was more likely a manifestation of his medication than an otherworldly visitor. Had Jared charmed Amy, too? Was she visiting him?

Did Kevin know?

Siobhan shot a glance at Amy. She owed it to Kevin to make an effort to like Amy, but there were too many red flags, starting with Mary's messages from the great beyond, followed by the familiarity that came from being confined with Kevin while they hid from a serial killer coupled with Kevin's inexperience with women. Now Amy knew about Jared's ghost.

Something didn't ring true.

Siobhan drifted from table to table, making her way toward Elsie.

"Bunco!" a woman called, followed by a "Damn!" from one of her partners.

Elsie wandered over to confirm, and when a second table shouted Bunco, Siobhan stopped to congratulate the winner. One by one, the rest of the groups announced their winners, prizes were awarded and wheelchairs were repositioned to begin again with new partners.

As the next round began, Siobhan sidled up beside Elsie. "I was surprised to run into Amy Benson here. She didn't mention volunteering before. She's engaged to my brother, you know."

Elsie cast an adoring glance at Amy, one that left Siobhan with a sick feeling in the pit of her stomach. "She's been volunteering here for years. We were so happy when she told us she was engaged. I hope she'll keep coming after she's married. She's such a sweet girl."

Not the answer Siobhan had been expecting. She took a second look at Amy, who was laughing and teasing with another of the old gentlemen. He gave Amy an adoring smile that twisted a knife of shame in Siobhan's gut.

She's a very nice woman. One who had obviously spoken to Jared. Why hadn't Jared mentioned that he'd spoken to Amy? The answer to that was fairly simple. Siobhan had made her opinions on ghostly encounters clear. On the other side of the coin, Amy talked to the dead. Or the dead talked to Amy. Siobhan still wasn't clear how that was supposed to work.

"You. Lady." Mr. Burke raised his hand as Siobhan neared his table.

"Yes, Mr. Burke?"

"I just remembered something. Amy was asking about the people who owned the house before Charlie and Lily. There was a young couple, I'm pretty sure the woman had been divorced and he was her second husband. She had children by the first man. Twins, if I recall correctly. Boys."

"I don't know if it matters, but I'll tell Amy."

He patted Siobhan's hand. "She's a lovely girl, Amy. And you, too. Much too pretty to be wasting your time hanging around us old folks, unless you're looking for a sugar daddy. I'm not dead yet!"

Siobhan laughed. "I appreciate the offer, but no, I'm not in the market for a sugar daddy."

Mr. Burke winked at her. "Just as well. My wife promised to walk beside me until it was my time to go. She always was the jealous type. I'd hate to have her haunting you."

More ghosts. Siobhan forced a smile, patted his hand once more and walked away.

By the third round of Bunco, half the residents were nodding off in their wheelchairs. One by one, aides escorted them to their rooms, and as the last of the tables concluded, Siobhan gathered the leftover prizes.

"For your game closet," she told Elsie. "Save them for next time, or give them out as birthday presents."

"I absolutely will. We'll have to make this a regular event. Monthly, at least, and maybe even weekly."

"It was a hit," Amy added. "When we've been here so long, sometimes we run out of fresh ideas."

"I'm glad I could help," Siobhan replied. "Oh, and Amy, Mr. Burke mentioned something about the family before the Sumners. He said a divorced mother with two boys lived there. Twins, he thought, and her new husband."

Amy crossed her arms and tilted her head. "Interesting."

"What made you ask him about the boy?"

"Jared mentioned it. He invited me and Kevin over Saturday morning to see if we knew any of the house's history."

"And to ask you about the ghost?" she asked pointedly. She blushed when Elsie turned to listen.

"You have time for a cup of apple cider?" Amy asked, changing the subject. "Goes great this time of year, and there's a café not far from here that serves pastries, too."

"Sounds good," Siobhan replied.

Ten minutes later, they sat across a round café table sizing each other up.

Siobhan had to lean forward to hear Amy's voice. "Kevin mentioned what you said to him. About the physical aspects of our relationship potentially clouding our judgment."

Straightforward. Siobhan winced, remembering that was the quality in Amy she liked, but right now, Siobhan was embarrassed. "It happens that way sometimes."

"The thing is, we're both close to 30, and for what it's worth, he's my first, too. Yes, it's pretty intense, but we're not teenagers anymore. We both have lives and a reasonable level of intelligence."

Siobhan let out a slow sigh. "I think I'm more concerned this has happened so fast."

"You and my dad, but he trusts my judgment. I hope you'll trust Kevin's." Amy's way of saying butt out.

"I do trust Kevin's judgment." As much as she hated to admit it. "But there's this other thing. As a reporter, Kevin's credibility comes into question if people think he's a whack job who believes in ghosts. The only job he'll be able to get will be with the scandal rags." *You're going to ruin his future in journalism.*

Amy straightened. "Are you calling me a whack job?"

Siobhan's breath froze in her chest. She was on shaky ground if she wanted to maintain her relationship with her brother. "No."

"And you don't believe in ghosts."

"No."

The bell over the door rang and Amy folded her arms.

"Hey, Sandra," a tall, well-built man said as he walked in. He went straight toward the cashier, the cute blonde who'd waited on them, and leaned over the counter.

Sandra, stepped back and cocked her head toward the table where Amy and Siobhan sat. Odd gesture.

The man glanced across and stood straight. "Hey, Ame. What's up?"

He knew Amy?

He sauntered over to the table and extended his hand. "We haven't met," he said to Siobhan.

"This is Kevin's sister, Siobhan," Amy said. "My brother, Garth."

One of the figurative football linemen Kevin had referred to. Siobhan shook his hand. "Nice to meet you."

Garth cleared his throat. "Getting a cup of cider, and then I have to go set that new stone in the cemetery," he told Amy.

"Don't let us keep you," she said with a half-smile.

"Here's your cider," Sandra called from the counter.

"Nice to meet you," Garth told Siobhan. He tipped two fingers to his forehead and returned to the counter, where he leaned over and whispered something to Sandra. Clearly, there was more going on there than anyone was talking about.

When Siobhan turned to Amy, she found Amy studying her closely.

"Your mother is Catholic," Amy said. "I don't think Kevin has mentioned where your faith lies."

Siobhan raised her eyebrows. "You want to talk religion?"

"No, I want to talk beliefs. Whether you're a Christian or you're Jewish, you adhere to a certain belief system. A way of thinking. Does that make one of them wrong and the other one right? Or politics. Whether you're a Republican or a Democrat or an Independent, does that make the other person wrong? Does your opposition to their platform require you to shun people of the other party?"

A laugh bubbled up. "My ma would certainly try to change your mind if you were on the other side of the fence," Siobhan said.

Amy smiled. "I believe she would."

Siobhan considered what Amy was trying to tell her. She folded her hands and stared at the cup of steaming cider on the table, at the zarf imprinted with the café's name that protected her fingers from the heat. There was an analogy there, one that could burn her.

"I know you don't believe in ghosts," Amy continued.

"And what you're saying is I don't have to." Siobhan looked into Amy's eyes, that odd amber color that seemed otherworldly. "And because I don't, I shouldn't judge other people for having a different opinion on the matter."

Amy smiled. "Yes."

Points to Amy. She wasn't afraid to speak her mind, and she wasn't angling for Siobhan's approval. She was secure in the fact that Kevin loved her, and he'd proven his family wasn't going to change his relationship status.

Instead of resenting Amy, Siobhan took a long look at her own shortcomings.

Amy *was* a very nice woman, and she put Siobhan to shame.

"In case I haven't said so, I'm happy for the two of you," Siobhan said. "I've never seen Kevin look at another woman the way he looks at you. He deserves to be happy, and from everything I've learned about you, so do you."

Amy's eyes glistened. "Thank you."

~ ~ ~

His cell phone woke Jared. He wiped his face, looked around for the source of the ringing and sat straight, setting both his feet on the floor, which sent a jolt of pain through his body.

"Damn," he muttered, as he reached for his phone. "Hallo."

"Jared, it's Amy Benson. Listen, I ran into someone today who told me the people who owned the house before your great aunt had children. Twin boys. Their mother was divorced from the children's father. She owned the home with a new husband. He didn't remember much more than that, but I thought you might want to know."

Jared elevated his leg onto the footrest and closed his eyes against the throbbing that continued to pulse into his groin. "Since my visitor seems to be looking for his brother, that could make sense. Did he mention the name Mason? Public records show them as the previous owners."

"He didn't remember."

"Divorced mother, you said? Assuming the boys had a different last name, I could check for a marriage certificate. That would be a matter of public record, like property records. If we get her name before she married Mason, that might give us a lead on the other boy—man now." The pain had receded, but Jared kept his eyes closed, hoping to keep it at bay.

"Did you see him again? The boy?"

"Yeah. He hugged the tree, the one that split in the ice storm."

"Oh."

Jared waited for her to say something more. When she didn't he asked. "Oh, what?"

"Well, we've already told you about my gift, Kevin and I…"

"Yes, ma'am?"

"Well, the epitaph makes more sense now, and if the tree marks a grave... One becomes two, two become one. If your ghost is a twin…"

Jared glanced around the dark living room. Because he'd fallen asleep, he hadn't turned on a light. His phone told him it was six o'clock. Was it too soon for the boy to appear? Did he want the boy to appear?

"Jared?"

"I might need your help with something. Maybe you'd tell me more about your gift. You see, I have a talent of my own."

Amy drew a sharp intake of air. "Does Siobhan know?"

He shifted in the chair, satisfied the pain had subsided. "No, ma'am, and for now, I think it best not to tell her."

Chapter 15

AS SIOBHAN STEERED ONTO Monroe Street, the snow fell harder. The thermometer on her dash showed the temperature was below freezing, which meant the snow that melted on the roads would be turning to ice. She hadn't had to deal with snow and ice in Virginia.

Good thing she'd volunteered to take Jared to his physical therapy appointment. A slip on icy stairs would land him back in the hospital and a cabbie wouldn't offer extra assistance. As she parked in his driveway, she grabbed the bag of Ice Melt she'd brought. She spread it along the sidewalk as she made her way to the house.

Jared stood inside the enclosed porch, a confused look on his face as he watched her sprinkle the steps with pellets.

He opened the door and asked, "Marbles to make me fall?"

"What doesn't dissolve with the snow will provide traction," she said. "You ready to go?"

"Making sure you're not trying to kill me," he said with a sly grin.

"Goes against my oath," she replied. She positioned herself in front of him. If he fell, he'd knock her over, but at least she'd give him something soft to land on.

He eased his crutches down, one step at a time, with a triumphant look when he reached the front walk.

"You still have to make it to the car," she reminded him.

He screwed his forehead up with concentration as he hobbled his way to the car, reminding Siobhan that despite his bravado, he was still a patient, and still in the early stages of his recovery.

She settled him in the passenger seat, watching every grimace, every hiss of Jared's pain. His reluctance to tell her about Amy and Kevin's visit could easily be due to an increase in his pain level, or the effects of his meds washing him out. She needed to stop looking for her own shortcomings.

"You should take pain meds before physical therapy," she told him.

"I did."

Siobhan settled into the driver's seat, glanced over her shoulder and backed out of the driveway.

"What's those squiggly lines on your dashboard?" he asked.

"The wheels are sliding."

He tensed. "Right. But you seem to be going straight."

"Some things you don't forget, like how to drive in the snow. If the car slides, you take your foot off the gas. Don't brake. Turn into the slide."

He nodded. "Makes sense. Would have been handy to know a few weeks ago. We don't get this kind of weather where I'm from."

"You slid off the road?" she asked. "Is that what caused the accident?"

"That and the other car that decided to join me in the ditch."

"You lived to tell the tale," she said.

"Wasn't so sure there for a while." He glanced out the window. "I must admit I feel better knowing you can drive in this stuff, and it's better than riding in a taxi. Nicer view, too." He was looking at her again, warming up those hidden spots inside her.

"You don't get snow in Louisiana?" she asked, trying to change the subject back to the weather.

"Not like this, no."

They arrived at the physical therapist's office, and Siobhan dropped him in front of the door beneath a portico. "I'll wait for you inside after I park the car."

He nodded, grimacing again as he unfolded and got out of the car. He leaned on his crutches and made his way inside.

When she walked into the waiting room moments later, Jared was watching for her. He smiled and waved her over. "Forgive me for not getting up," he said.

She took the seat beside him. "You can be gallant when you've healed."

The PT assistant stood in the door to the exercise room. "Jared?"

He pushed to his feet.

"You can come back, too, Mrs. Pierce, if you want," she told Siobhan.

Siobhan blinked. Was it worth correcting the woman?

Jared leaned toward her and whispered, "Wanna be my wife for an hour? Hold my hand while they torture me?"

Siobhan raised an eyebrow. "I'll wait here."

"Probably for the best. I might show too much leg." He gave her a wink and followed the woman to the equipment room.

Siobhan had already seen his leg, but not the body it was attached to. At least not undressed. Heat washed over her. She picked up a magazine and flipped through it, something to distract her from Jared's virility—and from the disturbing way she liked the idea of being his wife.

When she'd moved home to Edgarville, she hadn't figured she had anything to lose. She'd been without family for all those years. Now she had everything to lose—her brother, a soon-to-be sister-in-law who was growing on her, and a mysterious stranger who reached into those places she'd closed off.

Closed off had been safe. After a few short weeks at home, she felt more vulnerable than she ever had, even after living with an abusive father.

She'd flipped through two magazines by the time Jared returned to the waiting room.

"Take me home, woman," he commanded. His face was pale and he was draped over his crutches.

"Make sure to ice when you get home," the physical therapist told him, a man whose biceps bulged beneath a company polo shirt.

"After what you two did to me?" he said. "Gonna take more than ice to forget this pain."

"No alcohol while you're taking your meds," the PT added.

Jared forced a pained smile. "It takes a special kind of person to inflict pain on an injured man."

The therapist chuckled. "You'll feel better tomorrow. I promise."

"No lollipop?" Siobhan teased.

"Take me home, wife," Jared growled.

Siobhan guided Jared with a hand around his bicep, a well-developed bicep. "Wife," she sputtered. "As if you'd ever have a wife the way you flirt."

"I just might. One day. If I can find a woman feisty enough to put up with a Frankenstein monster." He leaned over his crutches and held his arms out straight, showing his bottom teeth in his best monster impression.

She chuckled. "If you want to wait here, I'll bring the car to the door."

"Yes, ma'am." He saluted her with two fingers and she shot him a glare.

What was it about the man that got under her skin?

She drove the car under the portico and helped Jared in. As she started driving, he winced. "We'll pack you in ice when we get home," she said.

"You're not the nurse of me," he said in a petulant voice, which he followed up with a grin.

"How about this?" She affected a southern belle voice. "Are you in much pain, honeybunch?"

"Oh, I like that," he said, wagging his eyebrows.

Siobhan shook her head.

"I hate being so weak."

"Did you work on foot touches?" she asked. "Partial weight-bearing?"

"I told you not to nurse me," he said, a more serious look in his eyes.

"My point being you should be making progress. If you're doing foot touches, they're teaching you to bear weight. You couldn't do that a week ago."

"And I can barely do it now," he snarled.

And Mr. Grumpy Patient was back.

The snowflakes were fat and fluffy, pretty to look at if she didn't have to drive through them. The plows kept up with the streets, but the grassy areas showed a couple of inches of accumulation. Any time snow fell in Virginia, the emergency room became crowded with accident victims. Siobhan missed the fast pace of the ER, the daily interaction with patients. Was that why she had attached herself to Jared?

No, her attraction to Jared ran well past the realm of professional. What was she doing with him? Even in high school, the boys hadn't affected her this way. She might have thought she was in love with Carter once, but even he had been the means to an end. Once she'd made the decision to take charge of her own life and stop looking for Prince Charming to save her, she'd had no use for men.

Until now. She wanted to use Jared, the one man who was presently unable to fulfill her fantasies.

As if he'd read her mind, he chose that moment to speak. "You should stay with me tonight. That way I don't have to worry about you driving home in this."

She smirked. "That's very hospitable of you, but I'm sure I can make it home."

"If you still want to play nurse, you could give me my meds and tuck me in."

"Does that ever work for you?" she asked.

The cheeky grin was back. "Worth a try, wouldn't you say?"

She laughed. "And I thought you were dangerous over the phone."

"Dangerous?" He raised his good eyebrow at her. "You mean you like me, just a little?"

"As long as I don't have to take you seriously." She concentrated on her driving, keeping an eye on her traction control. When she turned into his driveway once more, she breathed a sigh of relief.

"Now, you know I have extra bedrooms. I'm serious as the grave if you want to stay. And being a nurse, you know I'm harmless in this condition," Jared said. "These roads are waiting for someone to play with, and I'd hate to see you end up like me."

She was tempted, but she wasn't going to spend the night under the same roof with Jared. He was far from harmless. "I'll walk you in."

She opened the car door and stepped out, burying her foot in new snow. "I should shovel first," she said, half to herself. "At least a path to the door," she said to Jared.

His jaw was clenched, his skin still pale. "You shouldn't have to do that."

"Well, you're not in any shape to shovel. This is why I'm better than a cabbie." She grinned at him, but his face was still tight.

"When's your next pain pill?" she asked.

His eyes narrowed. Yeah, she knew. She was nursing him again. At least he didn't bother to reprimand her this time. "Not for another two hours."

"Then let's get you inside with some ice."

"Plenty of ice out here."

She smirked. "Now I know you're not from around here, but this white stuff? This is called snow. Sometimes it turns into ice, and sometimes it melts away."

Jared shook a finger at her, giving in to a smile. "Clever woman. One game of chess before you go? I'll let you beat me."

Yes, he was baiting her, but she wasn't biting. Jared Pierce was going back to Louisiana as soon as his doctor gave him clearance to travel. Siobhan was already too attached. She'd be smarter to walk away.

"Wait here," she told him.

Siobhan walked down the driveway and opened the side door to the garage, found a shovel, and cleared a path from the driveway to the house. She left the shovel inside the enclosed porch and went for Jared, walking beside him as he moved his crutches carefully through the trail she'd blazed.

Inside, she helped him out of his coat, settled him into his chair and retrieved an ice pack. Jared's head leaned against the back of the chair, eyes closed. Physical therapy took a toll on most people, and this was his first trip out of the house since he'd been released from rehab.

Siobhan refilled his cup of water, positioned the television remote where he could reach it and straightened the second table that held his tools and the chess pieces he was carving. When she looked at Jared again, his mouth was opened slightly, breathing in short, even bursts. She grinned when she considered kissing his cheek before she left, remembering the ploy he'd used the first time he'd kissed her. She wouldn't get caught this time, and if he wasn't faking the sleep part, she didn't want to wake him.

"I'll call you tonight," she said softly.

When he didn't answer, she let herself out.

~ ~ ~

Siobhan stood before the balcony doors in her bathrobe, arms folded, watching the snow fall. Snow had a way of making the world look fresh and clean, and the silence that came with it brought peace.

When she'd been a child, she'd loved the snow. Catching snowflakes on her tongue, making snow angels in the yard, sledding in the park. She and Kevin. They didn't have many friends thanks to their father's erratic behavior, but they had each other, and they had their other siblings.

When she'd walked away from the abuse, Siobhan hadn't realized how much more she'd left behind. All the years she'd been away, she'd buried herself in work so she wouldn't have time to think about how alone she was.

She loved playing with the animals at the shelter. Once she settled into a house, she'd adopt one. Or two. They'd keep her company.

And the assisted living center. Whether she wanted to admit it or not, she'd adopted them, too. Places to go, things to do.

Inside her pocket, her cell phone rang. Siobhan pulled it out and answered the call from her mother.

"Wanted to make sure you were out of the weather," her mother said.

"Yes, I'm in for the night," Siobhan replied.

"You'll be here for Thanksgiving, won't you?"

Siobhan smiled. This year, she had something to be thankful for. "Of course I will."

Her mother sniffled. "It's that glad I am you're home," she said, her Irish accent husky.

"Me, too."

"And your gentleman friend? The one you went out with Friday night? How did that go?"

Duncan Phelps. Friday night seemed so long ago, now. "He's looking for a replacement wife. Probably better not to date people I work with anyway."

"Probably so. And maybe that means he won't keep you from dinners with the family."

A tear snaked down Siobhan's cheek. She knew she was to blame for the uneasiness at the family dinner table. Her mother's point, the one she'd been trying to make since Siobhan's return, finally found purchase. Her family would always be there for her. It was time she allowed them back into her life. "I'll make the effort," she whispered. "I love you, Ma."

"I love you, too. Get some rest now."

Siobhan slipped her phone into her pocket with a sigh. The book she'd started lay on the coffee table, but in her current state of mind, she didn't want to invoke more images of a tall, handsome stranger, one who spoke with a deep, soft drawl. She pointed the remote, but before she could turn the television on, someone knocked on her door. She crossed the room and checked the peephole.

Kevin. And he was alone.

She opened the door. "Hey, little brother."

"Thought you might like some company," he said.

"Don't take this the wrong way, but where's the little woman?"

Kevin walked in and looked around. "I thought the two of you made peace."

"We have, and I think I've done an admirable job of minding my own business."

He smiled. "Yes, you have. I hope I'm not interrupting anything."

She closed the door and ushered him into the living room. "Just watching the snow fall."

"Making the world new again," he said.

Siobhan struggled to rein in the nostalgia.

Kevin sat on the couch and spread his legs, his arms wide across the back of the sofa, making himself at home. "We haven't had much time to talk, you and me."

Siobhan raised an eyebrow and sat in the chair across from him. She wouldn't point out that he and Amy had become inseparable. But he was here, and she'd be grateful for the company tonight. She'd even have been grateful if Amy had come with him.

"You okay?" he asked.

"Men don't like small talk. What's on your mind?"

He shrugged. "Feeling bad that every time you came looking for me I didn't have time to talk."

"I'm fine. I've been discovering that life you told me to grab hold of. Thankful, more than I can tell you, to be among family." Dammit, her eyes were watering again.

"You give any more thought to buying that house?" he asked.

"The haunted-not haunted one?" she teased. *The one Jared Pierce filled with his presence.* His presence would linger long after he'd returned to Louisiana. Siobhan blew out a breath and closed her eyes. He'd gotten to her but good. Jared was one spirit she needed to exorcise. "I think I'm going to have to pass."

Kevin leaned over his knees and stared at her, reading her.

"What?" she snapped at him.

"Is it the ghost? You're not going to run off again, are you?"

Her heart hitched. She deserved that. "Where am I going to go? I left everything behind in Virginia. There's nothing there to go back for." But he could obviously see she was considering her next move.

"So, not the ghost," he said, still watching her too closely.

She was willing to entertain someone else's opinions in regard to ghosts, but she still couldn't believe her level-headed brother would consider such nonsense. "Don't you worry someone will question your credibility?" she asked.

He straightened, his eyes wide with surprise. "So you still don't believe."

"I don't have to. That's the compromise. And I'd be lying if I didn't tell you I'm surprised you do."

Kevin assessed her again. "So it isn't about the ghost, and it isn't about leaving. That guy isn't going to be there forever, just until…" His face widened with a grin. "That guy who happens to be your patient, one you weren't supposed to meet face to face. But you did." He reached for the novel on the coffee table. "Nice looking guy, in a romance novel sort of way."

Siobhan grabbed the book and scowled at him. "I suppose he is."

Kevin nodded, his cheeks dimpling with a wide grin. "So what's the problem?"

She winced and rubbed her forehead, unable to meet Kevin's insistent stare. "There is no problem. He's recovering from a broken hip, and once he's able to travel, he'll be going home to Louisiana. End of story."

"Not even close to the end. He knew who you were, Siobhan. When we went over there, when you were so worried he'd find out you were his invisible nurse, he knew who you were. He said you talk on the phone every night."

Siobhan rose from her chair and reshelved the book. She'd be damned if she'd finish reading it now. "He's a patient, and he'll be going home once he's able to travel," she repeated.

"That night, when we left, he said 'Tell Siobhan I'll talk to her later.' And he didn't sound like he meant he'd be talking to his nurse."

"But that's what I am," she said. She faced Kevin, met his gaze. Mistake. She knew it as soon as his smile grew again.

"Shev, this is me you're talking to. No one knows you better. Just like no one knows me better than you. Isn't that why you sent me after Amy? You knew I was afraid to take a chance."

She raised an eyebrow. "Didn't figure you'd forget about the rest of us when you did." As soon as she said it she regretted it. She waved a hand in front of her face. "Forget I said that. I don't really mean it." She took a deep breath. "All those things you told me to go out and do? I found a couple that stuck. You were right." She managed a smile. "I have a life. For the first time in a long time, and it's thanks to you."

"What about Jared?"

"I don't need a man to make my life complete. I learned that lesson a long time ago, when Carter threw me back."

"No one since?" Kevin stood beside her and rested a hand on her shoulder.

"Nope. No gaping holes to fill, no need to chase after fairy tales that don't exist."

"That's because you haven't made room for anyone else. That doesn't mean you can't."

"He's a patient. It's unprofessional."

"Aha!"

Siobhan sighed. "Aha, what?"

"It *is* unprofessional. Present tense. Not the conditional form 'would be.'"

Leave it to her journalist brother to pick apart her forms of speech.

"Talk," he said, folding his arms.

"I have been. You're not listening. It *is* unprofessional. He *is* moving back to Louisiana. End of story. No future tense to be found here."

"He seems like a nice guy."

"He is a nice guy."

Kevin settled on the sofa, allowing Siobhan to resume her seat in the chair. "Broken hip means you probably aren't having sex, so at least I don't have to go threaten him or ask his intentions."

"Very funny," she said, but she couldn't meet Kevin's eyes.

"But you like him," Kevin said more softly. "And you're worried you'll commit your heart and he'll do the same thing Carter did. Invite you to move away with him and then pull out the 'only kidding' card."

She must be PMSing, because her damn eyes were watering again. "He's not like Carter."

"No, he doesn't live with his parents."

Siobhan looked up at Kevin's teasing expression and grimaced. "Ha ha."

"What does it hurt to spend time together while he's recuperating?"

"I already like him more than I should," she admitted. "I'm supposed to be rebuilding my life, not setting myself up for more heartbreak."

"And if he's part of that rebuilding?"

"Have to question his IQ. After all, he believes in ghosts," she said, fighting a grin.

"I know. He and Amy are talking through what to do about that now."

"He and Amy?"

Kevin nodded.

"A romance novel hero, and you sent your fiancée over there alone?"

Kevin grinned again. "I trust her. Besides, he's harmless in the condition he's in. And I don't know if you noticed, but he's scarred and bruised. She might not think he's quite the catch you do."

"But you just said he was handsome enough to be in a romance novel."

"No, I suggested it as a way to get you to tell me about him. You're the one who sees him that way." He leaned forward again. "And you do, don't you?"

Siobhan sighed again. "I don't know. That ghost thing? That might be a deal breaker."

"That house might change your mind."

Chapter 16

THE STORY AMY TOLD Jared was familiar. Restless spirits had a way of making their presence felt. What surprised him was that Amy had only seen the one ghost, Kevin's sister. Her gift, as she told it, was hearing the final thoughts of the dead, something she was able to put to use by adding epitaphs to gravestones.

"I never *saw* Mary until Kevin and I stayed here, with your great aunt," Amy told him, hands folded in her lap as she sat on the sofa. "Mrs. Sumner thought it might be a result of the two of us together, her abilities as a medium and my ability to hear the voices, although after the séance, I saw Mary other places."

"In my experience, spirits have a way of knowing who can see them," Jared said. "They can be persistent."

Amy drew her folded hands closer. "You mentioned you had a talent of your own."

"Yes, ma'am. It's why my family sent me to flip the house instead of my brother. You see, my father is considered something of a shaman back home. My grandmother, Aunt Lily's sister, thought of him as a ne'er do well because of it, and I suspect that's part of the reason we never heard much about Aunt Lily."

"Actually," Amy said, "according to Mrs. Sumner, her sister, Margaret, thought she was flighty, another ne'er do well like you were talking about. Your grandmother sounds like she may have been a tad judgmental, if you don't mind my saying so."

"That's for true. My father was a finish carpenter, same as my brother and me. His mama, my other grandmother, had the sight, so when he started seeing spirits in some of the houses he worked, she taught him how to help them move on. Now, you met my Aunt Melinda. She was sure this house was haunted, and she was afraid to come back here. The family sent me to make sure the house was cleansed of spirits so they could sell it."

Amy nodded. "You said you saw the ghost hugging the tree?"

"Yes, ma'am."

She nodded again. "I'm pretty sure that boy is buried either under or near the tree."

"I believe it," he said. "And when the storm took the tree down, his spirit was released." Jared grabbed his pad of paper from the tray table beside his chair. "I did more internet searching, public records. The people who sold the house to my great aunt and uncle were Stanley and Iris Mason. Dug a little further and found the record of their marriage right here in the same county. Assuming the boy and his mother shared the same name before she married her second husband, that gives us a starting point. You said the boy was a twin?"

Amy nodded once more.

"If we can find the new ghost's brother, we might be able to give his soul rest. You mentioned the séance before…"

"No more séances," she said. "I went along with Mrs. Sumner's suggestion because it seemed like the only option open to us, and it did give us the answers we needed to find the truth about Mary's death, but when we opened the door, dozens of spirits came through." She swallowed hard, her eyes shining. "Like being a rock star in a crowd of rabid fans, all clutching at you and vying for your attention." She shook her head. "I wasn't cut out to be a rock star."

"I hear that. Opening the door often creates more problems. No séance." Jared rubbed his thigh to ease a twinge. "And the voices? If you touch the tree again?"

"I'll get the same message. That's how my gift works. Not a conversation, more a trail of words left behind for me to hear." Amy glanced around the room as if searching for something.

"You're wondering if the two of us together would be like you and Aunt Lily together," he guessed.

"You read minds, too?" she asked, grimacing.

"Simple deduction. What's your conclusion?"

Amy rose from the sofa and walked into the dining room. She stopped halfway to the kitchen. "You said the boy spoke to you."

"That's right."

She heaved a sigh. "I don't know if I can help, but I'm willing to try, as long as it's just the one ghost."

Jared pushed himself upright and reached for his crutches. He walked to the bookshelves and took down one of the candles. "Spirits seem to like sandalwood. I'm guessing that's why my aunt kept these candles. Would you mind lighting it?"

Amy crossed the room and slid the book of matches from the shelf. When she took the candle from Jared, her hands were shaking. She set the candle on the dining room table and struck a match.

"Can you summon him?" Amy asked. "The boy?"

"He'll come when he's ready." Unconsciously, Jared touched his foot to the floor the way the physical therapist had taught him, testing his ability to bear weight on his broken hip. The pressure ached, but he didn't feel the shooting pain. He tightened his grip on his crutches so an unexpected breeze wouldn't knock them out of his hands.

The boy appeared between Jared and Amy, his head cocked to one side.

"Can you help me find my brother?" the boy asked in a hollow voice.

Amy gasped.

"What's your name?" Jared asked, the same way he had before.

The boy turned, took one step toward the kitchen and stopped. He asked Amy the same question.

She put her hands over her mouth, shot a glance to Jared. "What's your name?" She repeated, her voice shaky.

"Luke. Can you help me find Levi?" the boy replied.

"We'll try," she answered. "Can you tell me anything else?"

The ghost cocked his head again and walked past her, through the kitchen and through the back door.

Amy gasped, then followed and peered through the door's window.

Jared limped on his crutches to stand beside her. The boy wrapped his arms around the remaining tree trunk.

"He told you his name," Jared said quietly.

"And the name of his brother," Amy replied. "Now I'm wondering if he'd tell me more if I touched the tree." She turned to face Jared. "I don't have a lot of experience with this. The voices are benign, and Mary's ghost was the only one I ever interacted with." She paused. "I don't mind telling you I'm scared."

"Wise to be guarded," Jared told her. "Although he was much more forthcoming with you. Maybe he's more trusting of women. Personalities don't change much, even after you die."

Amy walked into the living room and put on her coat. She passed through the house once more, opened the back door and crossed the yard to the separated tree. After a moment's hesitation, she reached for the trunk.

~ ~ ~

Kevin's phone buzzed with an incoming text. He rubbed the scruff on his chin as he read it and scowled.

"What is it?" Siobhan asked.

"Amy. She's ready for me to pick her up."

"Why the face?"

He handed Siobhan his phone and she read the text. "The ghost talked to me."

"You don't believe that," Siobhan said.

"I've see a lot of strange things in the past several months," he told her. "I'm a believer."

"Listen, I don't care what Amy believes or thinks she can hear—or see—but you?"

"Then come with me to pick her up."

Siobhan took a step back. "Why?"

"You might see something that will change your mind."

She wasn't sure she wanted to change her mind. "I'm not dressed."

"Then get dressed."

"You know, I was there when he claimed to have seen the ghost the first time. I didn't see anything."

Kevin took her hand. "I didn't see Mary right away, either."

Siobhan waited for him to deliver a "gotcha" or start laughing about his joke, but his expression remained serious.

If she was going to see a ghost, she'd rather see Mary, to apologize for leaving and staying away all those years.

Kevin had told her Mary was at peace now.

"I think you should come with me," Kevin said again.

"Why?"

He chuckled. "Same reason you told me to call Amy when you first got home."

Siobhan sputtered. "That's different. Your feelings for Amy were written all over your face. I'm not in love with Jared."

"You sure about that?"

"I hardly know the guy." And yet part of the reason she didn't want to go with Kevin to find out about the ghost was because she didn't want to fall under the spell of Jared's southern charm. He definitely had an impact on her, and her resistance was waning.

"You talk to him every night, don't you? Didn't you drive him to physical therapy today?"

"We're friends," she said, hands on hips. "And in case you haven't been paying attention, he's not from around here, nor is he likely to stay, and I'm not about to chase a man across the country a second time."

Kevin reached for Siobhan's hand again. "Then come with me. If nothing else, you might learn something. Broaden your horizons. Who knows? You might even see a ghost."

Siobhan folded her arms. "Go get your fiancée. I'm in for the night."

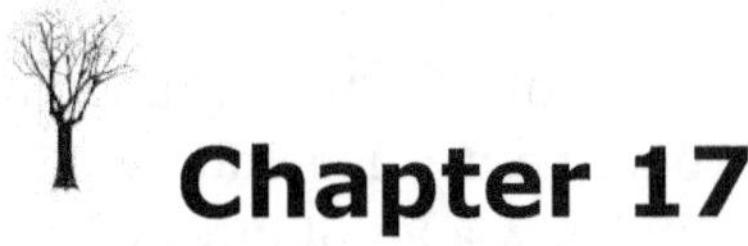

Chapter 17

ONCE, SIOBHAN HAD BELIEVED in the intangible things, in love and magic. The falling snow was one of the few magical things she hadn't outgrown. The short time between when snow covered the world with a fresh, clean blanket of white and the time the mud and the salt discolored it was a time of possibilities.

Possibilities that always ended up ruined and muddied. Siobhan's car added to the mud, soiling the perfection of the fresh layer of snow. The temperatures were predicted to rise so that by the end of the day, the snow would take on a gray, slushy appearance.

Siobhan parked in the hospital garage and rode the elevator up, but when she arrived at the administrative offices, she paused by the windows that lined the hallway overlooking Edgarville. When had her outlook become so gray and slushy? She continued to her office.

When she settled at her desk, she opened PHM on her computer, ready to check the progress of her patients.

"Siobhan?" Duncan Phelps came into focus over the top of her monitor. "Listen, I wanted to make sure our date the other night didn't make you uncomfortable. I meant it when I said no strings. Are we okay?"

Was he angling for another date? She'd have to choose her words carefully, remind him that she wasn't interested without getting herself fired. "Of course. And I hope I didn't offend you. I tend to be too straightforward sometimes."

"No, I appreciate your candor."

Then why was he worried about their relationship?

The phone on Siobhan's desk rang and she held up a finger. Kevin greeted her when she answered.

"Hey, have you ever heard the name Ketterhagen? From when we were kids?" he asked. "Luke, or Levi?"

"Luke Ketterhagen?" she repeated, shaking her head. "No, I don't recall that name."

"How about Mason? Luke Mason?"

"Should I know him?"

"Probably not. I'm going to call Ma. She might know. They would be her generation, anyway. Thought I'd give it a try, though. You knew a lot of guys when we were in school."

Heat rose up Siobhan's neck. Yeah, she knew a lot of guys, and there were lots of them whose names she didn't remember. Not the best time of her life. "Why are you looking for him?" she asked.

"The ghost told Amy his name last night."

"Did you say Luke Ketterhagen?" Duncan asked.

Siobhan shot him a glance. "Hang on a sec, Kevin." She put her hand over the mouthpiece. "Do you know him?"

"I did, when I was in grade school. I haven't heard his name in years. His family moved away sometime around fifth grade."

"Moved away?" Which meant he wasn't a ghost, wasn't dead.

"Yeah. Always wondered what happened to him. He was a twin. Luke and Levi. I think their stepdad's last name was Mason."

Siobhan held up a finger to him again. "Kevin, one of my bosses says he knew them. Twins? He says they moved away."

Kevin's voice grew excited. "Can I talk to him? Your boss?"

"He wants to talk to you," Siobhan told Duncan. "My brother. He's a reporter and he's chasing a story." At least she hoped he'd frame the question as a story instead of asking about a ghost.

Duncan took the phone and Siobhan folded her arms.

"Yeah," Duncan said. "We went to school together," he repeated for Kevin's sake. "They moved away during grade school. Fifth grade? The twins went to stay with their father while their mom and stepdad packed up the house. I remember thinking that was odd. Their real dad wasn't around much, so I had assumed he'd died." He paused. "No, we didn't keep in touch. Ten-year-old boys, you know? School friends, but that was about it." He nodded again. "Sure. Anytime. Just let Siobhan know and she'll get in touch with me." Duncan handed the phone to her with a smile.

"Talk to you later then?" she said to Kevin.

"Yep. Tell your boss thanks again."

"Will do." She hung up the phone and forced a smile for Duncan. "Sorry about that."

"No, I'm sorry. I shouldn't have eavesdropped on your phone call."

Why was he still lurking around her desk? But he'd apparently helped Kevin by doing so. "I'm glad you did. Seems like you've resolved a lead he was chasing."

"Wish I could have been more help." He put one hand on her desk. "This is the brother with the very nice fiancée?"

"Yeah."

Duncan smiled. "I'm sure it's nice to have your family nearby. I guess you'll be spending Thanksgiving with them?"

"Yes, everybody still lives here. What about you? Is your family close by?"

He shrugged. "No. Since the divorce, I don't have anyone to spend the holiday with."

There it was. The reason he was worried about offending her. The reason he was lurking. Duncan Phelps was lonely. Her nursing gene kicked in again. Why did she feel the need to take care of everybody?

What harm could it do to invite him to Ma's? One more mouth to feed wouldn't make much difference. "If you want a home-cooked meal, I'm sure my Ma wouldn't mind setting an extra place. Not a date," she emphasized, "and not meet the family. Somewhere to go if you want to be with people."

He gave her a sheepish smile. "Understood. And I'm just lonely enough to take you up on that. You sure she won't mind?"

"I'll call her at lunchtime to confirm."

"You'll let me know if it's a problem?"

"I'm sure it will be fine," Siobhan said.

Duncan retreated to his office and Siobhan reached for her phone, then thought better of it. She'd stop by Ma's after work. Jared, another of her strays, didn't have physical therapy today. She wasn't committed to either the animal shelter or the assisted living facility until after the holiday, so she had plenty of time to help her mother prepare. As if her mother needed help.

Was Jared's family coming north to be with him for Thanksgiving? He hadn't mentioned anything. She'd have to remember to ask him. Even if she couldn't invite him to her mother's now that she'd invited Duncan—one stray was enough—she could take Jared a plate of food.

And watch him eat.

And listen to him talk.

All by herself, without the interruption of family.

Siobhan shook her head. Romance novel hero. That's what Kevin had called him, and then he'd had the gall to say Amy wouldn't be attracted to Jared. A man with a handsome, if slightly scarred, face, a voice that sent ripples of pleasure to her core. That didn't mean she was falling in love with him. What she felt for him was easily dismissed as a chemical response. The days of indulging her hormones were long gone, and yet she didn't trust herself around him.

Not for the first time, Siobhan was glad Jared was currently disabled.

If she transferred to another position, he wouldn't be her patient anymore.

If she transferred to another position, she wouldn't have to feel awkward around Duncan Phelps every day.

Siobhan checked the human resources portal on her computer and browsed the open positions. ER nurse. Pediatrics. Operating room. All positions she'd filled before, and all of them demanding roles. She missed working with patients, but she liked the regular schedule she had in administration.

Clinical faculty. As a nurse educator, she'd have the best of both worlds. Couldn't hurt to apply. She had the requisite experience and education. If, by some chance, she was offered the job, she could decide then if she wanted to make the change. The more she thought about it, the more the idea appealed to her.

She filled in the application and then, content that she'd done something to resolve her current situation, focused her attention on the job she had.

By the end of the day, as expected, most of the snow had melted away. Siobhan drove straight to her mother's. Even after all these years, walking up to the door filled her with the dread of meeting her father in a foul mood.

Da had been gone almost as long as she had, but the memories lingered on.

Siobhan put a hand on the doorknob and hesitated, suddenly unsure of etiquette. This was the home she'd grown up in. She'd never had to knock when she entered, but she didn't live here anymore. Should she knock? Kevin's apartment had felt like home, but he'd expected—and deserved—that courtesy.

"What you waiting for?" Liam asked, barreling past her and through the door. "An invitation?"

Siobhan smiled. Nothing like a little brother to put things into perspective. "Waiting for you, slowpoke," she said.

He shrugged a duffle bag off his shoulder and went to the refrigerator as Ma walked into the kitchen.

"Siobhan, I wasn't expecting you. Are you staying for dinner?" Ma said.

Siobhan looked past her mother, into the living room beyond. Was Da in the study? Would Ma disappear?

Da wasn't here, but the ghosts remained. Were these the ghosts Amy saw?

"I stopped to ask if it would be okay to invite a friend for Thanksgiving," she said. "One of the doctors at work is alone and I thought he might appreciate being with family, even someone else's."

"A new beau, then?" Ma asked, her eyes sparkling.

"No," Siobhan told her. "Nothing like that."

"Lord knows we'll have plenty of food. Of course this doctor friend of yours is welcome." Ma gave her a hug. "Still bringing home the strays, like that cat in the basement."

The cat. She'd meant to keep it hidden for a day or two, and then one cat became five and Ma had discovered her secret. "I didn't know the cat was pregnant," Siobhan said.

Ma squeezed her arm. "And your Da never found out, not about the cat nor the kittens."

Reminding Siobhan once again that she'd misplaced her anger when she'd left home. Ma was as much a victim of her father's wrath as she was. "How did you live with it? All those years?" Siobhan whispered.

"I had the five of ye to worry about, didn't I? Even after he left, I wondered how I'd manage, but by then he wasn't bringing home enough to feed us all anyway." Ma smiled and turned away. "The Lord provides. I should have trusted in Him sooner."

Faith. Like Amy had pointed out. Everyone believed in something, and that didn't make the rest of the world wrong in what they believed. For too long, Siobhan had only herself to believe in.

~ ~ ~

Too many hours with nothing to do provided Jared ample time to finish the first set of chess pieces. He'd done an Internet search on Levi Ketterhagen, but he'd hit a dead end. No Facebook page, no Twitter account, no mention of him anywhere.

Jared turned on the television and flipped through the channels looking for something to capture his interest before he gave up, frustrated.

What he wanted was to see Siobhan's beautiful face, looking at him across the chess board, teasing him. He'd fallen asleep when she'd brought him home yesterday, and she'd left without saying goodbye. Their conversation last night had been distracted, on his end because of what he'd learned from Amy. How much had Amy told Siobhan?

Jared rose from his seat, gripped his crutches and limped into the kitchen. He opened the refrigerator looking for the last of his mother's casseroles, the one he'd eaten at lunch. He checked the freezer, also empty. Time to call for a pizza.

He returned to his chair, picked up his cell phone and called… Siobhan.

"I ran out of food," he told her when she answered, choosing to appeal to her nurse's sensibilities. "If you bring me dinner, I'll pay you for it. And then I thought you might like to stay for a game of chess."

"It's your lucky day," she replied. "If you make me a grocery list, I can run out after dinner. But the chess game…"

"You afraid I'll beat you again?"

She hesitated, then another breath told him she hesitated again. "I have to be honest. I'm uncomfortable with the flirting." Her voice grew hushed. "And the kissing."

Bullshit. Jared did his best not to call her out on the lie. The chemistry between them was white hot, which reinforced his original opinion that she didn't trust herself. Did he want to push her? Hell yeah, but there was more to Siobhan McCormick. She was the kind of woman he wanted to sit on the porch with. Hold hands with. Watch the sun set, or the snow fall.

He'd also seen her jump to a challenge. "I'll behave myself if you will."

She huffed and then asked, "What do you want to eat?"

"I'll have to trust you," he said. "I'm not from around here."

"What do you like?"

"Everything."

"I'll be there in half an hour," she told him.

"I'll leave the door unlocked," he replied.

"Is that your doctor friend?" another woman asked in the background. "You can invite him for dinner tonight if you want."

"No, Ma," Siobhan replied. "It's someone else."

Doctor friend?

"See you soon," Siobhan told him, and hung up.

He knew Siobhan was attracted to him. He'd heard it in her voice, saw it in her eyes. Hell, she'd made it clear when she'd kissed him. Why was she setting boundaries? His injuries should be proof enough he wasn't a threat to her.

Jared rubbed a hand across two days' growth of beard, then lifted an arm to sniff for body odor. If he had thirty minutes, he might do well to clean up.

Doctor friend?

He hopped to the bathroom, then lowered his second foot to the floor as he set one crutch against the wall and prepared for the shot of pain. The physical therapy must be working, because he was able to balance himself on the bad leg, as long as he didn't put too much weight on it.

He used his free hand to lather his face, then picked up his razor. Activities of Daily Living, ADLs they called them. Caring for himself. They wouldn't release him from rehab until he could show he was capable of doing ADLs. He could. That didn't make it easy. Every day seemed to bring him more strength. Two days ago, he hadn't been able to put his left foot on the floor. He should be able to give up the crutches altogether before long, surely before Christmas.

Ridges of shaving cream lingered along his jaw line. Jared scraped them away once more, then wiped his face with a washcloth. He might be clean shaven, but the bruises from the accident lingered, and the scar that puckered his eyebrow was still fresh. He was a sight. Battle wounds, Siobhan had called them, and he'd won the battle. He wanted Siobhan as his prize. A woman that feisty shouldn't be afraid of anything, but she was most definitely afraid of getting too close. Someone had left his mark on her.

Jared met his eyes in the mirror. Was he fooling himself? Siobhan had a doctor friend. What vanity for Jared to believe he had to crack her shell when she might be involved with someone else and perfectly happy.

Except she'd kissed him. Like no one and nothing else. Not the way someone who was perfectly happy elsewhere should kiss a stranger. He wasn't alone in this fascination they shared.

A car door closed outside. Jared reached for his second crutch and started for the living room, then stopped when Luke appeared before him.

"Can you help me find my brother?"

Jared grimaced. "Not tonight, kid."

The ghost flew into the air and circled the living room. Surprised, Jared lost his balance and fell on the hardwood floor in the hallway. Pain shot through his pelvis, creating white streaks at the edge of his vision. If he didn't pass out, he just might vomit.

Chapter 18

SIOBHAN KNOCKED. Yes, she was expected, but no, this was not her house. Except Jared had limited mobility. And he wasn't answering the door. He'd said he'd leave it unlocked.

She cracked the door open and called out. "Hello?"

Her greeting was met with groaning and several epithets uttered in a strained voice. Siobhan stepped inside. Jared wasn't in his chair. She glanced around the room. One crutch lay on the floor coming out of the hallway in front of the bathroom. She set the Italian beef sandwiches on an end table and rushed to the hall, where she found him on the floor.

"Jared?" She knelt beside him and reached for his left side.

Jared recoiled, sweat on his brow, his face a mask of pain. "Dammit, woman, leave me be."

Siobhan took out her cell phone and dialed 911.

"What the goddam hell did you do that for?" he growled.

"You fell and you're obviously in pain. The doctor will want to take x-rays to make sure you didn't do more damage. What happened?"

He glanced over her shoulder, to the ceiling, and scowled. "Must have taken a wrong step. Help me up."

"I don't think I'm strong enough. I'll leave that to the EMTs. We don't want to make anything worse."

"Ma'am?" the 911 operator asked her.

"Sorry," Siobhan said. "I'm a nurse, so we're fine here until the EMTs arrive, but I'll stay on the line, just in case."

"Is the patient stable?"

Siobhan grinned. "Irascible, but yes, stable."

She tucked the phone under her chin and reached for his leg once more. This time he turned his head away, but didn't try to stop her. "I'm going to take a look at your incision," she told him. She tugged on the elastic waistband of his sweatpants.

"If you wanted to take my pants off, all you had to do was ask," he said, trying to smile. His face was pale, letting her know he was still in pain.

Damn him! Her hands trembled as she uncovered his muscled leg. "No broken skin. The scar looks okay." She probed with her fingers, routine for a nurse, but Jared was not a routine patient. "Nothing seems to be out of place."

Jared winced and recoiled under her touch. "Then I don't need to go to the hospital."

"Oh, you absolutely have to go to the hospital," she said.

"You keep touching me," he whispered, his eyes squeezed tightly closed. "I'll tell you where to stroke."

"Really?" she asked sitting back. "You can still flirt with me with every bone in your body screaming in agony?"

"Not every bone."

A knock on the door signaled the arrival of the paramedics. "They're here," she told the 911 operator. "I'm going to hang up now." She dropped her phone into her purse, walked into the living room and let them in.

While the EMTs checked Jared's vitals, she told them about his broken hip. She stood out of the way when they brought in the backboard and eased him onto it. All the while, Jared lay with his eyes closed, one arm across his forehead.

When the paramedics lifted him onto the cot, he reached for Siobhan's hand. "You go ahead and eat without me, y'heard? And call Amy. Ask her to stop over."

Siobhan backed away. "Amy?"

He grimaced once more, looked away, and then nodded. "Yeah. Tonight. Tell her Luke's angry."

"The ghost?" She shot a nervous look at the paramedics. "You don't want me to go to the hospital with you?"

He shook his head. "No."

"Jared..."

He opened his eyes and tried to lift to his elbows, but dropped to the cot with another wince. "I said no."

"Stubborn man," she murmured.

"That's for true." He managed a wave as the paramedics wheeled him out.

Amy? Did Amy have magic fairy dust that attracted men? First Kevin, and now Jared. Siobhan scoffed. She watched the ambulance take off down the street and reached for her cell phone again. Why did he want Amy to come over? With a sigh, Siobhan placed the call and passed along the message.

"He said the ghost was angry?" Amy repeated. "I guess I'm not sure what he needs me to do."

Siobhan sat on the sofa. "When Kevin talked to my boss the other day, my boss said the boys moved away. How can there be a ghost?"

"Kevin's been trying to track down their parents to get the story."

"And what do you have to do with all of this?" Siobhan asked.

"Luke spoke to me."

Siobhan pressed the heel of her palm into her forehead. "Right."

"Listen, I'm coming over. Will you still be there or should I bring Kevin with me?"

"Because you're afraid of ghosts and you don't want to be here alone?" Siobhan chided.

"Something like that."

If Amy thought she could talk to the dead, Siobhan wanted proof. Firsthand. "I'll be here." She disconnected and retrieved the sandwiches. Jared's would be soggy by the time he ate it. She'd have to buy French rolls for him so he could transfer the meat to fresh bread.

He'd said something about a grocery list. Siobhan walked over to the tray table beside his chair and found one, but Jared might not be home for a couple of days, depending on if he'd reinjured himself. She tucked the list into her purse, figuring he'd need food when he did come home, and headed to the kitchen.

She paused once more, at the dining room table, to admire the set of chess pieces he'd completed. Half of the pieces, the pawns, were simply carved, but the other pieces, the ones that lined the back rows, were all detailed, from the horses' manes on the knights to the bricks on the rooks, to the helmets of the bishops. The pieces would sell quickly at a craft fair. More pieces took shape opposite the ones he'd completed, carved from a lighter shade of wood, a different texture. The woodsy scent carried and she lifted one of the new pieces and sniffed. Pine. Mint. Lemon. The wood had a unique smell, one that had a calming effect.

Siobhan set the pieces on the table and went into the kitchen. Alone in the house, she glanced around. Jared would be selling this house in a couple of months. Did she want to live here?

The house was different without him. She took the opportunity to look around, get the feel of it, and give it more thoughtful consideration. If she planned to stay in Edgarville, she should think about a more permanent residence.

Did she want to stay in Edgarville?

Siobhan carried the sandwiches to the refrigerator.

The kitchen was small, but large enough for one person. The appliances were all normal size, plenty of room to cook if she invited the family over. She returned to the dining room, picturing five people—no, six—sitting at the table. It would be tight, but they'd all fit, and there was room to expand into the living room, which wasn't much larger than a sitting parlor. With the open floor plan, they had room enough to be together whether they were eating or not.

Siobhan opened the attic door and took the steps to the second floor. Did she need the extra bedrooms? And walking upstairs to take a shower didn't seem efficient. If she remodeled the bathroom downstairs…

She paused by the window at the end of the hall overlooking the backyard. Amy had arrived and stood beside the fallen tree. She appeared to be talking to someone, but if anyone else was there, Siobhan didn't see them.

Siobhan made her way downstairs, into the kitchen, and opened the door.

Amy looked up, patted the tree trunk, and walked toward the house.

"Were you talking to someone?" Siobhan asked.

Amy hesitated as she took off her coat. "I don't think you want to hear the answer to that."

"Why?"

Amy draped her coat over the chair, put her hands on her hips and faced Siobhan. "When I was a kid, the mean girls made fun of me. Called me names. I can't change who or what I am and, like Jared, there are times it's better not to open myself up to criticism."

Siobhan's mouth went dry. "What do you mean 'like Jared?'"

Amy raised her eyebrows, her point made. Jared had shared something with Amy that Siobhan wasn't privy to, and didn't that just piss her off. "You might as well tell me," Siobhan said, her hands tightening into fists at her side.

"And if I told you I was talking to a ghost?"

Siobhan closed her eyes and drew a deep breath. This was Kevin's fiancée, and he believed the hocus pocus stuff. "Okay," she said, as much as it pained her to say so.

"When I stopped over last night, Luke told me his name, and he told me his brother's name, but Luke wouldn't tell Jared."

"Luke being the ghost."

Amy nodded.

Siobhan controlled her desire to roll her eyes. "And why wouldn't the ghost tell Jared his name?"

"Well, Jared thought he might be more comfortable around women." She glanced at the back door. "I saw Luke sitting on the tree branch tonight, arms folded, but he wouldn't say anything."

Siobhan bit her lip, fighting the urge to say something sarcastic.

"Did Jared tell you how he fell?" Amy asked. "I'm worried Luke might have hurt him."

"I don't believe ghosts can hurt you," Siobhan said. "I'm sorry, I have to draw the line there."

"But Jared didn't say?"

"He said he was clumsy," Siobhan said sharply.

Amy took Siobhan's hand and invited her to sit at the table. "He hasn't told you about his gift?"

"You mean the chess pieces?"

Amy furrowed her brow, then smiled. "No. His talent with the other side."

Siobhan sighed. "I don't suppose he has. You may have noticed I'm a tad skeptical."

"Why did you stop by tonight?"

Heat rose in Siobhan's face. "He's a patient."

"He's more than a patient. Kevin and I have both seen the way you look at each other."

"He ran out of food and asked me to bring him dinner," Siobhan said, waving toward the refrigerator.

"Why?"

"Because he was hungry?"

"He could have ordered something to be delivered."

Siobhan clamped her jaw tight. "He has a way of charming people to do what he wants them to."

"But you're smarter than that," Amy said.

Siobhan looked away. "What's your point?"

"He knows how you feel about ghosts, so he hasn't shared his talents with you. He's afraid you'll turn your back on him."

"I wouldn't turn my back." Siobhan bowed her head. She would, and she had.

"He's afraid he'll scare you off, or worse, you'll ridicule him for something that is woven into his DNA. Something he has no control over. When I was in junior high, we did a taste test in science. Some people tasted nothing, and for some people, the taste was bitter."

"You're back to faith and belief systems, aren't you?" Siobhan said.

Amy shrugged. "I thought you might relate to the science test more."

"This isn't science."

"In a manner of speaking, it is."

Siobhan huffed. "So why did Jared want you to come over tonight?"

"To talk to Luke. He said Luke was mad, right?" She leaned on the table. "I think Luke had something to do with why he fell."

"I still don't believe a ghost would have the... the... substance to cause physical damage."

"They don't need substance," Amy told her. "They only need a weakness. No, Luke probably didn't push Jared, but he knew how to throw Jared off balance." She rose and walked to the door once more, looking to the yard. "There was something different about Luke tonight. Something angry."

Siobhan stood beside Amy, still unable to see what Amy and Jared professed to see. "Kevin told me you hear the dead. He said Mary was the only ghost you've ever seen. How is it you can see and speak with Luke?"

Amy turned toward Siobhan with a sad smile. "There's something about this house, apparently. This is where I saw Mary, too." She laid a hand on Siobhan's arm. "Luke's disappeared again, but I have a bad feeling. You're not planning to wait here for Jared to come home, are you?"

"No. Why?"

Amy pursed her lips. "Until we understand what Luke wants— why he's upset—I'd be afraid to stay in the house alone."

A chill crawled along Siobhan's spine. "Then I guess we should leave, unless there's something more you want to say to the ghost."

Amy scowled. "Let's go." She opened the door, checked the lock and waited for Siobhan to pass through. "You going to the hospital to see Jared?"

"He said he didn't want me to," she replied. And she was still piqued that he'd told Amy something about himself that he'd withheld from her. "I'm sure they'll keep him overnight. I'll check on him in the morning, when I go to work."

As Amy closed the door, Siobhan glanced over her shoulder at the dark house. Was that a face in the window?

Nope. She was pretty sure she didn't want to buy this house.

Chapter 19

SIOBHAN SAT IN THE Wednesday morning administrative meeting prepared to present the status of her PHM patients.

She was first on the agenda so the social worker, Betty, could present her opinions on the one app patient who had been readmitted to the hospital, Jared Pierce.

"He was released from rehab 2 weeks ago," Betty said. "They agreed he was able to perform basic ADLs, but he has no one at home with him, and his recent fall raises concerns about how well he can care for himself. He stayed in the hospital overnight without complications, but I'm reluctant to release him without at-home care."

"What do his metrics indicate?" Dr. Phelps asked Siobhan.

"He hasn't had any issues prior to the fall," Siobhan reported. "His progress has been within parameters, and he feels his fall was an unlucky fluke."

Betty raised her eyebrows. "Our goal is to forestall re-admission. Fluke or not, I'd like to see him receive additional at-home care, despite his objections."

Siobhan bit her lower lip to keep from telling them she'd observed him at home, that she was sure he'd be fine, except for a certain ghost. If Amy was right, he shouldn't go home alone.

"If the fall didn't result in complications, I'd say the decision is his," Dr. Phelps said, "but you can certainly pass along your recommendation," he told Betty.

Betty shot Siobhan a suspicious look. Did she know about Siobhan's relationship with Jared? Would they question her professionalism, something she'd always prided herself on?

What *was* her relationship to Jared?

"I have to get back on the floor," Betty said, and left the meeting.

Dr. Phelps asked for the overview of the rest of the PHM patients, questioned Siobhan about triggers that might indicate risk during their recovery, and then moved on to the next agenda item.

When the meeting concluded, the vice presidents took turns slapping each other on the back and wishing each other a Happy Thanksgiving since they would all be leaving early to get a head start on the holiday. Siobhan gathered her things and prepared to do rounds to check that the right people were in the right rooms on the isolation ward—and to check on a certain patient from Louisiana.

All the patients were in their proper places, and when Siobhan arrived on the orthopedic floor, the nurses were giggling at their station. They were talking about the hunk in room 3313 who called everybody 'baby' and had the best accent.

Siobhan passed them, to room 3313, smoothed her blouse, and walked in. "Good morning, Mr. Pierce." He reclined on his bed, dressed in a t-shirt and shorts.

"Now there's my girl," he said.

A nurse, who followed close behind Siobhan gasped.

"Flirting with all the nurses again, are you?" Siobhan asked.

"These angels of mercy have all been very kind to me, but now I know I've made it to heaven. You know you're the only one I care about, don't you?"

Siobhan turned to the nurse behind her. "Is he this way with all the nurses?" she asked.

The nurse stared at her, wide-eyed. "No, ma'am."

Siobhan tilted her head. "He's not?"

A smile crept across the nurse's face. "He's been telling us how he's been waiting and hoping that his lady would show up."

"And so she has," Jared said.

Putting Siobhan front and center in the rumor mill. She wanted to disappear. And why was she stopping in his room? The gossip would be all over the hospital before the end of the day. *Not professional.*

"Imagine my surprise when I arrived in Edgarville and found my old friend, Siobhan," Jared continued.

She shot him a sideways glance designed to shut him up, but he continued.

"Like the old days, isn't it? But some women you never get over."

He'd known from the start she was worried about what people would think of her fraternizing with a patient, and he was offering her a cover story. A relationship that pre-dated his patient status.

The nurse nudged Siobhan, a decidedly unprofessional move and Siobhan gave her a stern look.

"Don't be hard on her, sweetie," Jared told Siobhan. "She's been taking real good care of me." He nodded to emphasize his point.

"You're all he's been talking about," the nurse said quietly. "About how he can't wait to play chess with you again and hold hands on the porch and watch the sunset. It sounds so romantic."

Siobhan glanced at Jared. "Yes, it does."

A couple other nurses loitered outside the door, checking charts, making patient notes on their tablets, sending secretive glances at Siobhan and Jared. She didn't see a way out of this. Siobhan shook her head and sighed. "Has the doctor made his rounds yet?" she asked the nurse.

"We're expecting him to release Jared around two this afternoon," she replied.

"I suppose you need a ride home?" she asked Jared.

"Would you mind giving us a minute?" he said to the nurse.

The nurse hurried out of the room to join the hoverers outside the door.

Jared motioned Siobhan to the side of the bed. "The social worker is being prickly about sending me home alone," he said quietly. "And I don't want to go back to rehab. Can you tell her you'll be staying with me? Of course, I wouldn't expect you to actually stay…"

~ ~ ~

He hated being so helpless, and he hated asking Siobhan, of all people, for help. He'd been talking up his girlfriend to the other nurses, in part to keep them at bay, and in part with hopes they'd track Siobhan down and she'd get him out of here.

"Amy told me about Luke," she said.

He nodded. "And I know you don't foster to ghosts. I'm not asking you to."

She pursed her lips and looked away. "Amy says its part of your DNA, part of her DNA. As much as I'd like to believe that, I have a real hard time…"

"Darlin', I don't care what you believe." The words came across harsher than he'd intended. "Look. I'm not a crazy. I have a real job and I have a real life. The cleansings? That's something I do to help people out."

"Cleansings?" she asked.

So Amy hadn't told her everything. Jared raised his chin. "If you don't want to hear about the ghost stuff, I won't share it."

"But you shared it with Amy."

Oh. Now he was getting somewhere. From their conversations, he knew Siobhan took issue with Amy. "I suspect Kevin had a hard time believing Amy in the beginning, too, but he seems to have found a way. Maybe you'd give me that same chance. If you want to know about the extra work I do, I'll tell you. But you haven't seemed too interested up to this point."

She folded her arms. Not a good sign. He might regret it, but he gambled on her feistiness to get her talking.

"So why'd you stop in?" he asked. "To tell me how ignorant I am?"

Her arms dropped. Progress.

"I stopped by to make sure you were okay. We discussed your fall in the app meeting this morning."

He nodded. "Don't want a bad mark on your record. PHM is supposed to prevent return trips to the hospital, isn't it?"

"Your hospitalization wasn't a result of poor care," she said with a defensive tone.

There she was. The sparkle was in her eyes, the fight in her voice. Her cheeks took on a rosy color. When Siobhan got all riled up, she stirred things inside him he didn't know were there, made him want to test her, to see how far he could take her, to let her drive him right to the edge and over. "Maybe I do need home care," he told her. "Can you recommend someone who'll stay with me a couple of days? Through the weekend?"

"I'll stay with you," she said angrily, then turned away. "Dammit."

Jared smiled, almost ashamed of himself for pushing her to the point where she made a commitment she didn't want to make, and yet if she truly didn't want to, she wouldn't have. He'd have to pay for his sins later. "I do appreciate it, ma'am," he said.

She narrowed her eyes at him. "I'll be back to check on you around two." And then she stormed out.

He might live to regret this.

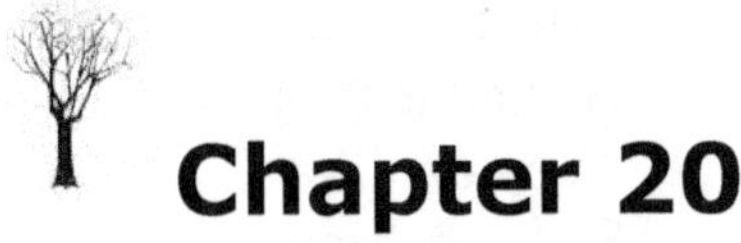

Chapter 20

THE WEATHER TOOK A Spring-like turn as Siobhan drove Jared home from the hospital. He hadn't said much since she'd offered to stay with him, didn't say anything on the ten-minute drive home, which was just as well. She was still stewing about her lapse in judgment.

She handed him his crutches and watched him get out of the car, limp his way up the front steps and into the house where he settled into his chair.

"Do you have to go back to work?" he asked.

"Most everyone left early with the holiday tomorrow," she said. "I can monitor my app patients from here, but I do need to pick up a few things from the apartment."

He nodded.

"I have your grocery list, so I'll stop at the store on the way. When's the last time you did laundry? I can do a load for you tonight."

"I can do my own laundry."

"I'm sure you can, but since I'm here, I'll take care of it."

"That's not necessary."

Siobhan turned to look at him. Jared wasn't smiling. In fact, he looked as if someone had kicked his cat. Probably the pain. "When are you due for more pain meds?"

"Not for a while."

"Do you need an ice pack?"

"Go get the groceries," he said, his voice deep and menacing. *Menacing?*

Siobhan put her hands on her hips, but was stopped when someone knocked.

"Tree removal," a man said when she opened the door.

Siobhan glanced at the street, where a truck and a wood chipper had parked. She turned her head. "You called for tree removal?"

"Yes, ma'am."

"The tree's in the back," she told the man at the door.

He nodded, walked out of the porch and trotted down the steps.

"You don't have to stay," Jared said.

Siobhan heaved an impatient sigh. "Is your family coming for Thanksgiving?"

"They can't make the trip."

"Would you like to join my family?" she asked through clenched teeth. "You already know Kevin and Amy, so you'd have people to talk to." As much as she hadn't wanted to invite him, she'd assumed responsibility for him.

He narrowed his eyes at her, his mouth set into a frown. "I'll be fine on my own."

"It's a holiday. You don't have to be alone."

"You can stop nursing me now," he groused.

Chainsaws buzzed in the backyard. Siobhan spared a glance toward the kitchen and caught a glimpse of three men attacking the felled tree. When she looked at Jared again, he was still glaring at her. What had she done to deserve that?

"Did you or did you not ask me to help you find someone to get you through the weekend so the social worker would release you?" she asked him.

"I did."

"And now?"

"I can care for myself."

She set her hands on her hips, all too familiar with truculent patients. "Here's the deal," she told him. "I signed off on your care, so now you're stuck with me. I won't be here all the time. I'm covering for someone at the animal shelter tonight and I want to stop by the assisted living facility on Saturday. You can sulk when I'm gone. I'll be attending Thanksgiving dinner with my family, and if you ask me nicely, I'll bring you a plate of food if you want to be antisocial. But you have to ask me nicely."

"And which of those places is where your doctor friend works?"

"My doctor friend?" she asked.

"Yes, the one who will be attending Thanksgiving at your mother's."

Siobhan blinked a couple of times before she remembered she'd been talking to Jared when her mother asked about her doctor friend. *He was jealous?* She didn't know if she should laugh or set him straight. Another knock kept her from having to decide.

"Excuse me, ma'am," the tree guy said. He shifted from one foot to the other and tugged the baseball cap in his hands. "We won't be able to finish the tree today. In fact, I had to call the police department."

"Police department?"

"Yes, ma'am. While we were trying to clean up the root ball—it pulled out of the ground when the tree fell—we found a skeleton tangled in the roots." He tipped his hat and jogged to his truck.

Siobhan shivered. Skeleton? It had to be a joke. "It's not real, right?" she asked Jared.

"What's not real?"

"C'mon. The joke's not funny."

"Why don't you tell me the joke and let me decide."

She stared at him, this man she hardly knew.

Jared tilted his head and narrowed his eyes. "Siobhan? What is it?"

"The arborist. The guy you hired to remove the tree. He says there's a skeleton in the root ball." She dropped onto the sofa.

"Then I guess Amy was right."

Amy? "We aren't going to start talk of ghosts again, are we?" she asked, struggling to find her breath. The hairs on the back of her neck stood up. She was *not* superstitious. She *was* creeped out, however.

Jared reached for his phone and placed a call. His focus remained on Siobhan. "It's Jared," he told the person who answered. "I thought you might be interested to know they found a skeleton under the downed tree."

"I have to go to the store," Siobhan said, rising from the sofa. She had to go anywhere but here.

Jared disconnected the call and held out a hand. "Siobhan. Wait."

She shook her head. "I don't know what game you're playing this time, but I don't want to be part of it."

"You know I'm not part of this. You said they found a skeleton, not a corpse, and I'm in no condition to bury things in the backyard."

She pulled on her coat. "Seriously. I have to go to the grocery store. You don't have any food in the house."

"You'll be back?" he asked.

She chuckled. "Didn't you tell me I didn't have to stay?"

His face softened with a smile. "But you will."

Damn that man! She scowled. "Yes, I will."

~ ~ ~

All the color had gone from Siobhan's face. She walked out the door, along with any chance he might have of establishing a relationship with her.

He leaned into the chair and closed his eyes, exhausted. Cautiously, he tapped his left foot on the floor, waiting for the streak of pain, which didn't come. A night in the hospital hadn't done any harm. In spite of his fall, he was able to measure his progress. He was getting stronger, and he could prove it to Siobhan. He didn't need anyone mothering him, taking care of him. He'd been taking care of himself since he was eighteen.

Another knock. He eased out of the chair and leaned into his crutches. A policeman greeted him when he opened the door. Jared looked past him, to the street, where several other municipal vehicles were parked.

"Jared Pierce?" the policeman asked him.

"Yes, sir."

"I'm Officer Lynch. The tree service said you'd called for tree removal, is that correct?"

"It is."

"Can I come in?"

Jared stepped aside and waved him in.

"Accident?" the policeman asked as Jared settled into his chair.

"Yes, sir. Not used to driving in ice and snow. Had a problem on the Interstate."

"Is this your house?"

"No, sir. My great aunt lived here until recently. She passed a month or so ago and the family sent me to help settle the estate. I ended up staying longer than I expected after the crash."

The policeman jotted down notes. "Any ideas about the skeleton in the backyard?"

Jared considered his answer carefully. "I heard a story recently," he began. "About twin boys who lived here before my great aunt and uncle. Someone mentioned they'd disappeared about the time they were ten. In fact, one of my friends is trying to locate the boys. Can you tell the age of the person from their skeleton?"

"That's up to the coroner."

"Any chance you could help me locate the missing boys?" Jared asked. "I'm guessing they'd be near to fifty years old now."

The policeman scanned the room. "I'm not sure what the tree service people told you. You said the boys were twins?"

"That's what I've been told."

The policeman nodded. "I don't suppose it would hurt to tell you there appears to be more than one set of remains beneath the tree."

Chapter 21

A SKELETON.

Siobhan threw clothes from her dresser into her overnight bag. Amy and Jared had to be playing a practical joke. Was that the reason Amy had been over there with Jared? And Kevin had been sent to keep Siobhan busy. That made more sense than ghosts and skeletons.

Tears streamed down her cheeks. Why would the three of them conspire to play a joke like that? Because she didn't believe in ghosts? Were they trying to make a point or trying to scare her?

She tucked her toiletry kit beside her clothes and zipped the bag closed, then sat on the edge of the bed. And why was she staying the weekend with Jared?

Because he needed help, but she didn't have to stay there to provide it. She'd take him his groceries, do chores for him, make sure he had what he needed, but he'd been taking care of himself before the fall, and the fall hadn't caused any additional damage. Amy's comments about not being alone in a haunted house suddenly sounded suspect. Was it a ploy to throw Siobhan and Jared together?

Siobhan looked at her overnight bag. Might as well throw it in the car, just in case, but she didn't *have* to stay. She was not going to fall prey to Jared's relentless flirting and she definitely was not going to kiss him again. She'd play her role of visiting nurse—she had experience with that—and not allow the patient to manipulate her.

The grocery store was packed with last-minute Thanksgiving shoppers. She should have waited until after the holiday, but she was here now. Siobhan looked over his list—apples, milk, bread, lunchmeat, eggs, bacon, soup. He'd also added microwaveable meals and pizzas. She loaded all the items into her cart and waited her turn in the too-long checkout line.

"He's a patient," she reminded herself, gripping the wheel as she drove to his house. She shot a glance at her nurse bag on the seat beside her and chuckled. As if he'd let her check his vitals. Jared was at the far end of her friend spectrum at the moment, and perilously close to falling off altogether.

As she turned the corner onto Monroe Street, she slowed. In the encroaching dark of twilight, two police cars were parked in front of Jared's house, and Kevin's car was parked in the driveway. Two police cars? That was overkill if this was a joke. One of the cars had a 'Forensic Anthropologist' sticker in the back window. A chill shook her.

Jared had seen the ghost in the backyard beside the tree, and now there was a skeleton.

She parked behind Kevin's car and took a deep breath to calm her jangling nerves. Her brother wasn't a prankster, and if this was a hoax, it was far too elaborate. Siobhan made a conscious decision not to react or respond to whatever was going on inside the house. She popped the trunk, grabbed a couple of the grocery bags, and walked up the front steps.

"I've managed to locate a man named Hank Ketterhagen," Kevin was telling the policeman, "but nothing's turned up yet on Iris or Stanley Mason. I'd planned to contact Mr. Ketterhagen on Saturday, after the holiday, to ask him about the boys."

Kevin looked up, then at the bags Siobhan carried. "Do you need help?" he asked.

"If you don't mind," she said.

Amy was there, too.

The policeman rose from his seat. "And you are?" he asked Siobhan.

"Mr. Pierce's nurse," she said stiffly.

Jared scowled and rubbed his jaw.

Siobhan carried the groceries into the kitchen. Through the back window, she saw a man in a white suit in the hole beside the tree and a second man brushing something on a tarp beside him. Bones? She shivered and turned away, putting away the groceries she'd brought in. Kevin arrived moments later and set the rest of the bags on the table.

"The policeman gone?" she asked.

"For now. They found remains under the tree," he said.

"Actually, the arborist did," she corrected him.

Kevin's eyebrows rose. "You know about that?"

"I was here. I brought Jared home from the hospital." She gave Kevin her best 'don't screw with me' face.

They glared at each other for several minutes, Kevin appearing to assess her the same way she measured him. Kevin broke first.

"Look, I know you don't believe in ghosts or the afterlife, but you have to admit it's kind of coincidental Jared says he saw the kid the night the tree went down, and now they've found bones under the tree."

"Coincidental," she repeated, folding her arms.

"No chance of opening that scientific mind of yours to possibilities?"

She rolled her eyes. "Look, I'm here to do a job."

Kevin quirked an eyebrow. "Is that what you call it?"

Ignoring his unspoken question, Siobhan put away the rest of the groceries, then pulled a couple pots and pans from the cupboards so Jared wouldn't have to bend to get them out. She wasn't getting drawn into a discussion about ghosts.

A soft voice whispered in the door between the kitchen and the dining room. "Did you find Levi?"

Siobhan turned around to see who'd spoken. Amy was crouched in the dining room in front of a young boy. The light hit the boy in such a way he appeared to have a halo around his body.

"Was Levi with you when you died?" Amy asked.

Shivers tingled Siobhan's skin.

"Not dead. Not dead. Not dead." The boy flew into the air as if he had rocket launchers on his shoes and circled the room before he evaporated through the closed back door.

Siobhan dropped the pan she'd been holding.

~ ~ ~

The crash didn't sound good, and when Amy rushed into the kitchen, Jared hauled himself out of the chair to see what had happened.

Siobhan sat on the kitchen floor, her legs straight out in front of her. She leaned away from Amy, spearing her with a wary glance. "Mass delusions," Siobhan said quietly.

"If that's what you need to believe," Amy said.

"Right," Kevin said acerbically. "Because that makes sense."

"He flew around the room like that the other day," Jared told Amy. "Took me by surprise. That's why I fell."

Siobhan's eyes glittered with fear. "He knocked you down?"

"I fell," Jared repeated. It was a fine distinction, but he was not going to let a ghost chase him away, especially when he considered his alternatives to living here. "You saw him?"

Siobhan cradled her head in her hands.

Amy cocked her head toward the living room. Jared limped to his chair while Kevin helped Siobhan to her feet and guided her to the sofa.

"As I was telling the policeman," Kevin said, "I found a man named Hank Ketterhagen who lives about 20 miles from here. If he's the boys' father, he can shed light on what's going on. According to Siobhan's boss, the twins were supposed to be staying with him when the Masons were moving, which raises the question of how Luke ended up here."

She pointed at Jared. "We don't know this man, or what his motives might be."

Jared ground his back teeth. "What do I have to gain by having a ghost haunt my great aunt's house? It isn't exactly going to boost the resale value, not to mention skeletons in the backyard."

She retreated into the corner of the sofa. Now that she'd seen a ghost, she was more freaked out than before.

Jared scratched the beard outgrowth on his chin. "I don't know whether to help Luke find his brother so he can find his own peace, or to help him move on alone."

"The ghost made you fall?" Siobhan asked again. "You made me call Amy because you said Luke was angry. He made you fall. You can't stay here. Not if that ghost is trying to hurt you, not when you're already hurt."

Jared eased to the edge of his seat. "Now, Siobhan, let's not make this more than it is. I'm not what you'd call transportable at the moment. I'm settled here. I'm fine."

"Your bones are still healing. Every time you fall, you risk permanent damage." She glanced around the room, searching out their invisible guest. "We can't stay here, Jared."

"I'm not going back to rehab," he told her. "You're free to go, but I'm staying. I can help the boy move on."

"I don't think he'll want to move on without his brother," Amy said. "If we could locate Levi, invite him here…" She squeezed Kevin's hand. "You said you're going to talk to the dad on Saturday?" She looked to Jared. "Tell Luke we're looking for Levi, that we're trying to find him. He was a young boy, and he's clearly prone to temper tantrums as you've seen when he wouldn't talk to you the other day, and today, when I reminded him he was dead."

Siobhan pushed off the sofa and walked into the dining room, to the spot the ghost had appeared. She glanced at the walls again, at the ceiling. "I'm not leaving you alone with a… with a…"

"Ghost," Jared finished for her.

She put her hands on her hips and glared at him. Even frightened, she was fighting back. He was that proud of her. She was something, that's for sure.

"Shev?" Kevin said.

She fingered the finished chess pieces on the dining room table.

"We could stay," Kevin offered.

Jared had reached the limit of his patience. "I've been through this before," he told them all.

"With a broken hip?" Siobhan shot back.

Well, no, and she did have a point there. He was at a disadvantage, but if she stayed with him…

"Are you staying?" he asked, to be sure.

Her hands went to her hips, her eyes flashing. "Yes." She turned to Kevin. "I'll call you if something happens that we can't handle."

Kevin scowled and pulled Amy to her feet. "I'd like to give you the benefit of my experience, in this very house, but I know you well enough that I wouldn't expect you would listen. I don't know if there's anything more we can do tonight." He turned to Jared. "What are you doing for Thanksgiving?"

"Keeping my own company, right here."

"In case my sister hasn't invited you, you're welcome to join my family."

"As a matter of fact she did invite me, and I gave her my regrets."

Kevin's brow quirked. "Oh, I think you should come."

Jared glanced at Siobhan, who shot her brother daggers with her eyes.

"You shouldn't be alone in the house," Kevin continued. "And maybe Ma would make up one of our old rooms and you could stay there."

The steam practically shot from the top of Siobhan's head. Jared didn't want to upset her more than she already was. He would wager their late-night phone calls had come to an end. She'd already assigned the blame to him for showing her a reality she didn't want to face. "I think it best not," Jared told Kevin.

"Are you going to be okay?" Kevin asked Siobhan. "One phone call and Amy or I can pick you up."

She rose to her feet slowly, closed her eyes and took a deep breath. "I'll see you at Ma's tomorrow."

He nodded. "I need you to move your car. You're parked behind us."

Siobhan grabbed her keys and stormed out the door.

Kevin grinned. "We'll see you tomorrow," he told Jared before he escorted Amy out.

When Siobhan returned moments later, she put her hands on her hips, her face set in a frown. "What would you like for dinner?"

"You're not going to burn it, are you? I can make my dinner, you know."

Her jaw tightened. "I'll start your laundry then."

"Did you tell me you're a nurse?" he asked. "Mrs. Brown gave me the name of a housekeeper, you know. You should be asking to take my temperature. Do you want to see my scar? Or you could help me wash up."

She stared him down, her lips pressed together as if opening them would cause an explosion. She opened her mouth, then shut it again, took a deep breath and spoke. "Do you feel ill?" she asked. "Are you experiencing any pain?"

Jared waved her to the chair beside his. "Come play chess with me."

"I'm your nurse, not a paid companion."

"Don't be angry with me." Because she'd seen a ghost? "Are you afraid? You don't have to stay."

Siobhan scowled and huffed. "I said I would."

He wanted to laugh, but he knew better than to piss her off more. "A woman of her word. That's admirable."

"Or stupid," she muttered.

"Let me make dinner for you," he offered.

She shook her head. "No. As long as I'm here, I might as well make myself useful." Siobhan stomped past him and into the kitchen.

Jared eased to his feet to follow and was stopped by yet another knock at the door. This time, it was a man wearing a jacket with the word CORONER printed on it.

"Mr. Pierce?" he asked.

"Yes, sir."

"I believe we've collected everything we need for the moment, but I'll ask you not to venture beyond the police tape we've used to mark the area." He glanced at Jared's crutches.

"I'm obviously not likely to venture out," Jared told him. "And I'll make sure to tell anyone else who visits to steer clear for the time being."

The coroner nodded. "We'll be in touch." He walked out of the porch and down the outside stairs.

When Jared turned, Siobhan stood on the kitchen side of the pocket door.

"Looks like they've all gone," she said. "Is your ghost going to be back?"

"Couldn't say."

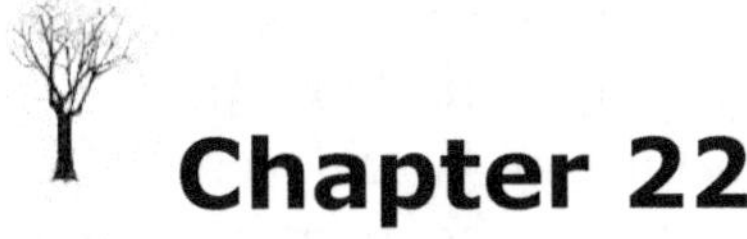

Chapter 22

DESPITE JARED'S INSISTENCE THAT she could have used one of the bedrooms, Siobhan slept on the sofa. She'd spent nights in less comfortable places.

She woke with a start to find a young boy standing in the dining room, staring at her.

"Is Jared a friend of Stan's?" he asked in a hollow voice.

Siobhan's heart raced. She blinked to make sure she was awake. Yep. Her eyes were open. She pushed herself to a sitting position to shake off any chance she was dreaming. Could the ghost hurt her? He was a ten-year old boy, and from what Amy had said, he didn't realize he was dead. She spoke softly and reassuringly. "I don't know Stan, but Jared is my friend," she told him.

"Did Stan take Levi?" the boy asked. "Do you know where Levi is?"

The boy waivered, like a hologram, which made Siobhan wrap her arms around herself and rub away the gooseflesh. "We're trying to find him," she told the boy. "My brother is going to ask your father."

The boy frowned and disappeared. *Disappeared.* Siobhan glanced around the room for something that might explain her ghostly visitor. The shades at the windows were drawn, and the room was too small to conceal anything. The light from a projection lamp should have been visible.

She'd spoken to a ghost. Why hadn't she seen the boy the night the tree came down, like Jared?

She sat upright for the next half hour, her blanket wrapped around her shoulders, but she couldn't stop shivering. When she'd convinced herself the ghost was gone, she snuggled into the couch and pulled the blanket over her head, where she slept fitfully until morning.

The squeak of rubber footed crutches on the hardwood floor told her Jared was awake and moving. He appeared in the hall a moment later wearing knit cotton shorts and a t-shirt as he limped into the bathroom, bearing partial weight on his left foot. Not bad for first thing in the morning. Siobhan rose from the couch, folded her blanket and went into the kitchen to start the coffee.

When Jared emerged several minutes later, he paused and met her gaze. Should she tell him about her ghostly visitor?

"Happy Thanksgiving," she said.

"Likewise."

"Can I get you anything?"

"Coffee." He glanced at the table beside his hip chair, where he normally kept his meds.

"You need a pain pill?" she asked.

"I'll get that if you'll bring the coffee."

She nodded and poured two cups, and when she carried them to the dining room, Jared was easing into the chair with the extra pillows.

"These new pieces," she said, picking one up and sniffing. "They're a different kind of wood. The color is lighter, and it's more aromatic. What is it?"

"Palo Santo," he told her. *"Bursera graveolens."*

"I've never heard of it before."

"The wood is more often used in incense. It's related to frankincense and myrrh."

"As in the Wise Men?"

"That's right."

She set the piece down. "But frankincense and myrrh are oils, aren't they?"

Jared nodded. "They make oil from Palo Santo, too." He sipped his coffee, leaned back and closed his eyes. "Since you're here, did you want to check my circulation this morning?" He opened his eyes, his brows drawn up with the question.

Siobhan let her gaze drift to his lap. He had a definite bulge in his shorts. "Didn't you just urinate?" she asked.

"Wasn't easy, either." He straightened in his chair. "You're very pretty in the morning."

Her heart raced and her womb clutched. Try as she might, she couldn't ignore him. "I wish you'd stop with the innuendo and the flirting."

"I can't seem to help myself around you," he said. "And calling you pretty isn't flirting." He set his cup on the table. "I like you, Siobhan. And I like kissing you. A lot. But I don't want to cause you discomfort. I had the feeling you didn't mind so much, that you enjoyed my company, too, but if I'm mistaken, I won't impose myself on you."

"You've already imposed yourself on me." She grimaced and turned away. "And I didn't mind so much."

"Can we call a truce, then? Maybe you'll stop being displeased with me."

What was she supposed to say to that?

"Look, Jared, in a couple of weeks, you'll be heading back to Louisiana and the chances we'll see each other again are pretty slim. You said you needed a friend, and I'm happy to be that for you while you're here, but kissing? That causes problems."

He made a vee with his hands over his lap. "You're telling me."

Siobhan shook a finger at him. "Stop. Even if we are consenting adults, sex is off the table until you're healed, and by that time, you'll be able to pick up where you left off with your girlfriend back home."

"Is that what's bothering you? The imaginary girlfriend back home? Or that I'll be leaving?"

The man was too smart for his own good. "Jared…"

"No, don't Jared me. I'm not asking you for the keys to the kingdom, just a chance to know you. And I'd be sad to think I'd never see you again once I go back home." He raised his eyebrows again, the scarred one puckering. "I'd at least hope we could keep talking. I do love the sound of your voice. For now, can we agree to be friends? Enjoy the time we can spend together and let the future take care of itself? Or do you need a commitment to be friends? You want me to promise I won't break your heart? I can't do that, no more than you can promise not to break mine."

Siobhan sputtered. "Break your heart? Please." And yet she was afraid of exactly that, that he would break her heart. She liked Jared way more than she wanted to.

"You might be the woman to do it," he said. He stared at her a moment before he rose from the chair, tucked his crutches under his arms and ambled to his bedroom.

She was an idiot. What was she expecting? He was right. Dating didn't come with commitments, and she could certainly enjoy his company while he was in Edgarville. If nothing else, it gave her practice for other dates, now that her schedule left her time to consider them. Not that anyone was lining up for the opportunity. Except for Duncan. She'd secretly laughed at him for being awkward, but was she any better? In high school she'd been looking for a boy to sweep her off her feet. Apparently, things hadn't changed all that much. She was still looking for a long-term commitment from a first date.

"Jared, I'm sorry," she called out.

The squeak and thump of his crutches indicated he was headed down the hallway. He came into sight wearing only a pair of boxers, carrying a change of clothes. "If you'll excuse me, I need to get cleaned up," he said.

She didn't miss the fact he hadn't invited her to help this time, but she was fairly certain the show of skin was for her benefit, and he'd achieved the desired effect. Her fingers itched to trace the muscles carved by hard work, and she had the oddest desire to kiss the greenish-yellow of the bruises around his ribs. He did a half turn as he closed the bathroom door and she admired the curve of his butt.

Yes, she was an idiot. Jared Pierce affected her far more than any man had since high school, and the damn man knew it.

~ ~ ~

"Cleaning up" consisted of using a pre-packaged, pre-moistened towel provided by the hospital. Jared couldn't lower himself into the tub, and he hated the seat on the side. He wasn't willing to negotiate the stairs on his own to take a shower, especially with a mischievous ghost lurking.

He absolutely was not willing to ask Siobhan for help. The new scars and the bruises that still hadn't healed were bad enough. He hated being less of a man, not being able to walk. Cajoling her into staying with him had been a mistake. He'd intended to use the time to win her over, but it seemed his efforts had backfired. She'd gone into full nurse mode and walled off her emotions.

Not that he was looking for emotions. Or was he? Truth be told, he liked Siobhan more than any woman he'd ever met. When he'd said she might break his heart, he might have spoken more truth than he'd considered. The idea they wouldn't see each other again after he healed produced a profound ache in his chest.

He finished washing and threw the disposable towel into the trash, brushed his teeth and considered his scruffy chin. Not long enough to shave yet, especially since his pain meds were kicking in and the familiar lethargy was taking over. He finished with the rest of his hygiene for the morning, sat on the raised toilet seat and used his dressing stick to pull on a fresh pair of boxers and his sweatpants. He tugged on a t-shirt and opened the bathroom door.

A rumble in the pipes told him Siobhan had turned on the shower upstairs. He glanced at the remaining blocks of wood on the dining room table, something to be thankful for. Jared would spend his holiday carving more chess pieces. He continued to his bedroom and threw his dirty boxers into the laundry basket.

Laundry. He could do that, too. He'd show Siobhan he wasn't helpless, even temporarily. He gave a sly grin as he considered starting the washer while she was in the shower, but a sudden change in the water temperature might darken her mood further.

On his way to his hip chair in the living room, Jared gathered a couple of pieces of wood and Great Uncle Charlie's tools.

"You're coming with me," Siobhan announced when she came downstairs.

"We already talked about this," he replied.

"I've pledged to take responsibility for you, at least until Monday, and I'm not leaving you alone."

"I really don't think…" Jared protested.

"Not taking no for an answer," she said. "I'm looking out for your well-being. Don't want you taking anymore falls."

"I promise to stay right here, in my chair."

"You're coming with me. If I had room at my apartment, I'd suggest we move there until you're back on your feet." She pressed her lips together. "That ghost of yours stopped by to chat with me last night. I'm not taking any chances."

Jared rubbed his jawline once more. Guess he'd have to shave after all.

Chapter 23

WALKING INTO HER MOTHER'S warm kitchen after all this time, Siobhan was assaulted by the familiar aromas, the cooking turkey, the spicy scents of cinnamon and nutmeg in the pumpkin pie and the rich smell of chocolate cake. Her eyes watered with the memories of happier times, and her heart clutched at the inevitable end to the holiday meal, when Da would leave to meet his friends and tip a few, leaving all of them to wonder what his mood would be when he returned.

In the years she'd been away, Siobhan had spent Thanksgiving either working at the hospital or volunteering at the homeless shelter.

Da was gone. And, now, so were Mary and Mick.

Siobhan had been away too long.

Liam sat at the kitchen table laughing at a joke Siobhan had missed hearing, and Kathleen bustled beside Ma preparing the side dishes.

Ma looked up and smiled. She wiped her hands on her apron and crossed the kitchen to greet Siobhan with a hug. "So happy to have everyone home this year," she whispered in Siobhan's ear. She stuck out a hand toward Jared. "Eileen McCormick. A Happy Thanksgiving to you."

"Jared Pierce," he replied. "I hope having me isn't too great an inconvenience."

Ma turned to Siobhan. "I thought your friend's name was Duncan something?"

"Jared's a patient," Siobhan told her, sending a silencing glare at Jared. "I didn't feel right leaving him alone. I hope you don't mind."

"Of course I don't mind. Help yourself to a drink, love," Ma said. "When will your other friend be joining us?"

"I told him eleven o'clock," Siobhan answered. "He should be here any minute. Where are Kevin and Amy?"

"Should be along shortly, and then they'll be off to spend time with Amy's family." A tear slid down Ma's cheek. "We are well and truly blessed." She hugged Siobhan once more before she returned to the oven and opened the door to check the turkey.

Blessed. The tear told another story, one that said two people would be missing from the table this year.

At the knock on the front door, Siobhan straightened her blouse and passed through the kitchen. "That's probably Dr. Phelps." She'd resorted to his title after their dinner date. Easier to think of him that way than the man searching for his next wife.

She opened the door and he held out a bottle of wine. "My contribution to the feast," he told her. "And I'd also like to thank you again for inviting me." He leaned down to kiss her cheek, a fatherly peck.

"Glad you could join us," she told him. "As with most family gatherings, all the action is in the kitchen, unless you'd rather watch the football game."

"I didn't come to watch television," he said. "I'd love to meet your family."

Siobhan escorted him through the living room, to the big country kitchen. "Dr. Duncan Phelps, my brother Liam."

Liam rose from the table and shook his hand. "Nice to meet you."

"My sister, Kathleen, and my ma, Eileen McCormick."

Dr. Phelps nodded to Kathleen, then took Ma's hand and kissed it. Siobhan controlled her inclination to roll her eyes. Ma's cheeks flowered from the attention.

"Enchanted," he told them. "Thank you so much for allowing me to intrude on your family celebration."

"Can't abide the thought that some don't have family to be with on a day like this," Ma said. "You're more than welcome."

"And this is Jared Pierce," Siobhan said, praying Dr. Phelps wouldn't recognize the name.

"The monitoring patient?" he asked Siobhan, shaking Jared's hand. "I'd guess from the crutches you might be he?"

So much for not recognizing the name. Would she be reprimanded? Fired?

"As a matter of fact, I am," Jared drawled in that easygoing southern drawl. "The accident left me far from home and my new friends insisted I join them for Thanksgiving." He shot a meaningful glance at Siobhan. "They wouldn't let me say no."

"No one should be alone on Thanksgiving," Dr. Phelps said, sending Siobhan an approving smile.

"Can I get you something to drink?" Siobhan asked, anxious for an escape.

Four voices called out their orders and Siobhan went to the collection of beverages on the countertop. While she opened the bottle of wine Dr. Phelps had brought, Kathleen sidled up beside her. "The patient?" she whispered. "He's the one?"

Siobhan grabbed Kathleen's wrist. "You can't say anything."

Kathleen twisted two fingers in front of her lips. "That guy's hot."

Not as hot as Siobhan's cheeks, and the heat was spreading all through her.

"What about you?" Siobhan asked. "No guest?"

Kathleen shook her head. "I'm not ready. Not on a holiday."

The back door opened once more and Kevin walked in. "Hey," he said.

"My brother, Kevin," Siobhan said. "This is Dr. Phelps."

Kevin crossed the room and shook Dr. Phelps's hand. He turned to look for Amy, "My fiancée, Amy Benson."

Kathleen helped Siobhan pour the drinks, and together, they delivered them. Siobhan offered Dr. Phelps a nervous smile, but he didn't seem to notice. He was in the middle of a conversation with Ma, engrossed in whatever they were talking about.

Siobhan cradled her drink, a cup of Ma's tea, as she watched the people gathered around her engage in conversation. Jared was seated at the table, and when she glanced at him, he smiled. Like her, he was outside the hubbub, watching. She returned his smile reluctantly as Amy sat down beside Jared to talk to him.

And Dr. Phelps? He seemed to have found a friend in Ma while she fussed with the food.

Siobhan was out in the cold again.

"Why don't you let me and Kathleen set dinner out," Siobhan said, stepping in front of her mother. "You've already done the hard work. Relax." Helping made her feel better, and Dr. Phelps appeared too preoccupied to wonder why Jared was here.

Everyone found a seat around the table while Siobhan and Kathleen set out the dishes of food. As Kathleen sat down, the last open chair at the table was the one beside Jared. Siobhan shot a glance at Kevin, who returned a smug grin. Subtle.

Ma quieted everyone and said grace, including a prayer for those the Lord had called home. When she finished, none of her siblings had a dry eye. Under the table, hands were clasped in memory of their lost sister and cousin.

Jared cleared his throat. "I'd like to thank you for your hospitality," he said to Ma.

Dr. Phelps raised his glass. "I second that."

"There's always room at the table for a couple more," Ma said, a rosy glow in her cheeks as she wiped a tear from her eye. She spared a shy smile for Dr. Phelps that sent a shudder along Siobhan's spine.

Siobhan dug into her food, the comforting tastes of home, and breathed a sigh. Even if she didn't fit in, she'd missed this. The conversation, the camaraderie, the sense of family. While she ate, she studied each of the faces around her—Liam had grown into a man, and Kathleen, well she already knew Kathleen had grown up. When she met Kevin's gaze, he smiled at her.

"It's good to have you home," he said.

Liam and Kathleen both looked up and raised their glasses. "Hear, hear."

A tear threatened from the corner of Siobhan's eye. "It's good to be home."

~ ~ ~

Siobhan hadn't told Jared why she'd left home. While he watched her interact with her family, he suspected there was something more to the story than she'd left to pursue a job. They seemed to be going through a process, much the same as spirits did when he helped them move on. Acknowledgement. Acceptance.

Would that make her more accepting of Jared? She'd seen the ghost, after all. At least she could stop looking at him like he was a mental case, which would give him a chance to crack through that shell she'd built around herself.

Her brothers and sister reminisced about Thanksgivings past, but any mention of their father was met with downcast eyes. He'd have to ask Siobhan about that later. Right now, he enjoyed watching the fabric of her family, from the good-natured ribbing, to the tender moments they touched on gently.

In Vacherie, his family would eat turkey sandwiches—his mother didn't like to cook—and then they'd go to the homeless shelter. Rarely did their Thanksgiving table consist of more than four people. Until now, Jared hadn't thought about what it might be like to be part of a large family.

He liked it.

Siobhan's "doctor friend" still puzzled him. Jared had envisioned someone she might be dating, but the doctor looked old enough to be her father, and he openly flirted with Siobhan's mother. When Dr. Phelps had commented on how nice it was of them to include Jared, Siobhan had seemed to exhale a sigh of relief. Was she still worried about the boundaries of professionalism? He didn't think of her as his nurse, but apparently she couldn't see past the fact he was her patient.

After the food had been cleared and the dishes cleaned, all without any of the guests leaving the kitchen, Amy looped an arm through Kevin's and nudged him toward the door to their next feast. Jared pushed to his feet.

"Would you mind dropping me home?" he asked. "I'm done in, and I'd hate to take Siobhan away from the family."

"I'll take you home," Siobhan said, appearing at his side.

"I don't want to cut your day short," he said.

"They'll retreat to the living room and turn on a football game, or a soccer game. I don't need to stay for that. You're probably due for your next pill."

"Yes, ma'am," he said. He was exhausted, but he'd enjoyed every minute of his day with her family.

She nodded. "Then let's get you home."

He said his thank-yous one more time and they walked out with Kevin and Amy. In the driveway, Siobhan hugged Kevin, then hugged Amy. Maybe it was the holiday spirit, or maybe whatever unresolved issues she'd been carrying had been relieved, but Jared smiled to see her at ease.

Kevin approached Jared and shook his hand. "Good luck," he said conspiratorially.

Amy rested her hands on Jared's waist and kissed his cheek. "Happy Thanksgiving."

"Same to you," he replied.

Siobhan helped him to her car and they made the drive to his house in comfortable silence.

She drove to the back door and he got himself out of the car, determined to show her he wasn't in need of nursing.

But he was in need of his pain pills.

He hobbled up the staircase in the receding daylight, grateful for the mild wave of weather. The wind rippled through the police tape around the oak tree, and branches creaked overhead. Siobhan followed him into the kitchen and flipped on the light.

"I'm going to change into more comfortable clothes," she told him. "And then I think it's time you and I had a conversation."

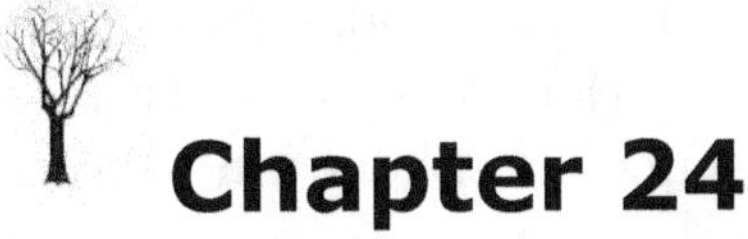

Chapter 24

JARED STARED DOWN HIS pain pills. The aches were still manageable, and if Siobhan meant to have a meaningful conversation, he'd do better to keep a clear head. He could only guess what might be on her mind tonight, and none of those guesses would come out well for him based on the past two days.

The stairs to the second floor creaked, announcing Siobhan's arrival. She came through the door wearing flannel drawstring pants and a light brown Henley shirt, both of which highlighted her curves in a way that made him hate how weak he was. Damn it all to hell, he wanted to cup those perfect breasts in his hands, to pull her hips against his, to let her know how very badly he wanted her in his bed, to bury himself inside of her… but he wasn't even able to support full weight on his left leg, much less maneuver the rest of his body in such a way as to give Siobhan the pleasure she deserved and he so desperately craved.

"Talk to me," he growled.

She eased onto the sofa warily as she picked up on his mood. "I want to know about you," she said. "Kevin said there was a reason your family sent you to flip the house."

"That's right."

She crossed her arms, which pushed her breasts up and enhanced the cleavage behind the buttons of her Henley.

"Kevin said you've been reluctant to talk to me about the ghost, and rightfully so, but things have changed, haven't they?" she said.

"Unless you've manufactured a scientific explanation for what you've seen," he replied testily.

"I deserve that," she said.

She deserved a lot of things, but his bad humor wasn't one of them. He sighed and turned away.

"I'd rather know who you are, all of it, than have you holding back for fear I'll make fun of you," she said.

"I am who I am," he told her. "I'm not worried you'll make fun of me, I'm more worried you'll turn away from me."

Her eyes grew large and the front of her shirt showed two pinpoints. She wasn't wearing a bra, which made his fingers itch even more.

"I've been struggling to find my bearings," she said quietly. "And for that reason, I may have been unreasonable and closed-minded. Clearly, I have a lot yet to learn."

Why had she left Edgarville? Or a better question might be why she came home. Instead, he asked, "What happened to your father?"

"There will be time enough to talk about me. Right now I want to know about you."

Jared winced. "Siobhan, I'm not sure I can be the man you want me to be."

"And who do you think I want you to be?"

"That guy," he said. "The normal one who doesn't see ghosts or do things other people might misconstrue as odd."

"And how do you know I'm not the odd one?" she said. "Maybe I'm the one who's too screwed up to see what's right in front of me. Jared, I don't want you to be anyone different than who you are, but I am asking to know who that is. If you don't feel comfortable sharing that with me, I'll go."

Was that what he wanted?

"Luke asked me if you were a friend of Stan's."

That's right. She said the ghost had paid her a visit last night. "He spoke to you?" Jared leaned forward in his chair when she nodded.

"Who's Stan?"

Jared rubbed his chin. "Luke's mother married a man named Stanley Mason."

Siobhan let out a slow breath. "You obviously know more about what's going on than I do. Why did you see the ghost the other night? And why didn't I? I want to know what you told Amy about yourself, to understand who you are."

If he was honest with her, she'd definitely paint him with her 'crazy' paintbrush. "I don't want you thinking less of me than you already do."

"I saw the ghost," she said. "I need to know."

At least she wasn't trying to rationalize what she'd seen. He folded his hands in his lap. "My grandmother was what people called a wise woman. I think Amy would call her a medium."

"Is Amy a medium?" Siobhan asked.

"No, ma'am. Not from what she's told me."

Siobhan nodded. "Sorry, go on."

"Folks would come to my grandmother for comfort, to talk to people who'd crossed over to the other side, who'd died. She didn't advertise herself, people just found her, as if they knew. The sight, it isn't something the family talks about with outsiders, for obvious reasons."

"And that's why you didn't tell me."

He nodded. "Well, my daddy, he inherited her gift. Often as not when he was working on a house—he was a carpenter, same as my brother and me—he'd stumble upon a spirit who'd lost its way. My grandmother taught him how to help the spirit along, to send it home."

"And by home you mean…?"

He grimaced once more. "I don't know that answer."

"And now you've inherited that trait? So you can help Luke move on?"

"It's not as easy as that." Jared eyed his pain pills once more. His leg throbbed now. "Some spirits remain behind because they have something they need to do."

"Ghosts can't hurt you, can they?" She glanced at his leg. "How did you fall?"

If he was going to tell her, he might as well tell her everything. "He was looking for his mother. The other night he knocked over my crutches while I was in bed. I had to call over Mrs. Brown to help. The boy doesn't know why he's here, and he's frightened because he's alone. He can't find his brother and his mother isn't where he expected to find her. I fell because he startled me."

Siobhan shivered. "Can he hurt you? Us?"

"Not if we keep our wits about us. How about you make us a pot of coffee and you can tell me about you."

"There isn't much…"

"Fair's fair."

She nodded and headed for the kitchen.

~ ~ ~

Siobhan glanced out the window as the coffee pot sputtered. The wind had picked up strength and rattled the windows. All this talk of ghosts gave her the willies, but not as much as talking about herself.

What could she tell him? That her father was an abusive drunk? That in high school she'd chased after a boyfriend in an attempt to escape her life? She'd been on a path to self-destruction and nearly succeeded. She wasn't sure she'd ever gotten off that path. She'd distracted herself before she did any real damage.

A gust of wind broke a large branch off the other half of the conjoined tree in the backyard, cradling it precariously in the remaining craggy limbs. Siobhan turned away from the window and poured two cups of coffee.

Jared had been honest with her. What did she have to lose? Baring her soul to a man who would be leaving in a few more weeks? She could tell Jared things she was too ashamed to tell her own family, even Kevin, and he could judge her all he wanted. After he left, she'd never see him again. She was emboldened, brave. Since they were sharing family secrets…

She carried the mugs into the living room and handed one to Jared before she resumed her seat on the sofa, a safe distance away. "Okay," she said, gathering the rest of her courage. "You asked about my Da. He left. Shortly after I left home." She paused to take a deep breath. One thing at a time, although now that she'd chosen her confessor, she found she wanted to tell Jared everything. "My Da was a drunk. He used to accuse all of us of various things and then beat it out of us. He started with my Ma until we grew older, and when I left, I blamed her for not protecting us. It wasn't until recently that I understood she suffered as much or more than we did." She swallowed down the lump in her throat. "When I graduated high school, I decided I'd had enough and left."

"Can't see as how anyone could blame you for that," Jared said quietly.

She nodded. "Maybe, but I left the rest of them behind, my brothers and sisters, to suffer his wrath. It was easier to blame my Ma than to accept I'd done exactly what I accused her of doing. She stood by them. I left them to deal with my sins."

"Running away isn't a sin, last I heard," he said.

She raised her eyes to look at him, at this beautiful, scarred man. "I behaved badly in high school," she told him. "I was so flattered by the first boy who asked me out, so grateful for an escape from the abuse, I didn't think to tell him to stop when he tested my boundaries." She licked her lips, reliving the fear of rejection, the need to feel loved. She winced, remembering how naïve she'd been. She glanced at Jared, who studied the cup of coffee in his hands.

"How old were you?" he asked.

"Fifteen."

He shook his head and set his mug on the table with a thump. "I don't suppose that boy who took advantage of you stuck around long."

"No, but right after that date, I became very popular."

"Teenage boys don't have any common sense," he said in a low growl. "They all think with their dicks."

"Not sure they outgrow that," she said, raising an eyebrow.

"I'm going to guess when you left home, you left with a boy?"

She nodded.

"And that didn't work out so good?"

She nodded again.

"At least he didn't leave you with a child to raise all on your own."

"I wasn't *that* stupid," she said. "After that first date, I went to the doctor. Made sure there were no accidents."

Jared shaded his forehead with a hand. "I'd like to kill that boy for you, and all his friends who lined up after him."

She chuffed. "You would have been right there with them. Just this morning you were man-spreading for me, showing me what you've got."

"I'm not gonna lie to you, Siobhan," he said, straightening in the chair. "Make no mistake, I want you something fierce, but I do know boundaries."

"Like tricking me to kiss you?"

He had the good grace to wince. "And now?" he asked.

"Now, what?"

"Are you still looking for validation when you sleep with a man? For someone to save you?"

"I saved myself." She swallowed down the doubt that snuck into her thoughts. Insecurities swarmed her once more. Why had she ordered whiskey when she'd had dinner with Duncan, Dr. Phelps? Why had she challenged Kevin to have a drink with her when he'd been worried about his relationship with Amy?

Why did she crave a drink? She'd been too busy to be an alcoholic before, but she had time now.

What was wrong with her, walking away from the life she'd made for herself? She'd been content, safe. Ever since she'd come home, she'd been off balance, one drink away from becoming her father. One boy away from prostitution. She might have thought she'd accepted herself, found her way, but now she was seeing ghosts, for God's sake!

The coffee cup shook in her hand as her nerves gave way.

"Siobhan?"

The sound of his voice rippled through her. She wanted Jared Pierce, as much as she'd wanted a shot of whiskey. Nothing had changed in all the years she'd been gone. All those years of denial hadn't changed anything.

Her voice was strained. "I shouldn't have said anything. I shouldn't have come home." She looked at Jared, who gazed at her with concern in his eyes. "I shouldn't have called you that night."

"Breathe," he said in that silky voice. "You're okay. You survived."

"No," she said. "I didn't." And suddenly she wanted to throw up. She ran for the bathroom and stopped dead in the hallway between the two bedrooms to wrap her arms around herself. The hallway was freezing cold, so cold it took her breath away.

The ghost stood in the doorway to the second bedroom.

Jared's hand on her shoulder startled her, but she couldn't look away from the door. "Fetch me one of the candles on the bookshelf," he said quietly. "And light it. Quickly, please."

Siobhan did as he said, but as soon as she returned to the hallway, Luke puckered his lips and a breeze blew out the candle.

The door to the back bedroom opened slowly, the room that should have been filled with boxes, but none of the boxes were visible.

"What in hell…?" Jared said.

Jared moved toward the open door. Siobhan followed.

Twin beds occupied two of the walls in the room. A boy lay curled on the farthest bed, facing away, his naked body flailing as welts opened on his back and his buttocks, until he gurgled and went still.

The images faded to be replaced by the boxes and the temperature in the hall seemed less cold.

"W-what was that?" Siobhan asked, shivering.

She turned around. Luke stood in the hallway entrance.

Jared glanced from the bedroom to Luke.

Siobhan knelt before the ghost. She was certain the boy in the bedroom hadn't been Luke. "Did whoever hurt Levi hurt you, too?" she asked.

The little boy nodded.

"He can't hurt you anymore," she said gently.

Instinctively, Siobhan reached for the ghost, but Jared stepped between them and Luke disappeared. She cast an annoyed look at Jared and hurried to the kitchen. When she looked out the window, two boys stood beside the damaged trees.

Chapter 25

THE COLD WAS A bad sign. The second ghost was a bad sign.

"I don't think Luke will be asking us where Levi is anymore," Jared told Siobhan.

"Then he can move on. Be at peace," she said.

Bless her heart. She didn't know any better. "You best go home," he said.

"Not this again." She put her hands on her hips. "Look, I told that social worker I'd stay with you through the weekend and I intend to honor that."

"This isn't about my safety anymore," he replied. "It's about yours."

"What on earth are you talking about?"

"Trust me."

Her eyes opened wide and she leaned toward him. "Trust you?"

"I've spoken true to you," he said.

"You're a manipulator."

He fought not to grin, but it was a losing battle. "Only when I want to bring someone to my way of thinking, when I'm trying to get something I want." He leaned over his crutches and took Siobhan's arms. "I'm dead serious right now. The cold in the hall, you felt it right? And the way the ghost blew out the candle? You saw that?"

She nodded.

"You'll have to trust me when I tell you those are bad signs."

"So the ghosts aren't going away? But Luke seemed so harmless, like a lost little boy."

"I'm not rightly sure what their intent is, or what those two boys can do."

She crossed her arms and huffed. "Then I'm definitely not leaving you alone with them."

Despite the uncertainty in her eyes, Jared recognized the empathy for what those boys must have gone through based on the vision they'd been shown. He'd seen the way she'd addressed the child and it had touched his heart.

Despite the abuse she and her family had borne at the hands of her father, or maybe because of it, the McCormicks were a close-knit family that pulled others into their fold. Jared would have liked more brothers and sisters, a brood of a family like Siobhan's. His family had been close, but they kept to themselves, as needs must, because of their unique talents.

The way Siobhan had spoken to the ghost of the little boy made him look at her in a different light. She'd make a good mother, and damn if that didn't make him want to help her on that journey. For the first time in his life, Jared wanted children.

He swallowed down the unexpected yearning. Nothing could be done to advance that idea today, and she needed to be aware of the problems at hand.

"Baby, Luke sees me as a threat, and based on what we saw, I'd wager Levi is even more hostile."

"They're little boys," she repeated quietly.

"Little boys who died a traumatic death. At least one of them did."

"So how do you help them find peace?" she asked.

"I originally thought to help Luke, to reunite him with his brother so he could finish his journey." He pointed to the tree outside the window. "His brother might have been buried with him. The police said they found two skeletons beneath the tree. The way it grew together like it did, that could be the spirits of those boys reaching for each other through the branches. One became two, two became one. The ice broke away half the tree, broke their connection. That branch there, the one that came down today, likely that's what released the second spirit."

Siobhan shivered beside him.

"Spirits seeking retribution for what sent them to their death are somewhat persistent," Jared told her. "Amy tells me that's what your sister needed to move on."

Siobhan held up a finger and ran from the room. Seconds later, he heard her in the bathroom. Jared limped behind her, his leg aching something fierce, and found her sitting on the bathroom floor, leaning against the toilet.

"Baby, I'm sorry," he said.

She shook her head. "I'm not going anywhere."

"It might not be safe for you to stay."

"And it will be safe for you?" she asked.

He could lie to her, tell her he'd be okay, but he wasn't whole. That left him vulnerable.

"I didn't think so," she said when he didn't answer. "I'm staying, unless you want to go back to rehab, or you could stay with my Ma." She hauled herself to her feet, leaned over the sink and splashed water on her face.

"I have to stay," he said. "Those boys need my help."

"And you need mine."

The woman had fortitude—that was for certain. He admired her even more for what she'd lived through, what she'd survived, and after what she'd told him, he understood why she kept such tight control of herself.

~ ~ ~

Abusive parents Siobhan could deal with—medical emergencies, hostile patients. How did one deal with angry little boy ghosts? She had no training for this, no point of reference. Jared was the self-proclaimed "ghost doctor," and Amy reportedly had experience.

If Amy could do it, so could Siobhan. She straightened her back but Jared blocked her exit from the bathroom. At least he hadn't been there to watch her throw up, although the aftermath wasn't much prettier. His expression was dead serious, and that made her nervous more than anything else that had happened.

Kevin had told Siobhan the days they'd spent trying to communicate with Mary had been the most difficult time of his life, but the threat to him had been a live person, the serial killer who'd murdered Mary and later, their cousin Mick. Ghosts couldn't do any harm, could they?

"You said you lost your balance," she said. "And that your crutches fell over. Obviously, that's an issue in your condition, but can the ghosts do any real harm?"

"They can," he replied. "And after what we've seen, I'm inclined to do a smudge, to bless the house and hope that sends them on their way."

"Okay." She swallowed down the taste of bile and followed Jared to the dining room.

Leaning on his right crutch, he moved the remaining wood blocks across the dining room table until he found a bag of small pieces, sticks. He extracted four pieces and handed them to Siobhan. "Hold onto these for a minute." He tucked the left crutch under his arm again and moved toward his bedroom. Moments later, he returned holding a ceramic bowl.

"The smoke can be intense. Your eyes will probably burn and the smell is what I consider sickly sweet. You don't have asthma, do you?"

Siobhan shook her head.

Jared gave her half a smile and nodded. "That's my girl. We have to prepare the rooms before we can start. Would you mind hanging a towel over the mirror in the bathroom? And we need to open all the doors, including the cabinets. Do you have your cell phone with you?"

She turned toward the sofa. "It's in my purse. Do you want me to call someone?"

"I want you to turn it off. And mine, too."

This would be a Thanksgiving to remember. Siobhan did as Jared asked, not stopping to ask why. She was already suffering from a case of too much information, including what she'd shared. "Now what?" she asked when she'd finished doing what he'd asked.

"This will go easier with two free hands." He waved one of his crutches in the air. "Would you mind lighting the sticks?"

Siobhan crossed to the bookshelves in the living room and retrieved the matches from the shelf. "These sticks smell like the new set of chess pieces. Palo Santo?"

"That's right." He inched toward the hallway, out of the dining room. "Sacred wood. Hold one end over the flame until the wood catches fire. Then you blow it out and let the wood smolder."

She lit each of the sticks, blew them out and placed them in the bowl.

"As I speak, wave the bowl so the smoke infuses the room. We're going to move left to right," he told her.

Tendrils of smoke rose from the sticks. Jared was right. Already the smoke was strong, the lemony scent of the wood, like furniture polish, growing syrupy sweet.

They stepped into the rear bedroom and Jared tilted his head. He spoke quietly, words too quiet to understand. Gooseflesh rose on her arms as she waved the bowl in front of her. The smoke diffused into the corners behind the boxes that lined the walls.

"Bless my gifts as I do your work here on earth." Jared said more audibly. He moved forward with his crutches. "I call to the Element of Air in the East. Inspire the child who remains behind to find his peace." He took another step and made a quarter turn. "To the Element of Fire in the South, encourage this child to the path that will lead him home." Another step, another turn. "Element of Water in the West, flow through me, help me to guide this young boy home." He turned once more. "Element of the Earth in the North, hold and support me, ground my work as I release these children from your sanctuary and to the arms of our Holy Father." Jared returned to his original position, his eyes closed. "Let your energy flow through me that these children might find rest. I am your humble servant." He took a bottle from his pocket, unscrewed it and tilted it to wet his fingers, then marked the windows with crosses.

Siobhan's eyes watered from the smoke. Jared worked his way through the hall, chanting more prayers while she followed. He stopped to mark the glass and the tops of the doorways along the way.

He continued to the back door, opened it, and held out a hand for the bowl. When Siobhan gave it to him, he held it in front of his face and blew smoke out the door. Then, one by one, he stubbed out the smoldering sticks.

Siobhan covered her mouth and coughed, choking on the thick smoke.

"Are y'all right?" he asked.

Siobhan nodded.

"Then I'm going to ask you to carry the ashes outside and spread them into the earth around the trees." He pointed to the hole in the ground that had been torn up by the tree roots.

She glanced into the yard, at the police tape surrounding the separated tree trunks. The glass in the storm door fogged over with the change in temperature. She considered going for her coat, but she wanted to get this over with, whatever *this* was.

Siobhan opened the door and carried the bowl outside. She got as close as she could without crossing the police line and sprinkled the ashes into the earth before she scurried into the house.

Jared had returned to his hip chair, his face pale as he sat with his eyes closed.

"What about you? Are you okay?" she asked, setting the bowl on the dining room table.

"It's all good," he said in a weary voice. "But I'd greatly appreciate a glass of water. I'm past due for my pain meds."

Siobhan retrieved his cup from the table beside his chair, carried it to the kitchen and refilled it.

"What happens now?" she asked when she handed him the cup. "The smoke. What does it do?"

Jared swallowed down one of his pills. "It's called smudging, or cleansing. Smudging is designed to restore peace, to remove the unhappy memories."

"So the ghosts are gone now?" she asked.

He gave her a strained smile. "Often enough, that's all it takes."

Siobhan wrapped her arms around herself. "So why am I still so cold?"

Chapter 26

SUNLIGHT STREAMED THROUGH THE curtains, shining a spotlight on Siobhan as she slept on the sofa. Jared had urged her to use one of the bedrooms upstairs, but she'd insisted the sofa would be fine, and he'd been too tired to argue with her. This morning, waking up in his hip chair, he was glad she'd stayed. He liked the idea of waking up with her, watching her in peaceful repose.

Most of the women Jared dated didn't know about the extra services he performed for homeowners. Siobhan was amazing. She'd helped him with the smudge, whether she wanted to believe in ghosts or not, and her concern for him didn't rankle as much when he considered it came more from her heart than from obligation. After what she'd told him last night, he didn't blame her for keeping a tight rein on her control, and he admired that, too. Siobhan had overcome more than most people ever faced, and she'd done it on her own. She was a powerful ally, or a formidable opponent. He definitely preferred her as an ally.

Jared tested his weight on the left side. It didn't hurt so much today. He leaned into his crutches and eased his way toward the bathroom to relieve himself, trying not to wake Siobhan.

When he returned to the living room, Siobhan was no longer on the sofa and the front door was open. He found Siobhan sitting on the wicker sofa inside the porch, her legs drawn up and wrapped in her arms.

"It's a nice day for November," she said. "Hard to believe we had snow and ice only a week ago."

"That's the beauty of the porch in the winter. Greenhouse effect." He eased over to the chair with arms and checked it for height. Would he be able to get out of it once he sat down?

"You don't have to sit out here with me," she said, dropping her feet to the floor. "I was thinking about what you said, about sitting on the porch…"

"We can move another chair out here," he suggested. "I'd like to sit on the porch. With you."

Siobhan rose from the couch. "I'm going to start the coffee, and then I should get dressed."

"I'll take that as a 'no, thank you?'"

She smiled. "I thought I'd take a walk to clear my head. If the weather holds, we can come out later."

She scurried into the house like a frightened rabbit. Jared shook his head. Sometimes things truly did work out for the best. As long as he was hobbled, he couldn't take her to bed, where he wanted her, where he was pretty sure she wanted to be. He'd judged from what she'd told him last night, satisfying their desires would have made him one more in a long line of bad decisions, and he wanted to be more to her than a bad decision.

"Oh, Jared," Mrs. Brown called as she crossed the front lawn, her voice muted through the glass windows.

He nodded a greeting. "Ma'am."

She walked up the steps and opened the porch door. "I thought I'd bring you some of our Thanksgiving leftovers. There's always too much food, you know? Would that be all right with you?" She sniffed and wrinkled her nose. "What do I smell?"

Jared studied his feet, curled his toes. "Well, I did have a lot to eat yesterday. I thought it best to burn some incense in the bathroom, if you know what I mean."

Mrs. Brown chuckled. "Are you already overloaded with leftovers?"

"If you want to share, I'd be happy to help you out."

She nodded. "Then I'll run home and be back in a jiffy."

Jared wandered inside, but left the front door open. Siobhan stood in the kitchen door with a mug of coffee.

"You want something to eat?" she asked.

"Not just yet. Will you sit with me a minute?"

Siobhan nodded and took a seat on the sofa while he eased into that damn chair, the same one he'd hardly moved from during the past couple of weeks. "You think you might want to buy the house?" he asked once more.

"No," she told him.

"Because of the ghosts?"

"No." She said it as if she dared him to pursue it.

He wasn't that brave this morning.

They had a world of time while he healed, and then they'd move forward from there. At least he hoped they would. First, he had to set her at ease. "Thank you for helping me last night," he said.

"Do you think it worked?"

"We'll see."

Mrs. Brown rapped on the porch door and let herself in. "I'll want the containers back when you're finished," she said, walking into the living room. She stopped when she saw Siobhan. "Oh, hello. I didn't realize…" She took in Siobhan's flannel pants and t-shirt.

"She's staying the weekend to make sure I'm fit to function on my own."

Mrs. Brown raised her eyebrows. "I almost forgot. I did see the ambulance here. No setbacks, I hope."

Siobhan folded her arms. "He's stubborn as a mule," she said. "Which is good for a patient's recovery. If you'll excuse me, I should get dressed."

Right back into nurse mode, but then he'd brought that on by trying to forestall unkind gossip. Jared scowled as she retreated up the staircase.

"I'll put this in the fridge," Mrs. Brown said, heading toward the kitchen.

"I do appreciate it," Jared replied.

"Jared?" Siobhan's brother rapped on the doorframe and stuck his head inside the room.

"C'mon in," Jared said.

"Everything okay? We tried calling, but there was no answer, from you or from Siobhan."

Jared picked up his phone. "I suppose we forgot to turn them back on."

Mrs. Brown bustled in from the kitchen. "More visitors. I'll have to make sure your mother knows you're well cared for," she said with a smile. "And you know to call if you need anything, right?"

"Yes, ma'am."

She nodded and walked out, past Amy who'd been hanging back on the porch.

"What's that smell?" Amy asked.

"Palo Santo."

"Which is…?" Kevin asked.

"Sacred wood."

"Luke?" Amy asked.

"And Levi, it would seem. The police told me they'd found bones to more than one body."

Siobhan's voice carried from the staircase as the steps announced her return. "But Dr. Phelps said the boys had gone to be with their dad while their mother and stepfather were moving."

"Either the boys came back, or someone was lying," Jared said.

~ ~ ~

Siobhan pulled one of the dining room chairs into the living room and sat.

"The police are waiting to identify the remains before they notify anyone," Kevin said. "I was going to call Hank Ketterhagen tomorrow, in case he was one of the unfortunate few who have to work the day after Thanksgiving, but I couldn't wait."

"It's awful early to be calling people." Siobhan reached for her phone, which was still turned off.

"It's ten-thirty," Kevin told her, glancing from her to Jared with an unflattering gleam in his eye. "Long night?"

"I'm guessing that's the reason for the palo-whatever-you-said-it-was," Amy said. "And you said something about Levi."

"There was a second ghost last night, a malevolent spirit," Jared told them. "We saw a vision of a naked boy who was beat to death."

Amy shivered and wrapped her arms around herself. "No séances."

"No séances," Jared said. "And I'm surprised my great aunt would do one. When you open a portal, you allow other spirits to come through, and they aren't all friendly."

Amy nodded. "She wasn't afraid, Mrs. Sumner. Maybe because she was a medium?"

Kevin put a protective arm across Amy's shoulders, sharing a secretive glance. Their ordeal with Mary's killer had clearly made them closer, brought them together. Siobhan looked toward Jared. Would last night's experience do the same for her and Jared?

She shook her head to clear her thoughts. "What did Mr. Ketterhagen tell you?"

Kevin frowned. "He said he wasn't proud of the fact, but he'd lost contact with the kids when they moved. Said it was easier to pretend he didn't have kids than to watch another man raise them. When I asked him to corroborate what Dr. Phelps told us, he said the boys hadn't been to visit him. He said something else that caught my attention, especially considering what we know now."

Siobhan waited for him to continue.

"He said Iris called him after she moved to say she was sorry. He figured she was apologizing for keeping the boys from him, for the animosity between them, but when he asked if he could spend time with the boys, she told him that wasn't possible and that she was sorry again." Kevin paused to draw a deep breath. "He asked me if I knew where they were, if that's why I was calling. He asked if they might be interested in meeting with him."

"You didn't tell him they were dead, did you?" Siobhan asked.

"We don't know whose bones those are," Kevin said. "Not definitely."

"Yeah, we do," she said.

Kevin chuckled. "Now you believe in ghosts?"

Her throat threatened to close. "Those boys were abused, Kevin, or at least one of them was."

"We need to find their mother," Amy said to Kevin. "Or their stepfather. They may be the only ones who know what happened."

"Oh, right," Kevin said. "And they're going to cheerfully tell us they chopped up the twins and buried them in the backyard?"

"Kevin!" Siobhan said, rising to her feet.

"Sorry," he said, meeting her gaze. "You have another idea?"

"Did you tell the police your theory?" Jared asked.

"Yeah," Kevin replied. "They're looking for Stan and Iris to find out what they might know about bones in the backyard."

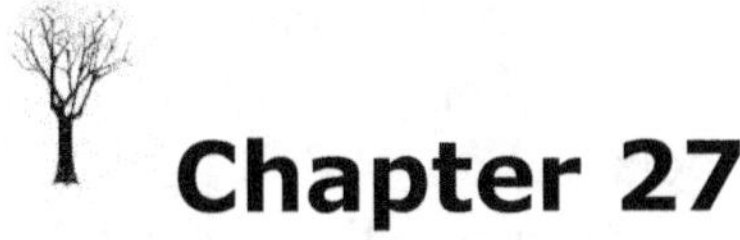

Chapter 27

SIOBHAN CLOSED THE BACK door behind her and walked into the sunshine, a 60 degree anomaly at the end of November. These days would be few and far between this time of year. She spared a glance at the police tape, at the hole in the ground.

She imagined the two boys buried there, growing with the trunks, reaching out to hold hands through the branch that grew between the two trees, the branch that conjoined them.

Tears slid down her face from the vision she'd seen, the little boy with welts on his back. *There but for the grace of God go I.* She stopped beside her car, resting her hands on the hood for support. A walk wasn't going to be enough. She reached into her pocket for her car keys, threw her purse into the car and drove to the animal shelter.

Coming home to Edgarville had been a bad idea. Yes, she needed to mend the relationships with her family, but there were too many shadows hovering at every corner. Too many bad memories. She'd ignored them when she'd moved away, or she'd been too busy to call them to mind.

Or her conversation with Jared last night had opened Pandora's box.

Siobhan never got the chance to know her baby sister. With the years between them, Siobhan had moved away before she knew anything about the person Mary had grown into. Now she'd never get that chance, the chance she had with Kathleen. But she had Kathleen. A sister. A friend. Siobhan didn't want to do anything to lose what she'd found.

And then there was Mick. He'd always attracted trouble, but it sounded like he'd been trying to do the right thing when he'd caught a bullet for Kevin. Could she have done anything to save either of them if she'd been home?

She pulled into the parking lot at the animal shelter, grabbed her purse and walked inside.

"Hey, Siobhan," the receptionist greeted her. "I didn't think you were on the volunteer list today."

Siobhan wiped at her eyes and smiled. "Needed some cat socialization. Didn't think anyone would mind."

"I'm sure the cats will be ecstatic."

Siobhan hurried through to the cat room, took off her coat and set her purse beneath it on a ledge. Immediately, cats curled around her legs and a kitten scurried up the leg of her pants and onto her shoulder, purring loudly in her ear. Nothing rivaled a warm ball of fur vibrating against your body when it came to comfort.

"See?" she told the kitten, pulling it from her shoulders and holding it while she scratched between its ears. "I don't need a man. I just need a roomful of cats." She gasped when she realized she'd said that out loud and laughed.

No, she didn't need Jared Pierce, but he was growing on her, getting under her skin. He'd asked to sit on the front porch with her, and for a brief moment, she believed he might actually enjoy talking with her, carrying on an intelligent conversation, as he put it. Except he'd stolen a kiss. She had no doubt he wanted to sleep with her, and if she was honest with herself, she wanted that, too, but she recognized that for what it was—lust. After they had sex, he wouldn't have any use for her. She'd lived that reality enough times in high school.

He'd said during their chess game he wasn't comfortable with the truth, as demonstrated when he'd told Mrs. Brown this morning he'd burned incense to sweeten the bathroom, a stretch of the truth, even if she didn't blame him for that one.

She wasn't sure what to make of the ghosts, but she didn't have a rational explanation for what she'd witnessed. Jared treated it like it was an everyday occurrence for him—not a comforting thought.

The kitten in her hands struggled to get free, extended its claws and jumped down. Siobhan settled into a chair and another cat immediately leapt into her lap. She stroked its soft fur absentmindedly, letting the low rumbling do its job.

Amy's apartment lease was coming to an end. If Siobhan intended to stay in Edgarville, she'd have to find another place soon or re-sign the lease for herself. If she intended to stay. The more she thought about it, the more she convinced herself she'd made another rash decision, moving home. She could come back for the holidays to visit. She hadn't second-guessed herself in years, but here, everywhere she turned she was reminded of the bad choices she'd made growing up—and one staring her in the face, waiting to be made. Jared Pierce.

Another cat crept up to curl around her neck and a third cat stretched its paws against her shins. Siobhan smiled, petted each of them in turn, set the cat from her lap on the floor and eased out from under the cat on her shoulders.

"Thanks, guys," she said to the cats. "I wish I could take you all home with me, but until I know where home is, you're better off somewhere else."

She left the shelter and drove to the cemetery, not realizing until she arrived that she had no idea where Mary's grave was.

The monument shop was across the street, the shop Amy's family ran, but Amy was with Kevin. Siobhan walked inside anyway and was greeted by the man she'd met in the café down the street, Amy's brother. He had washed-out brown eyes the same shape as Amy's, two-days' beard growth hiding his face.

"Can I help you?" he asked.

Siobhan managed a smile. "Garth, right? I don't know if you remember me? Siobhan McCormick. I wanted to visit my sister's grave, but I'm not sure where it is."

"Kevin's sister," Garth said. "I remember. I can take you."

"Thank you."

He extended an arm, inviting her to walk outside and followed her out of the shop.

"Must be hard, losing a sister," he said.

She nodded, not knowing what to say. She'd all but ignored Mary, leaving home when she did, and she hadn't come back when Mary died. The guilt produced a sour taste in Siobhan's throat. Yes, she'd been too busy to get away, but Mary was her sister. Her family. She should have made the effort. Siobhan had been a coward.

Garth led her through the cemetery gates and veered off the gravel road, up a hill toward a towering tree. "You know," he said, "this is where Kevin proposed to Amy. Out here, next to Mary's headstone. If you ask me, I think Mary gave him a push. He was trying to hide, but once he stumbled out into the open…" He shrugged. "The rest, as they say, is history."

"It certainly is." Siobhan forced another smile. Was she the only person who didn't believe in ghosts? How could she have lived thirty years without encountering anything like a ghost before?

She'd seen that little boy being abused. No one had suggested that image to her, in fact, she'd been told the boys were shipped off to visit their father and for all she knew, they should be alive and well. The ghost had shown them differently. Another lump rose in her throat.

"I'll give you a minute," Garth said, waving his hand toward the stone. "Do you want me to hang around? Help you find your way out?"

"Is my cousin's grave nearby?"

Garth cocked his head to the row behind.

"Thank you," she said. "I'm sure I can find my way out."

He bowed his head and trudged down the hill.

Siobhan knelt beside the grave, cold earth chilling her knees. "I'm sorry, Mary. I should have been there for you, if not in life, at least at the end to see you off. I'm not proud of myself, and I'll be honest, I don't know what to do from here. One step forward, two steps back, and all of that." More tears spilled down her cheeks. "If ever I *wanted* to see ghost, I think I'd want to see you now, to know that you can hear me, to know that you can forgive me—I hope you can." But Mary wouldn't appear. Kevin had told her Mary's spirit was at peace now. Mary had nothing tying her to this world anymore.

"Siobhan?" Amy's voice was little more than a timid whisper.

Siobhan rose to her feet and wiped at her eyes. "I thought you were at Jared's. With Kevin."

"We were, but Kevin ran off to check a story and I headed here. This is where I'm most at home."

Of course. She heard voices.

Siobhan immediately rebuked herself. She had no right to make fun of Amy's gift, especially not after what she'd seen at Jared's house last night. "I think I owe you an apology."

Amy smiled. "I thought we put all of that behind us."

Siobhan nodded. "You're a better person than I am."

"You're being too hard on yourself. Want to talk about it?"

Siobhan shook her head. She'd already said too much. With Jared. Last night. "No. I think I'm done talking for a while."

"How about a cup of coffee? Apple cider? There's that shop around the corner."

Again Siobhan shook her head. "I should probably get back to Jared's. I promised the social worker I'd make sure he didn't get into any more trouble." She smiled and hugged Amy. "And for the record, I'm glad my brother found you."

~ ~ ~

Jared sat on the front porch watching the squirrels chase through the trees. Despite being stranded here, he was content to have quiet time to enjoy the scenery. His great aunt had a peaceful neighborhood and a picturesque view.

He turned his attention to the block of wood in his hands, the final chess piece. He'd saved the queen for last. While he worked the design, he pictured Siobhan's face, the smattering of freckles and her easy smile. Her copper-colored hair was smooth—silky beneath his fingers.

Between him and Siobhan, she was probably the wiser of the two of them. Her kisses had been the sweetest he'd ever tasted, but she was right. In another month or so, he'd be on his way to Louisiana, and she wasn't likely to leave her family again.

He glanced around the porch. Should he stay? Buy his great-aunt's house and move to Illinois permanently? Not likely. He couldn't leave his brother that way, short-handed to run the business on his own.

It appeared all he and Siobhan had was this moment in time.

Jared set the half-finished queen on the table and closed his eyes. He tapped his left foot on the floor and ran through the exercises his physical therapist had given him that he could do seated. Each day was a little better, the pain dwindling.

Siobhan's car turned into the driveway, and when she got out, her eyes were downcast, as if she had something serious on her mind. When she looked up, her pace slowed. She was a sight to behold, so lovely, so graceful. She was in the right profession, caring for people. He'd seen the way she cried for Levi's pain—a dead boy.

Jared knew she cared for him, and yet he didn't dare push her. She had her own struggles to conquer.

She opened the porch door, her cheeks flushed with health.

"Thought you were going for a walk," he said.

"Changed my mind," she replied. "How'd you get the dining room chair out here?"

"You're not my only friend up here, you know." He winked as he patted the cushion on the wicker sofa. "Care to sit with me?"

"It's lunch time, are you hungry?"

"In a bit. What I'd like is a little conversation. Unless you don't want to talk to me." He shot her a challenging look which she answered with an indulgent smile. No comeback. The way she settled into the sofa triggered concern. She tilted her head back and closed her eyes. Something had changed.

"You okay?" he asked.

She didn't open her eyes. "Of course."

Where was her biting wit? Alarm bells sounded inside his head. "Talk to me, Siobhan."

She opened one eye and laughed. "Whatever is the matter? You look like someone kicked your cat."

"You're acting strangely."

She brought her hands together over her heart. "Me?"

"Something happen while you were out?"

She eased back again, closed her eyes again. "I visited my sister's grave. Saw Amy at the cemetery." She peeked at him once more. "I thought they were going to stay with you until I got back."

"I told them to go. There was no call for them to stay."

"Sometimes you say the funniest things," she said dreamily.

"Like what?"

She straightened again, taking in the landscape outside. "No call for them to stay." She shot him a mischievous smile, more like what he'd expect from her. "Or calling me 'ma'am,' or 'baby.'"

Something had her in an odd humor. Jared rolled the half-finished queen in his hand. Like the wood, Siobhan required special handling. "Nice day for a walk in the cemetery."

She twisted on the sofa to face him. "Kevin said Mary's spirit was at peace. Jared, I've never seen a ghost before I met you. Why?

Why am I seeing these little boys? And why didn't I see Luke that first night, when you saw him?"

"I can't say. Most likely it's because you weren't looking for them. Me? My daddy taught me how to look for them, how to see them when nobody else could. Another thought might be that Luke was troubled when you finally saw him. His energy was stronger." Jared held her gaze, trying to read her unanswered questions. "Were you hoping to see your sister when you went to the cemetery?" he asked.

She bowed her head, evidence enough for him he'd found the right question.

Siobhan's voice was little more than a whisper. "She was eight when I left home. A little girl."

"It's no consolation, I know, but Kevin says she's moved on."

Siobhan nodded. "Do you think, after last night, the twins are at peace? Luke and Levi?"

"I couldn't say." Levi troubled him. His death had been traumatic enough to show Jared and Siobhan. Luke, on the other hand, didn't seem to understand he was dead. How had he died?

"Jared?"

"Ghosts feed on negative energy. We need to stay positive." He framed his face with his hands and gave her a silly grin. "Be happy." The queen fell from his grasp.

She laughed as she bent down to retrieve it for him. She turned it in her hands and smiled. "You do nice work. This is beautiful."

"So are you," he said. He needed to tell her how much he admired her. "Inside and out," he added.

She pursed her lips, shrugging off the compliment. "It's not done yet," she said as she handed the queen to him. "A work in progress."

"Nearly done. Now that I have the model sitting beside me, I can add the finishing touches."

"Model?" she laughed again. "I wouldn't make much of a queen, I'm afraid."

"You're a queen in my eyes," he said as he scraped away corners of the block. "Talking to a stranger, helping people who can't help themselves, stretching the boundaries of your beliefs." He gave her a hooded glance that tweaked the scar in his eyebrow once more. "Inviting a visitor into your family's home for the holiday."

He concentrated on the intricacies of the crown, gouging gently, rounding prongs with the edge of the blade.

"I know what it feels like to be out of place," she said.

Jared stopped working to look at her. She was home. With family who loved her. How could she feel out of place?

She'd given most of her free time to him, something he was grateful for, but also telling. Was she avoiding her family?

"How about a game of chess?" he suggested.

She frowned. "Sure."

Where was her spark? As she rose from her seat to pass him, he tugged on her hand and beckoned her with a finger. Her eyes locked with his, a flash of uncertainty was replaced with an awareness that reached deep into his soul. Her lips met his in the kiss he asked for, a sweet buss, and then he cupped her neck to rest his forehead against her chin.

"Like no other," he said softly.

"How am I supposed to believe that?" she asked. "You said yourself you'd rather avoid the truth."

"I've never lied to you, Sweet Siobhan, and I swear to you I never will."

She pursed her lips, a look of doubt on her face.

He raised his hands. "You want the truth? Yes, I want to kiss you, more than I want to play chess with you. I want to lay on my bed with you beside me until you kiss me senseless. I want to be whole so I can make sweet love to you, to show you that making love doesn't have to be the end of a relationship. But, Siobhan, I'm not going to do any of that unless and until you want that, too."

She rolled her eyes and groaned. "You don't play fair."

"I play true," he replied.

She heaved another sigh. "Okay, yes, I want to kiss you. Yes, you turn my insides into mush, but there's nothing we can do about it at the moment."

"There's a lot we can do," he said, the possibilities running through his mind.

"No. Those things wouldn't be enough. I want it all. All of you. All of *someone*. Even if you could make love to me tonight, you'll be going home soon." Her eyes watered. "I've lost too much of myself already. I need a relationship I can hold onto. I've promised to stay the weekend with you, and I will. Please don't ask any more of me." With that, she walked inside.

Something had definitely changed in her. If he told her now that he loved her—*he loved her*—she'd think it was a ruse. A way around her defenses.

He reached for his crutches and eased out of his chair. Inside, Siobhan was setting up the chess board with the plastic pieces Mrs. Brown had brought over. Jared rested his hand on her arm. "Let's try the new pieces."

She looked up at him, wiping a stray tear from the corner of her eye.

"I made them for you. Something to remember me by." He handed her the finished queen and she raised it to her nose.

"Smells better when it isn't burning," she said with a smile. "But I can't take these. You made them. You could sell them at a craft fair if you don't want to use them."

He paused, considering his words carefully. He was pretty sure he'd already lost her. "It's a token of my friendship." He licked his lips. "Of my admiration for you. But if that's not what you want, then take it as a token of my appreciation for the care you've given me these past couple of weeks."

She started to protest. "Jared…"

He touched a finger to her lips. "No. I get to care about you, and I care a great deal more than you think I do. I can see there's something troubling you. I'd be happy to listen, but if you don't want to talk just now, we'll just sit here and be quiet together over a friendly game of chess. Can you do that?"

She nodded, her eyes welling with tears again.

For at least the hundredth time, he cursed his disability. Jared wanted to wrap her in his arms, to reassure her, to take over whatever burden she carried. But she wouldn't want that.

And that made him love her more.

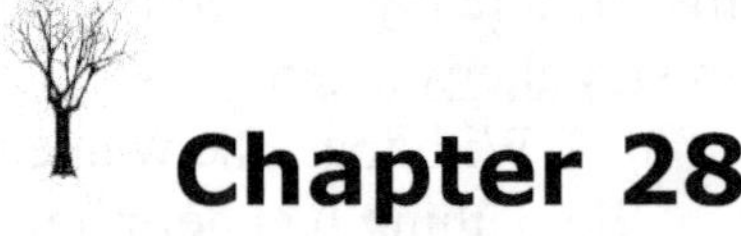

Chapter 28

THEY'D BEEN PLAYING CHESS for nearly four hours and the room was growing dark. Siobhan picked up her queen, contemplating her next move, studying the board. Was it a checkmate move or would she lose her queen?

She sniffed the chess piece. Something to remember him by. Siobhan knew she wouldn't forget Jared, even without the chess pieces. She turned the queen in her hand, studying it. Had he fashioned it after her? Not possible. Jared was the world's biggest flirt. She could allow a grudging acknowledgement that his work might resemble her. Siobhan snuck a peek at Jared, who was watching her intently, and made her move. "Checkmate?"

"Hard to do you justice with three inches of wood," he said.

"Is that a euphemism?" she asked.

Jared laughed loudly. "Just when I thought I'd lost you, there y'are." He leaned forward in his chair. "Maybe you do want to throw me back in the pond, but Siobhan, if that's for true, promise me we'll always be friends. I'd hate thinking this is all the time we have together."

"Throw you back in the pond," she repeated with a scoff. She rose from her chair and reached for one of the candles on the shelf. "I never fished you out of the pond," she said as she lit the candle and set it on the tray table beside his chair.

Jared reached for her hand. "You surely did, whether you know it or not."

Why did he have to be so charming?

The candle flickered with a chilly breeze, raising the hairs on her neck. She glanced first at Jared, then into the dining room.

Luke stood between the two rooms, the aura around him undulating like white smoke.

"How can we help you, Luke?" Jared asked.

"Levi says you tried to make us go away," Luke pointed at Jared.

Siobhan blew out a breath. She could do this. The ghosts were frightened little boys. "No, Jared wants to help you," she replied. "How can we do that?"

"Liar." The accusation came from another voice, another entity that flew through the room, knocking the candle to the floor before it disappeared down the hall.

Siobhan jumped to her feet and stomped on the flame where it burned the carpet, her heart racing. Yes, ghosts could be dangerous.

Jared reached for his crutches. "The back bedroom," he said.

"You'd better stay out here," she said. "They seem to have an issue with you. Or with men in general." She walked to the hall, the temperature dropping the closer she got to the bedroom.

Like the night before, the door was open, but there was no vision. The second twin wavered before her, naked, welt marks evident on his little body.

"Why didn't my mother stop him?" Levi asked. "She let him hurt me, let him hurt us. Where is my mother?" The aura around him grew stronger, brighter.

Siobhan's heart pinched. Hadn't she asked her own mother the same thing? She crouched. "I'd bet he hurt your mother, too," she said. "Maybe she was as scared as you were, do you think?"

The aura faded, an indication she was getting through? That he was less angry?

"Can you tell me what happened?" she asked. "So I can help you?"

Levi shook his head. "He told us never to tell or bad things would happen."

Something bad had already happened.

She'd survived her abuse. "My da used to hurt me, too," she said, "so I ran away. I know how you feel, Levi. Let me help you."

"Is he your dad?" Levi asked, raising a finger to point behind her.

Siobhan glanced over her shoulder, at Jared. "No. He's my friend. Not all men are bad, Levi. He wants to help."

"No, he tried to make us leave." Levi grew bright again and whooshed through the air.

Her heart pounding, Siobhan followed him into the living room where a gust of wind upturned the chess board. Pieces went flying, but there was no sign of either ghost. She continued to the back door, where Luke tended to disappear, and when she looked through the window, two clouds evaporated into the remaining tree trunk.

~ ~ ~

"Well that didn't go well," Jared said from the kitchen doorway. He leaned into his crutches, contemplating how he was going to help the boys while they viewed him as the enemy.

Siobhan glanced at the candle on the floor. "They could have burned the house down."

"We should avoid burning candles until we're sure the boys are gone." Jared smiled. "You did good. You'd make a fine ghost chaser, more of that caring I was talking about earlier. The key is to remain calm, and you did that."

"They knew you tried to get them to leave," she said. "They don't seem anxious to go."

But they trusted Siobhan. "As long as you're here, I'm going to let you talk to them," he said, "to help them find what they need to move on. You said Kevin was looking for their mother, right? If Luke or Levi or both of them come back tonight, you can tell them that."

He studied Siobhan's face. Her throat undulated as she swallowed. Her eyes blinked too many times. She'd been calm and comforting, because of the welts she'd seen on Levi's body?

She'd told him she ran away from home. Had she blamed her mother for the abuse she withstood?

Jared limped his way into the kitchen and put a hand on her shoulder. Hooking his right crutch at the back of his armpit, he leaned toward Siobhan and hugged her as best he could. As awkward as an off-balance hug was, he was grateful for the contact, and he hoped she was too. A reminder they were both alive.

Her hands circled his waist and she rested her head against his shoulder.

"It's true what you said to Levi, you know," he said into her hair. "Not all men are bad." She retained the scent of the Palo Santo they'd burned last night, a lemony musk. Fresh.

She nodded. "I know that, but some lessons are harder to forget than others." She stepped out of his embrace, closed her eyes and drew a deep breath. "I guess I should clean up the mess in the living room."

He followed, watched as she crouched to collect the chess pieces. She put them on the tray table and then picked up the candle.

"Did you blame your mom?" he asked.

"I did, until recently."

"And now?"

She shook her head. "Maybe we should give up on chess for the evening," she said, deliberately avoiding an answer. "And it appears we've missed dinner. Do you want something to eat?" She had a defeated look about her, the same look she'd had when she'd come home from the cemetery.

"Always trying to feed me," he teased. "I'm not fat enough?" He grabbed hold of his belly with one hand.

"There's not an inch of fat on you," she replied with a faint smile.

"Not technically true, but I'll take the compliment."

"Are you hungry?" she asked again.

"A turkey sandwich might be nice. I can help, you know."

"That's why I'm here. To take care of you. Go sit down."

He saluted her. "Yes, ma'am."

Another reluctant smile.

Jared eased into his seat, catching glimpses of her as she moved around the kitchen. He hated seeing her so subdued. She was a formidable sparring partner, one of the things he'd found most attractive about her. He wanted to hold her in his arms and promise her everything was going to come out right.

He could only hope that was the truth.

Chapter 29

AFTER THE LATEST GHOSTLY visitation, Siobhan didn't want to be alone in Jared's house, and she didn't want Jared to be caught alone, either. They played twenty questions, and as the clock marked the time from one day to the next, Jared's meds won out over his desire to stay awake.

Siobhan leaned her head against the sofa and pulled the blanket to her shoulders, closing her eyes for what she thought was a few minutes. When she opened her eyes to check the time, it was seven a.m.

Jared was still asleep in his hip chair, but with the arrival of the dawn, he'd be awake soon.

The ghosts had been quiet, and they seemed less menacing with the daylight. Siobhan needed something to keep her occupied, and Jared's laundry was in a basket on top of the washing machine.

Not all men are bad.

She'd said it, so she must believe it, but her father and the long line of high school dates insisted otherwise.

She loaded the washer and cleaned the dishes in the sink as quietly as she could before she started a pot of coffee.

Jared was still asleep in the living room. Siobhan folded the blanket she'd used and slipped upstairs for a quick shower between washing machine rinse cycles.

By the time she returned to the kitchen, the washer had finished. Siobhan moved Jared's laundry to the dryer, settled at the kitchen table with a cup of coffee and checked email on her cell phone. She read through several articles that had found their way to her inbox until the dryer signal announced the clothes were done—and woke her sleeping patient.

Siobhan set the basket of freshly dried clothes on the kitchen table and shook out a t-shirt. The squeak of a crutch tread followed by a step announced Jared's arrival.

He stopped in the kitchen doorway, his hair mussed and his jaw rasping as he scratched it. "I would rather do my own laundry," he said. "Not that I mind you seeing my underwear, but I'm used to doing it myself."

"You think I don't know how to do laundry?" she asked.

"I know you can. I don't want you to."

She raised her eyebrows, pulling out another t-shirt and folding it as she stared at him. Challenged him. Too late now. His laundry was all but done. She set the second t-shirt on top of the first on the kitchen table and nodded toward the counter. "Coffee's ready."

He grumbled something close to 'thanks' and moved toward the coffee. With one crutch.

"Where's your other crutch?" she asked.

He poured his coffee, took a sip and closed his eyes. As he turned toward her, that damn sexy smile woke up his face. "Weaning myself," he said. "I'm almost able to bear full weight. Which reminds me, you taking me to PT today?"

She put her hands on her hips. "I said I would, didn't I? Why do you keep asking me?"

He gave her a wink. "Just checking."

Siobhan pulled a pair of boxers from the basket. Heat rushed through her as she considered what she held, but she pressed her lips together and folded his underwear. Jared leaned on the kitchen counter, watching, looking so tempting. Too tempting. "Fine," she said. "You want to fold them, go ahead."

He grabbed her arm, halting her process. "Hey. Thank you."

And why did she want to kiss him again?

Her phone rang, saving her from an untoward impulse. She picked it up from the kitchen table and wandered into the living room.

"And the ghosts?" Kevin asked.

"Good morning to you, too," she said.

"Yeah, yeah. Did Jared's smudge work?"

"No."

"Damn. Listen. I have a friend at the police department. He tracked down the Masons. Stanley's in a memory care facility, but the police asked Iris to stop in for a conversation."

"The police told you that?" she asked. "Aren't you the press, and isn't this considered an ongoing investigation?"

"As I said, he's a friend. I'm going downtown, see if I can talk to her when they're done." Kevin's voice grew more subdued. "Amy suggested that if the boys are still hanging around, I might want to invite Iris over to Jared's house. Are you okay with that?"

Jared limped past her and returned to his hip chair, where he set his coffee on the tray table.

She put one hand around her cell phone. "Kevin says the police are questioning Iris Mason. He wants to invite her over here when they're done."

Jared nodded. "Might give the boys peace to see their mama."

Siobhan lifted the phone to her face. "Jared said okay. He's got PT this morning, but we should be back by lunchtime."

"I'll call you when I know more," Kevin said, and disconnected.

She glanced at Jared once more, who was replacing the cap on his pain pills. "If you're in pain, you should be using both crutches," she said.

"Quit nursing me," he grumbled. "I'm not in pain, but I am going to physical therapy, which means I will be in pain very soon."

He was right. One of the protocols was to keep the pain level manageable, and physical therapy would definitely raise it.

"You wanna help me get dressed, too?" he asked, raising an eyebrow.

She wanted to help him get *undressed,* but old memories continued to haunt her.

Not all men are bad.

She pursed her lips. "That would be considered nursing you," she said, struggling to keep her breath even. But her pulse was racing. And her breasts were tingling. And she wanted to kiss him again. Instead, she opened the door to the second floor and marched up the staircase.

~ ~ ~

Jared had flustered Siobhan, that much was apparent, but she'd had a ready retort this morning. He did love sparring with her. She kept him on his toes. If he could melt her defenses, get through that wall of hers, he might convince her to visit him in Louisiana. Or he could plan to visit her in Illinois. Or they could meet somewhere in the middle.

Except that wouldn't do. Siobhan wouldn't want a long-distance boyfriend. She'd said herself she wanted more. Could he be that man?

He hobbled to his bedroom, nearly able to walk on his own. If the information they'd given him at the hospital was right, in another month he'd be close to normal, doing all the things he was able to do before the accident.

A month didn't seem long enough to spend with Siobhan.

If he could talk her into sitting on the porch with him, they could talk things out. There had to be a way for them to be together.

He pulled off his clothes, all but his boxers in deference to Siobhan, dropped them on the floor and carried clean clothes to the bathroom. A smile creased his face as he remembered the look on Siobhan's face when he'd walked to the bathroom yesterday. He should lose the boxers, let her look to her heart's content. She wasn't immune to him, he'd guarantee that, but he'd wait until she was ready—lord, he hoped she'd be ready one day.

He dropped the boxers, nodded to the erection thoughts of Siobhan induced, and started washing. Floaters danced at the edge of his vision, marked by a spark of pain. Jared leaned over the sink and closed his eyes, trying to stave off the harbingers of a headache. Hopefully the pain pill would keep it under control.

With a deep breath, he finished washing and sat on the toilet with his dressing stick, slipping fresh boxers on one foot at a time and pulling them up with the hook. He followed suit with his sweatpants and then tugged the t-shirt over his head. One more month. Next month he should be able to get dressed without the stick.

When he finished dressing, he opened the bathroom door. An icy draft swept down the hallway. Was Levi making an early appearance today?

"Siobhan?" he called out.

"I'll be down in a minute," she called from upstairs.

The cold was gone, a draft after all. Jared carried yesterday's boxers to his bedroom and added them to the basket on the chair in the corner. He took his grabber stick and picked up the clothes he'd dropped to the floor, transferring them as well.

Siobhan tromped down the stairs. "Ready to go?"

Jared took one last look down the hall and nodded. "Need my shoes and socks."

She grabbed the socks from his hand and pointed to his hip chair. "Sit."

"I have my sock puller and my shoehorn."

She pointed a second time and knelt before him. "Might as well earn my keep since I'm here."

He did as she bade and watched her roll his socks over his toes.

"Are you swollen?" she asked.

Jared raised his eyebrows, resulting in a reminder the scar over his eye hadn't fully healed yet. "Isn't that a bit personal?" he teased.

"Your legs," she said.

He straightened his legs in front of him, but with his pants on, he couldn't tell. "I don't think so."

She palpated his calves. "Feels okay, but check with the PT when you get there." She pulled his socks up and slipped his gym shoes on. After she'd tied them, she rose to her feet and handed him his coat.

He hated feeling so helpless, and he hated that Siobhan was the one helping him. As much as he wanted to have the "when I'm better" talk with her, he imagined she saw him as a patient—as less than the man he was.

One thing he had in his favor was an abundance of time. He wasn't going anywhere anytime soon, not until after Christmas. Maybe the holiday season would work its magic and provide them both an answer for how they might turn his accident into something he and Siobhan would smile about in their old age.

Chapter 30

WHEN SIOBHAN AND JARED returned from physical therapy, Kevin's car was parked in front of the house. She glanced to Jared, who leaned into the headrest, his eyes closed. He was still pale. He'd been relatively quiet all morning.

She pulled into the driveway and turned the car off. Jared grimaced before he opened his eyes, then reached for his door. Siobhan bit her tongue, fighting the urge to ask him if he was all right. Clearly, he wasn't.

Jared hunched over his crutches, his left foot off the ground. For the past several days, he'd been bearing partial weight on that foot. Did the exertion of physical therapy set him back?

Kevin got out of his car and fell in step behind them.

"You're alone?" Jared asked. "I'm guessing Iris didn't want to stop over."

"According to her, 'I had nothing to share with the police and I have nothing to share with you,'" Kevin repeated, affecting a feminine voice.

"And?" Siobhan asked.

"I told her the boys aren't at peace and asked her over to help them move on. I also reminded her the statute of limitations for accessory after the fact expires, did expire years ago, if that was what made her hesitate. I suggested it wasn't too late to give the boys justice and turn her husband in."

"What'd she say to that?" Jared asked, pulling the front door key from his pocket. He handed the key to Siobhan before he worked his way up the stairs.

Kevin replied in that same female voice, "How dare you." His voice returned to normal as he continued. "Then she went on to tell me Stan is in a memory care facility and I should have compassion for a man suffering from Alzheimer's."

Siobhan unlocked the door and stepped aside as they passed inside.

"She also said she'd been divorced from Stan for thirty years," Kevin said.

Siobhan helped Jared out of his coat.

Jared sunk into his hip chair. "Which means shortly after they moved away."

Kevin nodded. "My hope is she'll consider what I said."

"I was hoping she'd come," Siobhan said. "From what we've learned, the boys don't trust men, and who could blame them?"

Kevin arched an eyebrow. "Which reinforces Stan was the one who beat them and potentially killed one or both of them."

"They were more receptive to Amy and Siobhan." Jared straightened his left leg and pumped his foot. "Siobhan, when they show up tonight, assuming they haven't had their fun haunting us and haven't decided to go on their own, you should talk to them. Encourage them to move on."

"I talked to them last night," she said. "And they were still angry."

"They were listening to you, though," he said. "You were getting through. Help them to understand where they are. Ask them if Stan hurt them, like we believe, and assure them he can't hurt them anymore. Tell them to walk away from the pain. Their mother loves them and wants them to find their peace. It's okay to move on. Just like you did."

Siobhan winced. "Except I'm not dead."

"I get the feeling I missed something," Kevin said, glancing from Jared to Siobhan.

"For someone who doesn't believe in ghosts, she did a fine job talking to them last night," Jared told him with a crooked smile.

She didn't feel like she'd done a fine job. The overturned candle might have burned the house down, and then there was the tumbled chessboard. "Maybe if Amy helped, if she was here when the boys showed up tonight…" Siobhan said.

"I could ask her," Kevin said. He took hold of Siobhan's arm. "Can you excuse us a minute?" he said to Jared. "I need to talk to my sister about something."

Jared waved them off, closed his eyes and tilted his head back.

Siobhan let Kevin lead her to the kitchen. Kevin pulled the pocket door closed behind them.

"What's this about?" she asked.

"Are you going to buy this house?"

For that he had to drag her to the kitchen and close the door? "No. Why?"

"You sure?"

Siobhan rolled her eyes. "For a house this size, I'd rather have a cottage-type layout instead of a bungalow. It doesn't have air conditioning or a fireplace." She didn't need to tell him that if she bought this house, she'd be envisioning Jared in that living room chair every day.

Kevin's eyes sparkled and the freckles on his face darkened. "Then Amy and I are going to make an offer."

Siobhan dropped into one of the kitchen chairs. "Even with the ghosts?"

"I'm assuming you and Jared can coax them to leave." He pulled up a chair beside her. "So what are you planning to do? Amy's lease is running out. You thinking of staying on? Signing a new lease?"

What *was* she going to do? Since her return to Edgarville, her past had taunted her. Life 'at home' hadn't turned out the way she'd imagined. She'd consumed more alcohol since she'd come home than she had in all the time she'd been gone. That couldn't be a good thing considering the family history. She'd had one date with a man looking for a trophy wife, and she had Jared.

And what exactly was Jared? Once he was healthy, he represented those high school boys she'd worked her way through. He had the same flirtatious manner, the same innuendos that slid right past her defenses. She thought she'd left that behind when she'd moved to Virginia, after she'd moved away from Carter's family. Or had she been too busy to get into trouble? Was she the same, mixed up girl she'd always been? Throwing herself into things before she took the time to see what she was getting into?

"Shevy?" Kevin asked, touching her arm. "You okay?"

She swallowed down the lump in her throat. For the first time since high school, she needed her mother. "I think I'll stop in and talk it through with Ma," she said quietly.

"Want me to pour you a drink?" he asked with a teasing smile.

She shook her head. "Probably not a good idea right now."

"Is it Jared?" he asked, nodding toward the closed door.

"Is what Jared?" She winced at the defensive tone in her voice. "He's a patient."

"He seems like a decent guy."

She folded her hands in her lap and stared at them. "My radar never did work so good."

"That was a long time ago."

She nodded.

"Nothing wrong with my radar," he said with a mischievous grin. "I think you ought to give him a chance."

Siobhan sputtered. "You're marrying the first girl to get into your pants. What do you know?"

"I waited for the right one," he said. "He seems pretty into you."

"He flirts with everyone." Except he hadn't flirted with the nurses after his fall. He might have charmed them, but he'd told every one of them he was waiting for Siobhan to show up. What if she hadn't?

"Yeah," Kevin said, "but he looks at you. Watches you. If he was goofing around, he wouldn't waste his time admiring you. He wouldn't waste his time, period."

She raised her gaze to meet Kevin's. "It's not about Jared. I've spent most of my life following the path in front of me. I never stopped to wonder if I wanted to go that direction. Now that I've stepped off the beaten path…"

Kevin reached across and hugged her. "I get it. But you do know you got somewhere when you weren't paying attention, right? From what I know, you're a pretty awesome nurse, so you did something right."

"Thanks," she said as she pulled away. "And as for that man in the other room, you do know he lives in Louisiana, don't you? His visit here is temporary."

"I get the feeling your visit here is temporary, too."

Siobhan set her hands to her hips. "I left my life in Virginia to come home. Everything." But he was right. She didn't belong here anymore. She didn't fit, and everywhere she turned, she had another demon to face. Once again, she'd gone "all in" before thinking it through. "Where do you think I should go?" she asked, half hoping he had an idea, because she sure didn't. The family had evolved, moved ahead, and Siobhan felt frozen in time, as if nothing had changed since she'd been gone.

Kevin narrowed his eyes. "You told me once life doesn't always follow a script, that we can't control the chaos around us. Aren't we the authors of our lives?" He rested his elbows on his thighs and leaned toward her. "Shevy, I'm not the one you should be asking where you should go." He poked her shoulder. "You're the one in charge of those decisions. Where do you want to be? What do you want to do?" He straightened. "It's third and nine. You gonna pass the ball or run with it?"

She gave in to a reluctant smile. Kevin had his football in high school to work out his frustrations. "You know me. I always throw the Hail Mary."

"Just make sure you have an open receiver."

"Maybe it's time I tried something different." She gave Kevin a playful punch to the arm. "If I want to visit Ma today, I'd better get going."

Kevin rose from the chair and opened the pocket door. "You want me to bring Amy over?"

Siobhan glanced into the living room, looking for Jared's input. He was asleep in his chair. "Can you stay with him until I get back? I don't want him to have any more accidents."

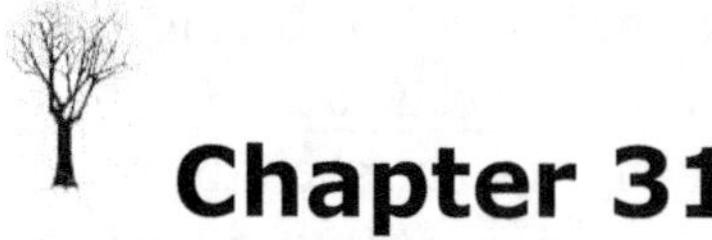

Chapter 31

SIOBHAN HAD LIVED WITHOUT her mother's advice for the past twelve years. And missed it. As awful as Siobhan had been, hurling insults and accusations when she'd walked out of the house all those years ago, when she'd knocked on Ma's door a couple of weeks ago, Ma hadn't said a word. Once she recognized Siobhan, she'd cried and held Siobhan tight, and oh, that had felt so good.

As she walked to the kitchen door, Siobhan was struck by that same uncertainty. This wasn't her home anymore. Should she knock? Or should she walk in?

Kevin had taken away her key to his place for walking in, but he hadn't known she was coming. Siobhan had called ahead this time, and yet she still felt like an outsider.

She raised a fist hesitantly, then rapped on the door. When it opened, Duncan Phelps was on the other side, sending Siobhan back a step.

"Hi, Siobhan," he said, his face flushed with color. "See you Monday." He turned toward Ma and waved. "Thanks for the coffee."

Not someone she expected to see at Ma's house. "Right," Siobhan said and walked into the kitchen.

Ma sat at the kitchen table, wearing a pale blue shirtdress—and slippers. She didn't look up right away. Siobhan took another look at the door she'd closed and then at her ma. No. It wasn't possible. Ma was… well she was her mother. Duncan wanted a trophy wife, not someone like…

"Surprised to see Duncan here," Siobhan said.

Still Ma didn't look up. "Well, you did say he was somewhat of a lost soul," she said quietly.

"Lonely," Siobhan said. "I said he was lonely."

Ma looked up then and took a deep breath. "And so am I."

Siobhan sputtered. "How can you be lonely with four kids running in and out of the house all the time?"

Ma rose to her feet and straightened her dress. "You're all grown and have your own lives now."

No. She had to be misreading something. "But he…" If Duncan was trying to date Ma, or dating her in fact, did Siobhan want to tell her mother she'd dated him? Only once, but still… "He's younger than you are," she said weakly.

"He's 49," Ma said. "And I'm 52. Three years at our age is not such a great difference." She crossed the room and took Siobhan's hands. "I've been alone a long time, Siobhan Iona. With you lot out of the house, it's time I looked after my own needs."

Duncan was older than she'd thought. Siobhan had definitely made the right call when she'd turned him down. No. She didn't want to discuss men with her mother, especially not if a certain man was sleeping with her mother.

Sleeping with her mother?

She raised her hands. "Not an appropriate topic of conversation to have with your daughter."

Ma laughed. "Does it shock you to know your mother is also a woman?"

"I've always known you were a woman," Siobhan said, lowering her voice.

"Of all of you, I'd expect you might understand better than the others."

Siobhan tugged her hands out of her mothers. Tears stung her eyes. "And what is that supposed to mean?" Her breath hitched. "A gentle reminder of what a slut I was in high school?"

"That's not what I meant, and well you know it." Ma's face immediately changed to concern. "You were always the one who knew what she wanted." She smoothed the hair from Siobhan's face. "Always so strong, so proud and so sure. You never hesitated to go after what you wanted, even as I was afraid for you." Her lips shifted into a sad smile. "Even when I didn't agree with you, I was always so proud of you, of your spirit. Even when it took you away from me. At least you were safe. I only wish you'd have come home sooner."

"But I'm not strong. And I'm not sure. I might even be reckless."

"Tea?" Ma asked.

Tea was the answer to everything, always had been, but a cup of tea wasn't going to fix all the things that were wrong this time. "No, thank you."

"Sit with me," Ma coaxed.

Siobhan took a seat at the table.

"What's troubling you?"

Because it was Ma, and because it was why she'd come, Siobhan shared her insecurities with her mother, including how she believed her life hadn't progressed in the time she'd been gone from Edgarville. Coming home made her feel she'd stepped into the empty shoes she'd left behind, shoes that no longer fit.

"It's not true," Ma said, handing her a tissue. "Look at all you've accomplished. You finished your schooling. You're a nurse, and I'm certain you've helped thousands of people through the years. Perhaps we were wrong to ask you to stay, to give up the life you'd built for yourself. The only things left here for you were bad memories."

"And family," Siobhan said through the tears.

"Aye, but you don't need to be near to keep your family close."

"Which brings me to the reckless part. I walked away from my life in Virginia the same way I walked away from my life here. I'm too impulsive."

Ma studied her a moment as if considering something. She pursed her lips and squinted the way she might if she tasted something unpleasant, then sighed. "The man Kevin brought to Thanksgiving. Your patient. Kevin seems to think there might be something between the two of you. Is that part of what's troubling you?"

Ma knew about the boys in high school. If not before, she knew by the time Siobhan left with Carter and his family. "I haven't been with a man since Carter broke up with me."

"In all these years?" Ma asked.

Siobhan shook her head.

Ma winced. "Should I assume you prefer women, then?"

Siobhan laughed. "No. You should assume I had too many bad experiences, that I don't believe a man would be interested in more than…" She hesitated. This was still her Ma, and they didn't discuss such things. "I have a hard time believing anyone would be interested in the person I am."

"You're being too hard on yourself. Maybe you've come for closure, to put memories of those boys behind you. They're older now, too, and I'll bet most of them feel poorly for ill-using you. The excuse is always that they were young and foolish, and you might consider that, as well. Excuses don't make everything right, but values are like Jell-O. They take time to set. It's from the choices we make that we gain insight into what we value as right or wrong.

"You had a difficult time growing up, and you went looking for another choice. It looks to me like you've found those things you value, things that represent right and wrong. You might have taken a darker turn with your life. I often wondered at what might have become of you. Oh, my Siobhan. Kevin never shared your private conversations, but knowing you were out there, alive, safe, I knew the Good Lord was looking out for you."

She took Siobhan's hands once more. "And you haven't told me about this patient of yours."

"I've never gotten involved with a patient. It's unprofessional."

Ma nodded. "So you've set standards for yourself, and now you're worried you're breaking the rules—your own rules."

"Maybe," she conceded. "That, and the bad memories."

"Darlin', if you've come for my advice," Ma's forehead creased by way of asking if that was true, and Siobhan nodded, "then I'll tell you to take a chance. If it's your own rules that are troubling you, set them aside. See what happens. It's plain you care about this man or you wouldn't be at odds with yourself. No one understands better than I do how frightening it is to trust a man again, but it's time. For me and, I suspect, for you as well. We're not getting any younger, you know."

Siobhan chuckled. "Speak for yourself. I'm glad you feel comfortable trying again. I'm not there yet."

Ma nodded. "You will be. When losing your chance is more frightening than stepping away from your fears, you'll move forward."

~ ~ ~

Jared straightened his leg and flexed his toes once more. The cramp in his calf was back.

"You know, you don't have to stay and babysit me," he told Kevin.

Kevin leaned back in his chair. "Is that what I'm doing? I thought we were having a nice game of chess."

"Call it what you will. I told Siobhan and I'll tell you, too. I've been taking care of myself just fine since I came here from rehab."

"Until you fell," Kevin reminded him.

"I was surprised, that's all, and I didn't get hurt any worse."

"I'm not babysitting you, and even though Siobhan said she came to stay the weekend because of the social worker, I'm inclined to believe it wasn't to nurse you."

"What, then?" Jared flexed his ankles again. That damn cramp wasn't going away.

"Be careful with her," Kevin said. "She's had a rough go of it. If you're a player and this is all a game to you, let her go."

Jared pushed on the seat of his chair to reposition himself. "I'm not playing. I'm for keeps, but she doesn't seem so sure."

Kevin eyed him, taking his measure. Jared held out his arms to show he was in earnest, or inviting Kevin to ask more questions.

"I made this board and these pieces for her," Jared told him. "A keepsake. I chose the wood because it symbolizes cleansing and healing of the soul. She's been in an odd humor lately. You'll see that she gets this if something should happen?"

Kevin nodded, his expression confused.

"I can't force her into something she doesn't want, and she may choose to burn the whole thing, but even then, I'd hope the smoke would bring her the resolution she needs to move on."

"I'm hoping you'll bring the resolution she needs to move on," Kevin said with a laugh. He rose to his feet when someone knocked on the door.

Judging by the arms that wound around Kevin when he opened the door, Jared figured Amy had arrived. He was proved right a moment later when Kevin pulled her into the room.

"We had an offer for you," Kevin said. "I know you're planning to move back to Louisiana, that you were planning to sell the house. Would you consider selling it to us?"

"I expect we can work something out." He bent over as far as he could tolerate and massaged his leg.

"Then let's make a deal." Kevin put one hand on the door to push it closed and hesitated. "This should be interesting."

"What should be?" Jared asked.

"Iris Mason. She's pacing beside a car on the street." Kevin stepped outside and called out. "Would you like to come in?"

Amy flipped on the living room light, calling attention to the fact the room had been growing darker. Jared checked his cell phone. Siobhan had been gone most of the afternoon.

Kevin returned a moment later, inviting the woman in. "Mrs. Mason," he introduced.

She was a tiny woman, smaller than Siobhan, and she had short gray hair. She wore a wool peacoat, so Jared assumed the temperature had dropped again.

"My fiancée, Amy Benson, and this is Jared Pierce. His great aunt was the woman who bought the house from you," Kevin said.

"Ma'am," Jared said. "Forgive me for not getting up."

She looked around the room and spoke in a subdued voice. "The house looks much the same."

"They remodeled the upstairs," Amy told her. "In hopes of having children."

Amy cast a significant look at Kevin that cut through to Jared's heart. He remembered the way Siobhan had spoken to the troubled little boy ghost, and for the second time in as many days, he envisioned a family of his own.

With Siobhan.

And there she was. Siobhan walked in the front door.

"And my sister, Siobhan," Kevin introduced. "This is Iris Mason."

Siobhan tucked her purse into the bookshelves inside the front door. "Mrs. Mason."

"I can come back, if you're busy," Iris said.

"No, ma'am," Jared told her. "We've all seen the boys. They're lost and afraid and aren't sure how to move on. I believe if you could tell them Stan can't hurt them anymore, that it's okay for them to move on, they might find peace."

She shook her head. "No. I can't believe after all these years…"

"Will you tell us what happened?" Kevin asked.

She shook her head again.

"Mrs. Mason, as I told you at the police station, whatever happened all those years ago, unless you killed your own children…"

"No, I wouldn't have done that," she said. She looked frantically at each of them. "I didn't know, I swear. I was a single mother and when Stan paid attention to me, I was flattered. It happened so fast. I didn't know…" Tears fell down her cheeks. "I had no idea he was more interested in little boys than he was in me, and here, I had two of them."

Siobhan helped her to the sofa and sat beside her. "Levi showed us a vision. He had welts on his back that I assume were inflicted the night he died."

Iris nodded. "I worked at the factory, and I was just getting home. I saw Luke race down the hall and followed." She closed her eyes and brought her hands to her face. "Stan was standing there, wearing nothing but his underwear. Luke went after him like a boy possessed, pummeling him with his fists. I was so shocked until I saw what happened next. Stan picked him up off the floor, and threw him—*threw him*—against the wall. That's when Stan saw me." She swallowed hard. "He said it was self-defense. Told me that surely I'd seen how the boy had run at him. He didn't mean to hurt him, he was defending himself. And then I saw Levi. Lying naked on the bed, Stan's belt on the floor with blood stains where it had cut Levi's skin."

Amy gasped and sat on Iris's other side.

"Stan convinced me it was all an accident. He said the boys hated him and tried to hurt him and if I told anyone he'd killed them, they'd arrest us both." Iris stopped to take a breath.

Which more or less confirmed the vision Levi had shown Jared and Siobhan.

Kevin grimaced.

Iris looked to him and rushed on. "I didn't know what to do. He buried them in the backyard. We were moving. He said no one would know." Tears streamed down her face. "But I knew."

"That must have been horrible for you," Siobhan said gently.

Jared twisted in his seat and another cramp clenched his calf. He grunted, leaned forward and pumped his ankles. Maybe if he stood up…

Siobhan rose to her feet and stood in front of Jared. He could see her struggling not to ask if he was okay. Maybe he wasn't.

"Just a cramp," he told her, worried it might be something worse.

She crouched down in front of him and squeezed his calves. The hiss of pain he gave her led her to roll up his pant legs.

"Jared, your leg is swollen. Did you ask the PT to look at your leg while you were there like I asked you to?"

He bit back the joke he'd made earlier, allowing for the company. "I didn't think it was worth mentioning."

"This might be a DVT, a blood clot. You know you have an increased risk after your surgery. This could be serious. I'm calling the paramedics."

"Now, Siobhan," he started to protest, and then, over her shoulder, Luke appeared. No sense wasting his breath, she was already talking to a 911 operator.

She narrowed her eyes and followed his gaze. Could she see Luke?

"I can't leave," he said. "We don't know what they'll do."

"A blood clot can kill you. The ambulance is on the way."

He was afraid for her, and for the rest of them.

The ghosts knew Siobhan, and they'd responded well to her. He had to hope for the best. Jared took her arms. "Stay with them. Help them find their way home."

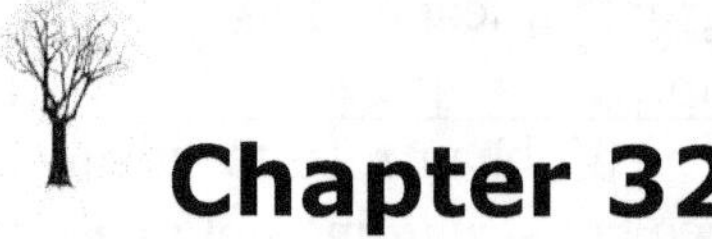

Chapter 32

SIOBHAN HANDED HER PHONE to Kevin and closed the door behind them as Kevin helped Jared to the front porch to wait for the paramedics. She squeezed Amy's hand and they faced Luke.

Ten year-olds prone to temper tantrums, Siobhan reminded herself. She could do this.

"Is the room getting colder?" Amy asked.

"That will be Levi, in the back bedroom," Siobhan said.

Iris paled, shivering as she stared at the specter in front of her.

"Mom?" Luke's hollow voice echoed in the small rooms.

Siobhan knelt in front of the ghost. "She's come to tell you Stan can't hurt you anymore. You don't have to stay here any longer."

Iris clasped her hands in front of her mouth.

Muted voices indicated the paramedics had arrived. The clatter of wheels on the steps and subsequent closing of the porch door let Siobhan know they'd taken Jared to the hospital.

Iris walked to the back bedroom, where an eerie glow shimmered.

"It's definitely cold," Amy said softly.

"Jared says that's Levi's anger," Siobhan told her.

Like before, the boxes in the room seemed to have disappeared, showing the small bed where a naked boy lay curled up. As the welts appeared on his back, Iris stepped forward.

"No! Stop. Leave him alone! He's just a boy…" As she reached for the ghost, the vision evaporated and Iris's hands landed on a box. She turned to Siobhan, tears streaming down her cheeks. "I swear I didn't know…"

"Am I dead?" Luke asked his mother.

Iris looked at Amy and then at Siobhan. Siobhan nodded.

"Yes," Iris squeaked out.

Levi appeared beside his brother, his eyes glowing red. He pointed to his mother, his mouth curled into an angry frown. Iris's eyes grew large, one of her arms half raised, as if frozen in place.

"Iris?" Amy said. She reached for her, but Levi raised his other hand and pointed to Amy. The room grew colder. Both Iris and Amy looked like mannequins, unable to move.

"She let this happen," Levi said, his voice echoing in the small room. The bedroom door slammed shut.

Siobhan gulped, closed her eyes and drew a deep breath. She knelt before the two ghosts. "She didn't know," she said quietly.

"Your mother did," Levi said. "You told me so."

"Yes, that's because my father hurt my mother, too."

Levi's aura wavered beside her.

"Did he hurt you too, Mom?" Luke asked.

Iris nodded, teeth chattering.

"Stan won't be coming back here," Siobhan said.

"I don't believe you!" Levi shrieked, flying around the room. "She let him kill us."

Iris sagged and reached for a box to steady herself. Amy rubbed her arms.

"I didn't know he was hurting you," Iris told them, tears streaming down her cheeks. "Not until that night."

Amy tried the bedroom door, then turned to Siobhan and shook her head. They were trapped inside.

Siobhan rose to her feet, hands on hips. Little boys having temper tantrums. Terrifying little boys, but little boys just the same. "Open the door," she told the ghosts.

The door flew open and both spirits sailed through. The cold dissipated.

"Are they gone?" Iris asked, teeth still chattering.

"Yes," Amy told her. "Can't you feel it? I'm warmer now."

"I couldn't move! How did Levi do that?" Iris asked Siobhan.

"I don't know."

Iris's eyes shone with fear, she gave Siobhan one more glance and darted for the living room. A minute later, the front door slammed shut.

"Should we go after her?" Siobhan asked, taking a step toward the hall.

"No," Amy said. "I don't think she'll come back. Ever."

"What happened?" Siobhan asked.

"I have never felt so much fear in all my life," Amy told her. "The cold. It was paralyzing."

"But they're her children."

"They were her children. If she allowed her husband to bury them in the backyard, she's not going to help them now."

Siobhan had to do something, but what? She didn't know how to banish ghosts the way Jared did. She glanced down the hall, to the open door of Jared's bedroom. He'd done that thing with the incense. Would it work if she tried?

She hurried to his room and looked around, searching for the bowl they'd used. She found it on the dresser, snatched it up and carried it to the dining room. Three incense sticks were left in the bag. How many was she supposed to use? And what was she supposed to say?

Amy laid a hand on her arm. "They trust you," she said. "The ghosts."

"And that helps how?" Siobhan asked.

"Jared said the smudge didn't work last time."

And Levi had told Siobhan he thought Jared was trying to send them away. She set the bowl and the incense on the dining room table and dropped into a chair. "I don't know what to do."

"Jared will," Amy said.

~ ~ ~

Jared flipped channels, looking for something, anything, to distract him. He hated being in hospitals, and he most especially hated that he wasn't allowed to leave his bed. He was dying to know what had happened after he left the house, and he'd been praying Siobhan was safe. A shadow at his door caught his eye, and when he looked, as if he'd conjured her, Siobhan hovered looking uncertain whether to enter.

"Thank God," he said. "Baby, tell me what happened."

She glanced over her shoulder and then walked in, her lips set in a grim line. This didn't look good.

"I was worried about you," he said as she sat in the chair beside his bed.

"I don't know how to help them," she said in a small voice.

"Tell me what happened," he repeated.

Siobhan looked nervously toward the door, rose, and closed it.

"Siobhan?" he asked, her actions making him more worried.

"They were angry," she began, and then she related what had happened, including the way she'd spoken to them, and the way they'd listened to her. His heart swelled with pride.

"How did Levi do that?" she asked when she finished. "Freeze them like that?"

"It's a form of possession," he told her. "More commonly known as fear. In that moment, he controlled their thoughts, shared his rage and his fear, fear of his experiences and of the end result. Of being dead."

Her eyes glistened. She swiped at one of her cheeks. "Why wasn't I afraid? Paralyzed with fear?"

Bless her heart. The ghosts had responded to her. "They trust you."

"What do I do? Every day they return to that house is another day of suffering for them. We can't wait for you to come home to show them the way, for whatever hocus pocus you do. How can I help them?"

Yeah, the doctors had told Jared his hospital stay would last a while this time—a week or more. And when he was able to return to the house, he'd still be hobbling along. He hated being helpless. Could Siobhan help the ghosts?

Jared straightened in the bed. "You don't go in there alone, y'heard? You take Amy with you."

"But she was frozen, too," Siobhan reminded him.

"You tell her everything I tell you," he said. "Don't let them scare you. Don't let them fill you with fear of any kind." He raised his eyebrows, asking for confirmation she understood. "You tell them you're not afraid, that their time on earth is over and if they let go of the anger, of the fear, they will find their peace."

"I don't know if I can. I still can't believe what I saw, what Levi did to his mother, and then to Amy. What if he does that to me?"

Jared smiled. "First, he could have done that today. He didn't. That means he trusts you. Second, you won't let him. You are in control of your thoughts and feelings." He waited for her to meet his gaze again. "Y'heard?"

"But I am afraid," she whispered.

How did she not see how truly fearless she was? "I don't think so. Didn't you tell me you told him to open the door, even when the other ladies were paralyzed with fear? You are the voice of authority to those two boys. You remember that, and they'll listen to you."

"And the smudge?"

"No, Amy was right. It didn't work, and Levi viewed that as me trying to hurt him."

"I don't want to go back there," she said, meeting his gaze once more.

"But you will. You're not the type to give up, now, are you?" He grinned at her and was rewarded with one of her reluctant sighs.

"You need to go back," he said. "I forgot my phone, and my mama will be worried if I don't answer when she calls. I don't want her on the next plane out, so if you'd be so kind as to bring my phone to me, I can call her and ease her mind."

Siobhan chuckled. "All right."

He reached for her hand. "And you take Amy with you. I don't want you alone with those ghosts."

"You're scaring me again."

"Don't be scared, be wary. Levi is a troubled soul, which makes him unpredictable," he said. "But you are the voice of authority. If anyone can get through to him, you can, and Luke will follow his lead. Trust your instincts, Siobhan. You might be the only one who can help them move on."

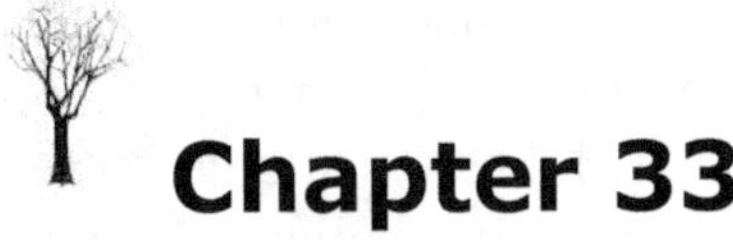

Chapter 33

NO MATTER WHAT JARED told her, Siobhan was not going to take Amy to the house. He hadn't seen the way Levi had frozen Amy and Iris. Amy had said she'd never been so afraid.

No, taking Amy was a bad idea. Siobhan would do this alone. The ghosts hadn't hurt her. She'd been frightened by what they'd done, but not paralyzed by fear.

She hesitated as she walked inside the porch of Jared's house, key poised to open the front door. Siobhan took a moment to admire the wicker sofa, thoughts of sitting beside Jared, holding hands, carrying on what he'd deem an intelligent conversation. As seductive a picture as it presented, it was a dream she couldn't quite grasp. If they continued on the road they were on, as soon as he was physically able, she'd succumb to his charms, sleep with him, and he'd disappear—like all the rest.

Except she'd never fallen in love before. Carter had been an infatuation.

When Jared walked out of her life, he was going to leave a gap she feared no one else could fill. Her only hope was to leave before he did, before her feelings went any deeper.

Way too late to worry about her depth of feelings, but one thing Jared had said rung true. She was in charge of her thoughts and feelings.

Once inside, she located Jared's cell phone along with the charger. In his bedroom. She dropped them in her coat pocket and paused to look around. At the too-small closet. At the unmade bed. At the pile of laundry in his basket.

Siobhan crossed to the bed and picked up a pillow, holding it to her nose and breathing in the scent of him. Squeezing the pillow to her, she closed her eyes. This was a close as she dared get to Jared and his bed. She lay the pillow down and smoothed the case, gave it one last, lingering look.

She wasn't his nurse, or his housekeeper, or his paid companion. The time had come to walk away from Jared and his house, but not before she did what she could to help the ghosts on their journey.

Siobhan sputtered. Ghosts. A month ago she didn't believe they existed. She believed in ghosts now, and she wasn't going to let a ghost with a temper frighten her. At the heart of it, they were little boys.

"Luke," she called out as she returned to the dining room. Would he come when she called?

Her fingers brushed over the carved chess set on the table and she lifted one of the lighter pieces to her nose, inhaling the spicy, citrusy, pine scent of the Palo Santo wood. She set the piece down and turned in a circle, searching the room. Nothing.

She walked to the back bedroom, took a deep breath to steal herself and walked inside. "Levi." She glanced at the boxes in the corner where the bed had appeared. "Frightening your mother was wrong," she said to the empty room. "She was afraid of Stan, like you. Instead of blaming her, you should have understood."

A cold breeze swept past her. So he was here.

"Levi," she said again. "It's time to let go. Leave the anger and the pain behind."

"You want to send me away, too," a hollow voice echoed behind her.

Siobhan turned to face the wavering form.

"I want you to be happy," she told him.

"No," he said impetuously. "I don't believe you."

The room grew colder. If Jared was right, that meant Levi was frightened and wanted to share that fear.

"You don't have to be afraid." She rubbed her arms. "You've been scared long enough."

"I want to go back to the tree," he said. "We were happy inside the tree, Luke and me."

"The tree is broken," she replied. "But you and Luke will always be together."

Luke took that moment to appear beside his brother, looking uncertain. "Am I really dead?" he asked.

"Yes."

He cried. "I don't want to be dead."

"If you send us away, we won't be together no more," Levi said, the cold increasing. "I don't want to be alone."

"Any more," Siobhan corrected.

Levi's voice grew in volume and echoed in the tiny room. "No more."

Siobhan covered her ears and winced. "You won't be alone."

"I don't believe you." His voice thundered. A fracture in one of the windows crackled as it grew in size.

"Stop," Siobhan shouted. She paused to regain her composure, calmed her voice. Yelling at a child seldom helped the situation. "You don't have to be mad. They can't hurt you anymore," she repeated. "Once you stop being mad, the pain will go away. Until you stop reliving the past, you can't move forward."

One of the windows imploded. Siobhan took a step backward, tripped on a box and fell. The pain in her ankle told her she'd likely sprained it, but that wasn't her worst injury. A long shard of glass had embedded itself in her leg. Bad time to consider she probably should have brought Amy with her, after all.

The boys stood side by side, Luke looking forlorn and Levi trembling with rage.

Siobhan winced with the pain. "Your mother loved you," she said. "She didn't know how to protect you. It's time to forgive her. It's time to move on."

"I want to be happy again," Luke said.

"We're together," Levi said.

"And you'll stay together," Siobhan told them.

"You promise?" Luke asked.

She was bleeding. Heavily. She needed help.

Levi hovered beside her. His eyes faded to a shade of gray and his expression was less certain.

"You don't have to be afraid," she told him one more time.

"But where will we go?" Luke asked.

Siobhan closed her eyes and winced with the pain. She didn't know the answer, and she was fading fast.

"Shame on you boys. Come along," another ghostly voice called out. "We are going to have such an adventure!"

The ghost of a woman smiled and extended a hand to each of the twins. She had braids wrapped around her head. "I'll guide them home," she told Siobhan. "And I expect Amy will be here shortly to help you. Forgive them, dear. They didn't mean to harm you." She turned to the twins. "Did you? Apologize to the nice lady."

Luke, head bowed, scuffed a ghostly foot. "Sorry."

Levi looked less sure.

"Enough of that, Levi," the woman said. "After all she's done to try to help you."

"Sorry," he mumbled.

Siobhan nodded, spots dancing at the edge of her vision. "Are you their grandmother?" she asked.

The woman laughed, an odd bark of a laugh. "No, dear. In life, I was known as Lily Sumner. I always wanted children of my own, but it wasn't meant to be. I'll take good care of them on the other side." She shook her hands toward the boys again. "Come along now."

The boys each took one of Mrs. Sumner's hands and turned to walk through the back wall. Luke waved one last time as they disappeared.

Tears streamed down Siobhan's face. She tried to push to her feet, but couldn't support her weight. She reached into her coat for Jared's cell phone—dead battery—and then remembered she'd left her purse, and therefore her phone, in the car.

She dragged herself along the floor and got as far as the bathroom before the spots at the edge of her vision joined together and her world went black.

~ ~ ~

The phone beside his bed rang and Jared nearly dropped it in his hurry to answer.

"Jared, honey, what happened?" his mother asked.

Not Siobhan. He sighed. "I'm fine."

"You're not fine. I've been trying to call and when I didn't get an answer, I finally thought to call the hospital. What's going on? Do you need me there?"

"No, Mama." He rubbed his forehead. "I have a blood clot. They're likely to keep me in the hospital another week."

"And why didn't you call me?"

"Can't make long distance calls from the hospital room, and I left my phone at the house." He looked up when someone stood in the doorway, Amy. She held up his cell phone.

"Praise be," he said. But why was she bringing it, and not Siobhan?

"What's happening?" his mother asked.

"Someone just brought me my phone. I'll call you back, Mama." He hung up the phone. "Where's Siobhan?"

"She's okay," Amy told him, handing him his phone and his charger. "The twins are gone. From what Siobhan told me, your great aunt walked them home."

"From what she told you? You weren't there?"

Amy took a seat beside his bed. "Well, you were right to call me, because she never did."

"She went there by herself?" he asked.

"She did." Amy met his gaze. "And she did what you asked her to."

"Is she okay?"

"There was an incident," she said. "Siobhan's in the emergency room, but they don't expect to hold her once they fix her up."

"Amy," he said impatiently. "What happened to her?"

"She stumbled and sprained her ankle."

Why did he get the idea she was leaving something out? "That doesn't sound like an incident."

Amy wrung her hands. "One of the windows at your house had to be boarded up. It broke."

"How did it break?"

"A loud noise? The cold weather? I'm not sure."

"Amy!"

She huffed. "She said it was cracked, and Levi made it break."

"And?"

"Siobhan caught a shard of glass in her leg." Amy held up her hands. "But she's okay. She lost some blood, but not enough to be a problem. They're stitching her up and giving her crutches for her ankle and the leg, and then they're sending her home." She put her hands on the edge of his bed. "She's okay."

Jared scrubbed his face with his hand. A shard of glass? It could have struck her anywhere. "I want to see her."

"Well, considering you can't leave this bed, and considering she's being attended to downstairs, that's not possible right now. Let her go home, rest up after her ordeal." She smiled. "She did what you asked her to do. The boys have gone."

"How can you be sure?"

"I'm sure."

He leaned into his bed and closed his eyes. "Amy, I need to see her."

"I'm pretty sure she's planning to come to work tomorrow, so I'll let her know she should stop in and see you."

Work. Then she must be okay. Jared swallowed down relief, his eyes stinging. "She's a brave girl," he said, his throat thick.

"Yes, she is," Amy replied. "I couldn't have done it. Not after what Levi did to me."

"She told me," Jared said. "I deeply regret putting you in that situation. And her."

"It all worked out." Amy smiled and rose to her feet. "And now I have a fiancé waiting for me. Talk to you soon, huh?"

"Amy." He mustered a smile. "I'm much obliged."

"I know." She fluttered her fingers in a wave and walked out.

He closed his eyes again and took a deep breath. Siobhan might be okay, but she had been injured, and it was his fault. Would she blame him? Would she visit him?

He hated being helpless.

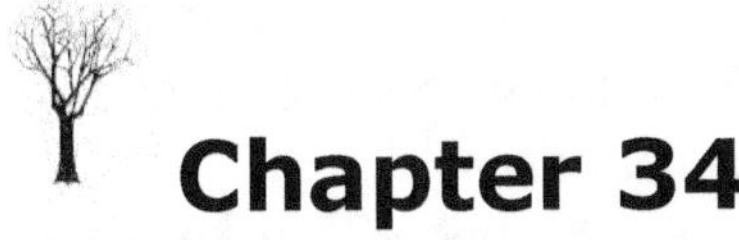

Chapter 34

THE WEATHER HAD A perverse sense of humor. Monday morning brought the return of more snow.

Siobhan navigated the slippery streets to the hospital, dreading what the next couple of months might bring. A white Christmas was worth coming home for, but she could do without the hazardous driving conditions during the rest of the winter.

After their conversation, Ma had reinforced Siobhan's notion to move away, get on with her life somewhere else, but where did she want to go?

The app was a good monitoring tool, but Jared was a perfect example of 'what can go wrong, will.' The tool was designed to prevent readmissions. Jared had been readmitted twice, once after his fall and now with the blood clot, neither of which could have been prevented with the app.

She drove into the parking garage, noticing two of the four vice presidents' cars were already there, one of them being Duncan's. One more reason to leave this job. How was she supposed to work with the man who was dating her mother? Thank heaven she'd developed the sense not to sleep with every man she dated.

Maybe she had grown up—a little.

She hopped out of her car and grabbed her crutches, grateful she didn't have to cross the snow with them. Once inside the elevator, her mind wandered to what she could do with her life. She'd fallen into her nursing career, making what had seemed like the only available choice at the time. Since then, she'd added to her resume of experience. For the first time in her life, she was taking charge of her future, deciding what she wanted to do and pursuing it.

Siobhan chuckled as she slid out of her coat. She could now add helping ghosts to her resume, not that she ever would. Taking a seat behind her desk, she opened a drawer and tucked her purse inside.

Ghosts. Would she see ghosts in the ER? Spirits leaving bodies as lives ended? She wasn't sure if that would be a good thing or a bad thing. She should cross ER nurse off her list of desirable positions.

She booted up her computer and opened PHM. Three patients were flagged as being readmitted, one of them being Jared.

No. She didn't want to be Jared's nurse, and he'd demonstrated another reason not to fall in love with a patient. They tended to be sick or hurt. The DVT he'd developed was serious, and Jared didn't take anything seriously. If the clot travelled, a pulmonary embolism could kill him. Even if she'd considered a serious relationship with him—and let's get real, Jared in a serious relationship?—with her luck, he'd die from the complications his accident caused.

She clunked her forehead on her desk.

"I hope I'm not responsible for your frustration," Duncan said from his office door.

Siobhan closed her eyes and pulled herself together. She smiled as she sat up straight. "Good morning."

"Doesn't look like it." He stepped aside and waved her in. "Would you step into my office for a minute?"

No. "Sure."

She straightened her sweater, grabbed her crutches and limped to the chair beside his desk. Duncan closed the door and, head bowed, returned to his chair. He opened his mouth, grimaced and tried again.

"If this is about you and my mom, you don't need to say anything," Siobhan said, helping him out. "If this is about the phone calls on the PHM phone, I forgot to turn it off that night and answered it out of habit. And I'm not dating a patient. Not really."

Duncan's eyebrows drew together. "What?"

Siobhan winced. "What did you want to talk to me about?"

"Did you apply to be a nurse educator?"

Oh. That. Siobhan's pulse raced. Had she violated protocol? "I miss being with the patients."

"But you do deal with patients in this position."

"Peripherally. I like to be more directly involved in their recovery." *Just ask Jared.* She closed her eyes and grimaced.

He leaned over his desk. "I hope this isn't personal. And if this is about your mom, because I do want to discuss that with you…"

"No," she said. "It's about me. I took this job to be closer to my family and to have regular hours and a more reasonable facsimile of a life. I have to admit, that part is going to be difficult to give up, but I think I'd like to try teaching for a while. That way I can help and be with patients at the same time."

Duncan sat back and steepled his fingers in front of his chest. "Closer to your family," he repeated. "You do realize you'll have to relocate if you take the teaching position?"

"The listing didn't mention where the job is." Another case of leaping before she looked, but she'd been thinking of leaving Edgarville anyway.

"I'd be happy to give you a recommendation if this is what you want."

Was it what she wanted?

"They have a shortage of nurses in Louisiana at the moment."

Siobhan closed her eyes. "Louisiana?" she asked hesitantly. With her luck, the hospital was in Vacherie, where she'd see Jared every time she went to the store. Every time she drove down the street.

"That's where the job is."

She swallowed down the trepidation. "Where in Louisiana?"

"Baton Rouge." He leaned over his desk once more. "You sure you want to do this?"

"I came home to reconnect, but this isn't where I belong." She snickered. "And I definitely don't miss the snow." She didn't know her Louisiana geography, but Jared had mentioned he lived near New Orleans.

She didn't have to avoid the state because he lived there.

~ ~ ~

As yet another person came at him with a needle, Jared turned his head away and grimaced. Yes, he understood the dangers of deep vein thrombosis, understood that they needed to test his blood regularly to check that he was responding to the Heparin, understood that although his blood needed to be thinned, if it was too thin he ran the risk of bleeding out. He didn't have to like being a human pincushion.

He'd hoped Siobhan would have stopped by before work this morning, but she had a job to do. When she didn't show up at lunch time, he began to worry.

After the phlebotomist finished taking his blood, Jared pressed the call button for his nurse. Like magic, she appeared in his door. Funny how quickly they showed up.

She flipped her hair and smiled broadly. "What can I get for you? Are you in pain?"

He didn't have the patience for a flirty nurse today. He was only interested in one woman's attentions, and she seemed to be avoiding him. "I'm fine," he said. "Listen, you know Siobhan McCormick? She works in administration. I need to talk to her."

The nurse's smile disappeared, to be replaced with a pout. "I'll call and see if she's available."

"Much obliged." He watched her walk away, then pointed the remote at the television once more and flipped through game shows and talk shows. After surfing the channels a second time, he clicked the television off and stared at his cell phone, trying to decide if he should call Siobhan. Amy had promised to ask her to stop in. Surely Siobhan knew he wanted to see her.

He was already pushing by asking the nurse to track her down.

And then he heard crutches in the hallway, followed by Siobhan hobbling through his door.

She gave him a guarded look. "I meant to stop down sooner, but it's been a busy day."

"Are you okay?" he asked.

She nodded and waved a crutch at him. "Learning empathy for my patients." She smiled weakly.

"You have lots of empathy. Unlike those sadistic physical therapists." He'd hoped to coax a bigger smile from her.

"Speaking of physical therapy, and home healthcare," she said. "You're going to have to make other arrangements after they release you."

"You're angry with me?" he asked.

She smiled. "No.

"Then…?"

"I've been offered another job. Or at least an interview." She bit her lower lip. "I'll probably be moving."

"Where?" He couldn't let her slip away, not like this. Jared was powerless, trapped in a hospital bed. "Surely you have time before you leave, enough time we can sit down and talk?"

"I'm not sure what my schedule will be like. I have an interview next week, and if that pans out, I'd be starting the first of the year."

"But that's still a month away. You'll want to be with your family for Christmas."

She nodded. "Yeah, I'll come back for Christmas. By then you'll probably be cleared to travel. You'll want to spend the holiday with your family, too, I would imagine."

He wanted to spend Christmas with her, wherever that was. He wanted to spend a lot more time with Siobhan, like maybe the rest of his life, but if he told her that, she was likely to bolt. "We're still friends, aren't we?" The question was lame, but he didn't know how else to hold onto her.

"Sure." She didn't sound convincing. In fact, her words sounded like a brush off.

"I'd like to keep in touch," he said. "You mean the world to me, Siobhan."

"It's that nurse thing," she said. "Patients get confused about that."

He shook his head. "No. That's not true and you know it."

"Jared…"

"Look, I know I've been a pain in the ass, but we have something special, don't we? You and me?"

She turned toward the door. "I have to go."

"Wait. We have so much more to talk about."

"This is something I have to do," she told him. "Something I want to do. For the first time in my life, I'm making a conscious decision about my future. I have to go, Jared."

How was he supposed to argue with that? "You'll keep in touch?"

"I'm not sure that's a good idea." Her voice took that breathy hitch he loved and her eyes welled with tears. "Get well, Jared. I wish you all the best." A tear slid down her cheek and she brushed it away with a nervous laugh.

"Can I call you?" he asked, his last option.

She took a step closer to the bed, leaned over and pressed a kiss to his forehead. "Bye." Siobhan turned and limped out of his room.

Damn, if she didn't take his heart with her.

But she hadn't told him not to call.

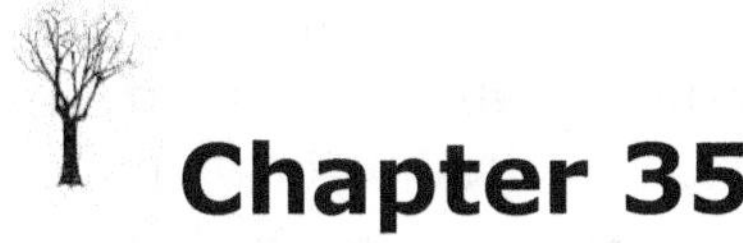

Chapter 35

"I DON'T UNDERSTAND what the hurry is," Kevin said over dinner.

"It sounds like a great opportunity," Amy said.

Siobhan waited while the server brought them each a glass of wine. "The new semester starts in January. I'd like to get settled in before that." She raised her glass. "Here's to making conscious choices and directing my own fate."

"Still feels like an impulsive decision to me," Kevin muttered.

"It's an opportunity," Siobhan said, nodding to Amy. "And who knows? I might be back here in six months if it doesn't work out."

"Somehow I doubt that. Didn't you say the hospital is an affiliate of St. Francis? And with Dr. Phelps's recommendation, I'm guessing the job is yours for the taking. The hospital already employs you." He took a sip of his wine, and when he set his glass down, Amy laced her fingers with his.

"You know she'll be back," Amy said. She turned to Siobhan. "You'll be home for Christmas, right?"

"Yes, ma'am." As soon as she said it, Jared's voice echoed inside her head. If she had any regrets about leaving, he would be the one.

"And what about Jared?" Kevin asked, as if he'd read her mind.

"He'll be leaving soon, too." She leaned across the table and pointed a finger at him. "Do *not* tell him where I'm moving. You hear me?"

"I think you're making a mistake," Kevin said. "He cares about you, and you're leaving him helpless. He needs you."

Siobhan fiddled with the napkin in her lap. "I do feel bad about leaving him the way he is, but he'll have help. And maybe the people buying his house will stop in from time to time until he goes?" She speared Kevin with a look, letting him know she was counting on him.

"You know we will," Amy answered for him.

Kevin shook his head. "And for someone who doesn't believe in ghosts, you handled the twins pretty well. What if Jared needs help with his ghost busting business? Seems as if you two make a good team. You sure you don't want to stick around a while?"

She took another sip of her wine, let it swirl around her mouth and then swallowed it before she answered. "All this free time you insisted on so I could get a life? It highlighted all the things I haven't dealt with. I need to get my life in order."

"You could do that with Jared," Kevin went on. "I can't help but feel you're making a mistake."

"You've said that." Siobhan took a deep breath. "Look. He's going home. Even if I stayed, he wouldn't be here for long. Besides, he's not the serious type. He flirts with everyone. He'll get better and then he'll move on to the next girl."

"I wouldn't be so sure." He stared at her, reading her the way he always had, making Siobhan squirm in her seat.

"Speaking of the twins," she said, changing the subject. "Have you heard from Iris? Are the police going after Stanley?"

"The coroner said the remains were consistent with those of two ten-year-old boys," Amy told her. "The police invited Iris back and she gave them a statement."

"Charges will be filed against Stanley," Kevin said, "but he probably isn't competent to stand trial. Most likely, he'll spend the rest of his life locked in the state hospital."

Siobhan poked at the salmon on her plate, the meal she hadn't ordered when she'd gone out with Duncan. "What do you think about Ma's new boyfriend?" she asked.

"Didn't realize you'd been trying to set her up," Kevin said.

"I wasn't."

"Then why did you invite him to Thanksgiving?"

Siobhan didn't answer for several minutes, not sure how much to share.

"Shevy, you didn't… with Duncan…?"

"No, I didn't," she said, allaying his obvious worries that she'd slept with him. "But I think he was hoping I would."

Kevin set his utensils on his plate. "Eww."

"Yeah," she whispered.

"Nothing happened," Amy said, looking to Siobhan for confirmation. Siobhan nodded. "And look how happy your mother's been lately."

Kevin and Siobhan exchanged uncertain glances.

"I don't want to think about my mother with a man," Kevin said.

"I already covered that with her," Siobhan added. "As she pointed out, she is a woman, and she's set aside her needs for a long time."

"I don't want to hear about her needs," Kevin said.

Amy laughed and Siobhan shook her head.

Kevin asked the server for a box to take his food home and Siobhan settled the bill.

"My treat," she told them. "To thank you, for giving me a place to live," she told Amy, "and for giving me back my family," she told Kevin.

"You'll come back for the wedding, too, won't you?" Amy asked.

"Wouldn't miss it. This guy in a tux?" She reached across the table and shoved Kevin's elbow.

"Who says I'm going to wear a tux?" he asked.

"Right," Siobhan said sarcastically.

"Will you stand up for me?" Amy asked. "Be my maid of honor?"

Damn her. She really was a nice woman. "I'd be honored."

Chapter 36

DECEMBER 23.

While it was sweater weather in Baton Rouge, Siobhan needed her parka when she got off the plane in Chicago. The landscape was covered in snow, and the clouds overhead looked heavy with more. Snow was pretty for Christmas, but she'd be happy to leave it behind again after the holiday.

As she climbed into the taxi, her phone rang.

"Did you make it okay?" Jared asked.

In the three weeks she'd been gone, she'd convinced herself the phone calls fell into the nursing category. Jared was still a stranger stranded in unfamiliar territory during his recovery period in need of a friendly voice. She could provide that. The fact his voice still gave her shivers didn't signify anything.

"Yep," she told him with a smile. "Did you make it to Vacherie?" Which was much closer to Baton Rouge than she'd expected. If he was going home, she could end their phone friendship gracefully. He'd be back with family and friends. Why did that idea tug at her heart?

"Not quite home yet," he replied.

"I'm glad you've recovered enough to get back to your old life. And I know Kevin and Amy are excited to have a place to start a family."

"I hope they're happy there," Jared said. "My family's glad to have Aunt Lily's estate settled. Will you be staying with the happy couple? Or are you staying with your mother?"

Siobhan smiled. "With my Ma. Christmas holds good memories. I'm sure I can stand it for a couple of days."

"You'll love every minute of it," he said.

"Yeah, I will. I'm sure you're anxious to be with your family, too, after being away from them so long. Sorry our schedules didn't work out better so I could wish you a Merry Christmas in person."

She still hadn't told Jared where she'd moved, afraid to fall under his spell once more.

"Would you?" he asked in that lazy drawl that wrapped itself around her. "Wish me a Merry Christmas in person if I was there?"

They'd made it through three weeks without any overt flirting. "Of course I would." Except memories crowded around her return trip to Edgarville, memories of playing chess and sitting on an enclosed front porch. Yeah, he was still way too potent to see in person.

Maybe if she saw him one more time, the ache in her chest would go away and she'd put an end to the fantasy that accompanied those faceless phone calls. "I'm thinking about going to Baton Rouge. What are you doing New Year's Eve?"

"Baton Rouge? Now don't you tease me, baby," he said. He pronounced the name of the city the way the French would, with the dialect the Baton Rouge locals used.

"I'm not sure how far it is from Vacherie," she said, knowing Baton Rouge was less than an hour's driving time. She'd checked. A dozen times. She'd even considered making the drive to be sure she wouldn't accidently run into him. She'd chickened out, every time.

"I'll tell you what I'll be doing New Year's Eve," he said. "I'll be waiting to kiss a certain nurse at midnight if she has it in mind to spend time with me."

Three weeks of benign phone conversations melted away. Siobhan hugged herself, warmed by the memory of how spectacular Jared's kisses were. She could be strong. She could resist engaging in verbal foreplay. He was a patient, and she'd been his nurse.

The taxi veered into Ma's driveway. "I have to go now," Siobhan said. "Talk to you later?"

"Count on it," he said.

As she unloaded her suitcase and paid the driver, Siobhan glanced at the place she'd grown up. Home. She remembered the Christmas mornings she and her siblings had gathered outside their bedrooms and planted themselves on the steps waiting for Da to tell them it was okay to come downstairs. Those early years were filled with fond memories. Even after Da's drinking had gotten out of control, Christmas mornings were still "safe" times.

The taxi pulled away, shaking Siobhan from her reverie. Kathleen's and Liam's cars were in the driveway. Kevin's was still missing.

She heaved her suitcase up the two porch steps and raised her hand to knock, but the door opened before she had a chance. Kathleen let out a squeal of delight and wrapped Siobhan in a hug.

"Merry Christmas," Kathleen said.

Siobhan set down her suitcase and squeezed her sister tight. "Merry Christmas."

The Christmas tree stood in the corner of the room, the same place it always had. Dozens of boxes wrapped in brightly colored paper were tucked beneath it and candles were lit on the mantle.

Liam tapped her on the shoulder, waiting his turn. Siobhan hugged him close and looked over his shoulder.

Ma's eyes glistened with unshed tears. "It's that happy I am ta have ye all here this year."

Siobhan hugged her mother tight. "Feels good to be home."

Ma pulled away, swiping at her eyes. "Are you happy?"

Siobhan nodded. "I am."

Ma hugged her once more and then took Siobhan's hand, pulling her into the kitchen. "I have to finish the soda bread," she said. "Come talk to me while I work."

The scents of cinnamon and cloves rose from the kettle of wassail steaming on the stove. Kathleen ladled out a cup and handed it to Siobhan. Liam plopped down at the table and grabbed a couple of cookies from a holiday plate. Siobhan sat down and helped herself to a cookie, as well. The lonely Christmases she'd lived in Virginia, often spent working at the hospital, melted away with the warmth of her family.

"And the place you're living, how is that?" Ma asked as she turned the mixer on.

"It's a studio apartment. I'm renting month to month until I find the right place," she said. "I don't need much. I'm hoping to find a house. A place with a fireplace and a front porch…"

"I'll come visit and help you look," Kathleen offered. "I don't have to go back to school until the middle of January."

The back door opened and Kevin stomped his feet before stepping inside. A few snowflakes flew in ahead of him. "It's snowing again," he said, unnecessarily.

Siobhan met him at the door with a hug. "Thanks for taking care of Jared," she said softly.

Kevin shrugged. "He's not a bad guy to hang around with. Besides, he gave us a great price on the house."

She peered out the door. "Where's Amy?"

Kevin's eyes shifted, taking on a guarded look. "She, uh, she was coming in the front door."

"Why?" Siobhan turned, but Liam blocked her view.

"Secret presents or something," Liam said.

"Yeah, or something," Kevin added.

Siobhan tried to sidestep Liam, but he continued to block her way. "What's going on?" she asked.

"Give her a minute to get your surprise ready," Liam told her.

"What surprise?"

Liam cocked an eyebrow. "If I told you, it wouldn't be a surprise."

Siobhan huffed and pushed Liam to one side. "Move." She hesitated before she crossed into the living room.

Amy still had her coat on, her cheeks flushed red and a silly grin on her face. "Merry Christmas."

"Merry Christmas," Siobhan replied. She crossed the room and hugged Amy. "So what's the big surprise?"

Amy's eyes flitted to the staircase. Siobhan turned to look and Jared stepped into view. Her heart nearly jumped from her chest. He looked so good, so handsome, and no crutches. No cane. Siobhan folded her hands over her heart. She was definitely not over him. "I thought you went home," she whispered, a catch in her voice.

"I wanted to see you first. I hope you don't mind," he said in that oh-so-sexy voice.

She swallowed hard, her fingers itching to hug him—and why shouldn't she? It was Christmas after all. She crossed the room and wrapped him gently in her arms. Jared snuck his arms around her, strong and sure.

"Now this feels like about the best Christmas present I've ever had," he said, his voice rumbling against her. He rested one hand on her cheek, his deep brown eyes reaching into her soul, and bent to kiss her.

"Are you still leaving?" she whispered against his cheek. "Still going home?"

He nodded. "First thing tomorrow. I promised my mama I'd be home for Christmas, but I had to see you. I hope you don't mind."

She nodded, unable to speak.

"And you'll be in Baton Rouge for New Year's?" he asked.

She nodded again. "That's where I'm working now." She shouldn't have told him. Hadn't meant to tell him. Her pulse raced. What would he say now that he knew?

A slow smile crept across his face. "For true?"

She looked for reinforcements, but the family had retreated to the kitchen, leaving her alone with Jared.

"You look happy," he said. "At peace."

She nodded. "I am."

"At peace with me?" he asked.

She'd forgotten the hypnotic effect of this man. Her body thrummed, begging to feel more of him, his skin against hers, and yet she'd abandoned him. "I feel bad for leaving when I did."

"Why? Because you wanted to nurse me some more? You know how much I hate not being able to do for myself. I'm happier you didn't have to put up with me any more than you did."

"I'm a nurse. It's my job to put up with my patients. Even the stubborn ones."

He grinned. "Yeah, but I don't want a nurse. I want you."

Siobhan's lips had become too dry. She ran a tongue across them as something deep inside pulsed to let her know she wanted him too. "Do you need to sit?" she asked breathlessly.

"I need to hold you in my arms, now that I can, the way I've been wanting to do since I met you," he told her. "But if you'd rather I didn't…"

She slid her arms around his waist. "I'd rather you did." He felt so good. Solid. Strong.

Jared played with her hair. "I had Amy wrap up the chess set for you," he said. "My present to you. But I had another present, in case you were happy to see me."

Siobhan grinned. "I am happy to see you, but I don't have anything for you. I wasn't expecting to see you."

"Then I'm going to take a chance I won't frighten you off again," he said, his face a mask of seriousness. "You think that's a safe bet?"

"I'm scared to death, but I'm not going anywhere. I just got here." She smiled, hands trembling. Where was her meddling family when she needed them? Was he going to ask her to spend the night with him? Could she? Everyone would know. She knew from the moment she'd met Jared he was the man she wanted to invite to her bed, but she was staying at Ma's, and Ma wouldn't allow them to sleep together. Siobhan swallowed down her questions. "I'm guessing the doctors have lifted your restrictions."

He raised his eyebrows and chuckled. "I do appreciate your enthusiasm, and yes, the doctors have lifted my restrictions." He glanced over her shoulder and put an extra inch between them.

The family had gathered in the kitchen doorway, watching. She stepped out of his embrace as heat flushed her face.

Jared cleared his throat. "In case I haven't told you before," he said quietly, "I love you." He managed a wobbly smile. "But I think the proposition you might be expecting isn't the one I have in mind."

Had she misread his intentions? Now that they could finally sleep together, was he telling her he didn't want to? Did he have permanent damage from the accident? He must have seen the questions running through her mind because he chuckled again.

"While everything's in fine working order, at least as near as I can tell without actually taking things for a test run…" he glanced at the family hovering in the doorway, cleared his throat again, and raised his voice. "I'm not able to drop to one knee quite yet." He dug something from his pocket and opened a small box. "But I hope you'll consider marrying me anyway."

Stunned, she grabbed his arm.

That's when she realized her mouth was hanging open.

"You need time to think about it? Get used to the idea?" Jared asked.

And then the tears started. Jared wanted her. All of her. He could have gone to Louisiana, could have taken an earlier flight.

He'd led her to believe he'd already left. But he hadn't. He was standing in front of her. Waiting for her. Wanting her.

"I'm not going anywhere," he said, and then leaned in and lowered his voice. "And once I get you in my bed, I intend to keep you there for a good long while. I'll even vow to those make-out sessions you talked about. I want us to spend the rest of our lives together. If you'll have me."

"Sometimes life takes you where you're meant to be," Kevin said, his arm around Amy. "Seems as if there's a reason that job in Louisiana turned up when it did."

"You going to give him an answer?" Liam asked.

She nodded, tears spilling down her cheeks.

Jared laughed. "Is that a yes?"

She gasped out a "Yes" and then she chuckled. "In case I haven't told you, I love you, too."

Dear Reader:

Thanks so much for reading this book. If you enjoyed the story, I hope you will encourage others by "liking" my books on Goodreads.com and everywhere the option is offered, and by posting an honest review to the site where you bought this book and/or at other book blogs/reading sites so you can help other readers decide whether it's worth their time. Authors like and need to get feedback to make each new book as good as it can be.

—Karla Brandenburg

Please turn this page for an excerpt of
Epitaph 3: Man in the Mirror

Chapter 1

SANDRA MEYER READ NICK Benedetto's text one more time. He was home, on leave, and he needed to talk to her. She preferred to leave him in the past, where he belonged. Anything Nick had to say couldn't be good.

As she tucked her phone back into her pocket, Garth Benson walked into the café and her mood improved. His jeans were covered in dirt, most likely from the cemetery if he'd come from work setting another stone for the family business. His shoulders strained the seams of his flannel shirt and he'd rolled the sleeves to display corded arms. The man oozed testosterone. He cocked an eyebrow and offered up a silly grin before he glanced around the empty café. "Hey, beautiful."

A thrill ran through her at the compliment. She couldn't take it seriously, but a girl did like to have her ego stroked. "Cup of coffee?" she asked.

He sauntered up to the counter and leaned over. "Yes, please. Sweet. Just like you."

"You know your compliments are wasted on me," she said as she poured his coffee. She flipped her hair over her shoulder and leaned toward him while she slid the cup across the counter.

Garth handed her a bill and she rung up the sale.

"How's the studying going?" he asked, nodding toward her computer.

"My final project is almost done."

"You should have gone to a regular four-year college," he told her, not for the first time.

"Wasn't so easy after my father died." Sandra turned away, picked up a cleaning cloth and wiped down the counter.

"How is your mom?"

She forced a smile a turned to face Garth. "She's getting along. Still goes to the real estate office every day."

"Gotta be tough, but I'm sure she's glad you're around to help."

And what else was Sandra supposed to do? She was the reason her parents got in the car that night, the reason they were arguing, the reason her father lost control. But Garth wasn't done dredging up old memories today.

"Rumor has it Nick's back in town."

Since she had the cloth in her hand, she slipped around the counter and wiped down tables. "So I hear."

Garth followed close behind. "Think you'll see him while he's home?"

Sandra straightened. "Small town. He'll probably be hard to miss." One lapse in a high school tutoring session would haunt her the rest of her life. Living with the guilt was hard enough on her own without Nick Benedetto holding it over her head. That was precisely the reason she had to get her degree, had to get out of Edgarville. The reason she could never do more than flirt with Garth Benson.

"You deserve better. You know that, right?"

Sandra folded her arms. "Did you want something to go with your coffee?"

Garth stepped inside her personal space. His voice rumbled. "Just don't want to see you get hurt."

"Been taking care of myself for a long time," she replied.

He nodded, turned and left the café.

Sandra closed her eyes and relaxed. Of all the people in town she might confide in, Garth would be her first choice, but she didn't dare. She'd learned about men the hard way.

~ ~ ~

Garth Benson stormed back to the cemetery, where his brothers were setting a grave marker, and shoved his younger brother, Brian.

"Hey," Brian complained. His eyes went from the cup of coffee in Garth's hand to Garth's face and he smirked. "Got shut down again, did you? When are you going to give up on that one?"

Garth fixed him with a murderous glare and Brian laughed.

"You tell her you saw Nick?" Thad, his older brother, asked.

Garth shoved Thad for good measure. "Didn't have to."

He spotted his sister Amy, her face turned toward the rays of sun beaming through the trees while she wandered through the headstones. Nick had charmed Amy once, and yeah, Garth might have overreacted when he'd taken it upon himself to beat the hell out of Nick for kissing her, but Amy had seemed more embarrassed than mad when Garth had backed Nick off.

What did women see in Nick Benedetto? Garth set his stride and intercepted Amy by the cremation niches.

"Yes?" she asked, brows up.

He slowed his pace. No, he couldn't ask her. "You know what? Never mind."

She folded her arms. "Too late."

Garth cupped the back of his neck. "You remember Nick Benedetto?"

She flushed slightly. "Yeah?"

"Well, he's back in town."

"And why do you care?" Amy's arms were still folded, and her eyes narrowed.

Sandra had been the one who started the whole Crazy Amy thing. He couldn't blame Amy for not liking her, even if that had been back in high school, but there were things about Sandra and Nick that Amy didn't know. There were things nobody else knew. Except Tammy Calhoun. Garth wasn't going to be the one to tell.

Amy took a step closer, staring a little too closely. "You're worried he's going to stake a claim on Sandra. You know, Kevin tried to tell me there was something between you and Sandra, the way she flirts with you, the way you flirt back." She lowered her hands to her side. "He's wrong, right? I mean, you wouldn't be chasing after a woman who humiliated your sister, would you?"

He grimaced. "Well, when you put it like that…"

"Garth," she said in a dangerously low tone. "Of all the women in town who want a piece of you, she's the one you give it to?"

His face suddenly felt warm. "Sandra and I have never dated, and you know it." Although if it were up to him, they definitely would.

Amy closed her eyes and shook her head. "Kevin's right. How is it that I couldn't see it? Honest to God, you gave me grief over every man I even looked at, and you're chatting up the woman who bullied me in high school?"

He winced again. Guilty on all charges.

"You know she's stupid in love with Nick, always has been. They probably hook up every time he comes home. You know that, right, Garth?" She rose up on her tiptoes, nose to nose. "Right?"

Wrong. He didn't know what hold Nick had over Sandra, but Garth was pretty sure it wasn't what Amy thought, not based on what he knew. He grunted, turned on his heel and headed for the cemetery gates, back to the family's monument shop.

Amy caught up with him before he hit the sidewalk outside the stone gateposts. She shoved him, the same way he'd shoved his brothers earlier, and he laughed.

"She's going to break your heart, and I refuse to feel sorry for you," she told him, hands on hips.

"What about you?" he asked. "You going to look up Nick now that he's back in town?" He couldn't help baiting her, even though she was punch drunk in love with Kevin McCormick and counting down the weeks to her wedding. Thank heaven for that.

She rolled her eyes. "It was one kiss." She held up a finger to emphasize her point. "One. Even if I wanted anything more from him, which I didn't, you took care of that when you gave him a black eye." She stormed back into the cemetery, fists swinging at her sides.

Yeah, based on what he knew, Garth had been only too happy to warn Nick away from his sister when Sandra told him she'd seen Amy and Nick kissing in the stairwell at school. Other people might believe Sandra had been motivated by jealousy. Garth knew better.

www.ingramcontent.com/pod-product-compliance
Lightning Source LLC
Chambersburg PA
CBHW061030120726

47910CB00006B/2182